three, seventeen

A Novel

Kerri L. Bennett

PUBLISHING
First Print Edition, 2012
Published in the United States of America

ISBN-13: 978-0615688367 ISBN-10: 0615688365

Dedication

This novel is dedicated to my grandpa, Lee Bennett, who loved science fiction and fantasy stories and who always told me to think for myself and never let others hamstring my imagination. It is also dedicated to my family and friends for their constant support.

I would also like to thank fellow novelist and Jedi, Sarah Wofford, for helping me understand my characters better, another fellow novelist, Slade Dupuy, for talking werewolf mythology with me, and Aaron Anderson for faithfully answering all my annoyingly random questions. To the members of my thesis committee: Dr. Jerry Ball, Dr. Rob Lamm, and Dr. Rick Lott; I would like to express my gratitude for your willingness to devote so much time and patience to me and this novel. I love you all.

A trek through the trees—
Superstition comes to life
Loup-garou is born.

Contents

Prologue

Massachusetts Bay Colony, 1690

Jacob Abbot knew that to look at this savage with an eye that was any other than wary was a sin. Abbot knew too that the pleasure he got from watching her as she gathered berries, occasionally sampling their sweetness, was a sin. Yet he could not help wondering if her lips would be as soft upon his as they were against the berries she put to them. He shook his head and turned to make his way from the woods and back to the settlement. His Leah had been gone too long, he supposed, if he had begun to think of an Indian in the same way as he would a Christian woman.

Why this was so, he could not fathom. Leah had been fair haired and blue-eyed, with skin so white it was like new butter. She was nothing like the red woman with hair as black as the soil that Jacob had come upon thrice now at the edge of the wood where he had been hunting wild game. At first, he had thought nothing of finding her; the Indians were a common enough sight now that they had made peace with the settlers and had helped them survive the winter. But when he went to his little house at night and laid in the cold feather-tick alone, the dark one came back to him, haunted him and his dreams the way Leah had for so long after she was gone. Jacob had thought that he would never see her face again, once the sailors had wrapped her body in canvas and tossed her into the sea, but he had been wrong. He had seen her face every night without fail until he first laid eyes on that heathen. Since that time, he could think of nothing else.

"Alsoomse," he whispered, and her name was almost a prayer. It was something he knew he needed, but since she had come to him that afternoon a fortnight ago, when she had finally caught him watching her, it was something he had been unable to do. Jacob knew by the signs she made that she was the squaw of some Wampanoag brave, but that was of little matter to him. What could one savage do? Threaten him with a hatchet? When he was honest with himself, he knew that he was willing to die to keep this dark beauty with her shy ways. But was he willing to face eternal damnation? He told himself that she was not a married woman, since there was no Christian law among her savage race. He was guilty of fornication, which he admitted, but only when he was alone in his cold bed. It never occurred when she lay next to him, and the only sound save the birds and insects was the breath they drew almost as one, but every time he left the forest empty-handed, his conscience met and plagued him until the next time he was able to lose himself in the wild freedom of her love.

The only answer he could ascertain was to marry her. Marry her in the eyes of English law, and then there would be no sin left to deprive him of sleep and the ability to pray and worship with a pure heart. If the Almighty could forgive King David for coveting Bathsheeba, surely He (and the community for that matter) could forgive Jacob for wanting Alsoomse. Once they were together, he was sure she would learn to live a Christian life and leave the pagan idols of her fathers in the past. The only thing that stood between them and heavenly bliss was her husband. Jacob knew that she would not go with him so long as she was bound to the savage, for he had taken her hand in his many times and tried to lead her out of the forest and into the settlement, but each time she had stood in the shadow of the trees and refused to step into his world. He saw the sorrow in her eyes, and he knew, though she had spoken no words, that she would never leave, so long as the other still claimed her.

That was why he had told her, in a fashion, that he wanted her to bring the Indian to the woods with her when she came to meet him. That, too, was why he came bearing a loaded musket at his side for the first time in many days. And that was why as soon as the savage stepped away from Alsoomse, Jacob took aim and fired into the russet chest of the one who stood between him and what he loved.

As the smoke cleared and the smell of the burning powder gave way to the dark scent of earth and death, Jacob watched her kneel at the body of the man whose hut she'd shared but would do so no longer. Her tears mixed with his blood and she rocked as she murmured over him while he struggled for each gurgling breath. He answered her in kind and lifted his voice in a plaintive cry that came out so strongly, Jacob began to wonder if the Indian truly was dying. The chant rose above the trees it seemed and sent birds and other small creatures scurrying from their dens, and with their departure, the forest became terribly quiet.

Chapter 1

Raleigh, NC, 2007

Logan Michaels was never one to believe in superstitions. There were those who would have made much of the fact that he was born on St. Patrick's Day and was of Celtic descent, but not Logan. He knew well enough that there was no such thing as luck–good or bad. "Luck" was up to each person and how he chose to handle the situations life threw at him.

So far, Logan thought that he'd handled things pretty well. He'd made it out of that small, stifling town he was born in and all the way to the second half of his junior year in college. It didn't matter if he hadn't actually gotten out of the state as he'd hoped. He had a full ride at North Carolina State because of his ACT score and only a year-and-a-half left before he earned his business degree. Where he went from there was anybody's guess.

He wasn't focused on the future because the present semester promised to be the best ever. He and three of his Kappa Sigma brothers had scored an apartment in Wolf Village that had been vacated in December. Its previous occupants having graduated, Logan was able to snag the sweet little third floor setup when the spring semester started. Not only was he pumped because of his new apartment, but he was also stoked because this

Spring Break he would be turning twenty-one in the Colorado Rockies and snuggling with a group of snow bunnies in tight sweaters. There was nothing better.

Spring term was fairly easy, since he was only taking twelve hours. He was slacking a little, but the other hours could be earned during the summer, and that would give him all the excuse he needed to stay on campus and away from home.

Logan looked at the calendar and confirmed what he had hoped: It was Saturday, March 10. That meant he was going to be leaving for Colorado in five days. Presently, his four-bedroom apartment in Wolf Village was filled with sorority girls who'd come to cook for him and his roommates. The place might be trashed by the end of the night, but the boys didn't care as long as they were getting home-cooked meals that did not involve a box of Hamburger Helper.

He decided to go out on the balcony after he had to dodge two blondes who were rushing back and forth, torn between looking the part of the happy homemaker and fighting over who was going to get the next make-out session with Andrew. Andrew, meanwhile, was lounging on the couch and giving his lips a little break. Logan looked at Andrew and shook his head. The boy could draw chicks like flies, and all he had to do was sit there looking stupid. He didn't even try to be smooth. He didn't have to, once the girls heard he was a pre-med major who inherited all his Italian mother's good looks.

He pushed his way past the crowd of people who were blocking the doors and stepped out onto the balcony. The weather was good—warm and breezy. He plopped into the hammock that the guys before them had strung up last fall and pulled his shades down over

11

his eyes, prepared to vegg until the cooking craziness subsided inside.

He'd just drifted off to sleep when he was disturbed by Mark opening the door. "There you are, my man! Pretty cold of you to slip off by yourself, don'tcha think?"

"What makes you say that?" Logan raised a brow, but otherwise made no movement that acknowledged Mark's presence.

"You know I've got no chance of bagging a chick with 'The Italian Stallion' in there, unless you help a brotha' out!" he said, using the *Rocky*-esque nickname Andrew had "cleverly" bestowed upon himself. Again, Logan said nothing, only shook his head.

Mark was short, with an average build. He had sandy brown hair that was currently buzzed and a crazy streak that manifest itself in his love for karaoke and practical jokes. Logan guessed he was nice enough, but it was true that the girls usually preferred Andrew or himself over Mark. "One of these days, you're gonna have to learn how to get chicks on your own. I won't *always* be at your disposal."

"You fixin' to die or somethin', Michaels? 'Cause if you are, I want your Alpine, a'ight?"

"You are not touching my stereo. And I am not dying. I only meant that we aren't always going to be roomies. We are going to graduate . . . sooner or later." Logan yawned.

"What are you screamin'? I'm on the decade plan! I got like seven more years left! I won't be done with college 'til I'm like forty!"

"Uh, dude, if you add that up, you'll actually be more like twenty-eight when you graduate."

"Whatever. Anyway, I need your help. I need a woman NOW, while I've still got–whatever I've got workin' for me . . . I guess that would be you."

"Fine. Give me a minute," Logan stretched. "If you're that desperate for some lovin', I'll see what I can do."

"Thanks, Logan. You da man!" he grinned and dashed back inside to scope out which girl he wanted Logan to sweet-talk into being his date for the night.

After a few seconds, Logan dutifully got up from the hammock and left it swaying slightly as he went back into the apartment. Mark immediately approached Logan in a way that he guessed Mark meant to be covert. "Dude," he whispered. "I want that one," he said, nearly pointing before Logan's sharp look stopped him. Instead, he inclined his head in the direction of the counter where three girls stood, busily chopping things. "The little redhead," he said out the side of his mouth. *Jeez! It **had** to be the one with the biggest knife, didn't it, Mark?* Logan thought as he nodded and began to head in the girls' direction.

"Hey good lookin', whatcha got–" he began with a grin when he was standing nonchalantly in front of the girl in question. He knew it would be taken as stupid and light, exactly the way he meant it.

"Logan, you are *such* a player! I honestly don't know why we put up with you and your corny pick-up lines!" she smiled, obviously enjoying the hit, even if her words said otherwise.

"Yes you do. You put up with me because you know it'll be worth it," he tilted his shades so that they made direct eye contact, and he knew she could see the hint of danger in his steel gray eyes. "And you put up with my corny pick-up lines because they work," he

13

immediately lightened the tension he'd just created. When she laughed easily, he continued. "Got plans for tonight, Melissa?"

"Nooo," she drew the answer out, trying to be as tempting as Logan was. "What'd you have in mind?" she punctuated her question with a smile.

"See that couch over there?" he looked in its direction and filled his voice with innuendo.

"Yeess," she replied.

"That guy on the end all by himself is my buddy, Mark. I wonder if you'd consider hanging with him a while tonight," he continued to smile. Her smile, on the other hand, vanished, and a pout began to form.

"And *why* would I do that when I've got you?" she asked, trying to revive the spark that Logan had just extinguished and using her pout as best she knew how.

"Because if you go with Mark tonight, you have me all to yourself on Tuesday," he said flatly. He'd found that to de-emphasize the punch line actually gave it more power. She looked enticed, and her smile returned. *Works every time*, he smiled back.

"Okay. But if I do this, does that mean that I have to . . . with–eww," she glanced in Mark's direction.

"No, no, just keep him company tonight." Logan leaned in to her ear, "You need to rest up and save your strength for Tuesday, right?" he whispered, the tip of his tongue grazing the rim of her ear. He felt her shiver and knew that she'd be good on her word. He gave her a knowing glance and went to sit with Mark.

As soon as Logan's body hit the couch, Mark snapped to attention. "Mission accomplished, pal," he told the questions in Mark's eyes. "You can thank me later."

"Really? That's awesome, Michaels! You rock!" Mark's grin split his face.

Logan glanced over at Andrew who was now on girl number four. At least he didn't need any help.

Logan took one last look at himself in the bathroom mirror. The fog from his shower had framed the edges of the glass, and the sheen of water droplets reflected on his skin gave him a dangerous look. His already dark hair was a dripping black. He was tall and athletically built, though he'd never been as committed to sports as most guys. He enjoyed a game of football in the front yard of the Kappa Sig house, but the winning or losing didn't matter.

He toweled his hair dry and reached for a razor and some shaving cream. He was smoothing the Colgate over his cheeks and chin when Rob entered the bathroom without preamble.

"Dang, man, it's like a freakin' sauna in here!" he said, waving a hand and trying to help some of the steam drift into the hall.

"You got a problem with it, you can always use *your own* bathroom. There is one on the other side of the apartment, you know."

"Yeah, but Mark just came out of there," Logan's third roommate replied.

"So go in there, if he's just left," Logan told him, beginning to shave the right side of his face.

"No. *Mark* just came out of there, man," Rob insisted.

"Look, I'm in the middle of something here. If you don't wanna wait for me to finish, *go use **your** bathroom!*" Logan's voice betrayed his irritation, but the hand holding the razor was steady and methodical. It was moving in smooth, even strokes, and after every second stroke, he tapped the excess foam into the sink. He was carefully tackling his upper lip when Rob spoke again.

"Man, can't I just pee while you're standing there?"

"Whatever. Just don't get it all over the lid like last time. I swear, you have worse aim than a two-year-old with no Fruit Loops to shoot at. Girls *do* come to this apartment occasionally, and they *do* wanna have a clean place to go if they need to. Though, from the looks of y'all's bathroom, it's obvious that you two don't understand that."

"Look, we don't have girls coming over and cleaning our side of the apartment like you do!"

"Maybe if you lived a little less like pigs and tried to be nice to them for a change, they'd wanna clean for you too," Logan muttered in a tone that held no sympathy as he made another stroke with his razor. "You're lucky they even go spray air freshener on your end, the way things are now."

Rob zipped his fly and flushed, then squeezed by Logan and the open door. "You think that girls come over here just because the place is spotless? You're stupider than I thought you were, man." Logan caught one glance of Rob's bitter smile as he went out into the hall.

Of the three of them, Logan liked Rob the least. He was tall and lanky, and he wore his hair in a style that was oddly reminiscent of *Ace Ventura: Pet Detective*. As for his eyes, Logan wasn't sure. Rob had an annoying habit of wearing his reflective pilot sunglasses everywhere he went, even indoors and after sunset. Rob was lethargic, even for a college student. He never got excited about games or girls or anything that Logan

16

ever knew of. He'd rather sit on the couch, watching *SportsCenter* and drinking scotch. In fact, the only reason he'd even made it into Kappa Sig was that his old man had been a member a couple centuries ago.

Andrew was a blast to hang with, and so was Mark, come to that, if you could look past the fact that he was a natural chick repellent. But Logan would have just as soon lived without Rob except that they needed a fourth person to secure apartment 317.

When he finished shaving, Logan wiped his smooth face with his towel, draped it loosely around his hips and went to his room to find something to wear. Fifteen minutes later, he emerged wearing jeans and a polo. He gelled his hair and combed it the way it suited him. It was quite a bit longer in front than it was in the back, but he didn't wear it down in his face very often. There was something distinctively repulsive to him in looking like Leonardo DiCaprio in his *Titanic* years, and he meant to avoid it at all costs. When he finished with his hair, he put on his cologne and left for the library and his weekly study session with his frat brothers.

He thought the study sessions an extreme waste of time, but they were required, and sometimes he got a couple dates out of the deal. Besides, it was Tuesday, and it wasn't like he had any plans, except the ones he had with Melissa that night. As he made his way to the study room that was reserved for Greeks, he passed the main circulation desk and nodded politely at all the "Hi, Logan"s he received. He was used to people speaking to him and having no idea who they were. It was just part of college life if you were Greek. Because you were required to be active in various clubs and social events on campus, 75 percent of the population knew your face and name before the third week of the semester. That was why he never paid too much attention to them either, especially if they worked behind the desk in the library.

By this point in the semester, Logan knew the way to the study room that was reserved for the Kappa Sigs, so he walked in that general direction without seeing anything or anyone he passed. Inside, he found a table off to the side that no one had taken yet and sat down, leaning back and propping his feet on the table in front of him, prepared to endure the next hour of brain-bruising boredom.

When that hour of his life was over with absolutely no way of getting it back, Logan roused from his comatose state, left and was more than glad to be gone from it, at least until the next day, and who knew, if things went well with Melissa, he might find tomorrow's study session a lot more interesting.

Logan had always been good at school but had never needed to apply himself to do so. Generally, if he read about or heard a concept, he remembered it without too much effort. This gave him the latitude to develop his social life without much of a toll on his grades. It also meant that he spent much of the time being uninterested in the happenings around him.

As he made his way back to the library's main entrance, Mark fell into step beside him. "Man, I sure am glad we've got that over with for the week," he nudged Logan, jerking him into consciousness. "Got any plans for the rest of the day?"

"Not until tonight," Logan shrugged. The boys walked together past the circulation desk, and he heard the hiss of air that Mark shoved through his teeth in lieu of a whistle.

"Did you see the girl behind the counter? Man, does she have eyes . . ."

Logan couldn't help himself, "Dude, chill. I'm still working off the last favor I called in for you!"

Logan left Melissa's at seven thirty on Wednesday morning. She'd shooed him out after he'd made breakfast for her while she was in the shower, and then they'd shared it. It was the least he could do after what she'd done the night before. What good did it do a guy to know how to make omelettes if he never got to prove he could? He walked out the door with the taste and scent of her still on him and jogged the short distance to 317. When he opened the door, he saw that Mark was the only one up yet and since he seemed to have a death grip on his coffee mug, it was clear that he wasn't awake.

"Gotta say, man, that was the best favor I've ever done for you," he grinned.

Mark's only answer was a grunt, but his scowl had lessened somewhat, and Logan took it as a positive response. "Gonna hit the sack. Later," he called as he headed for his room and some sleep before his ten o'clock class.

When his Advanced Database Management class was over, Logan shook off his apathy and tried to wake himself up before SAD (Systems Analysis and Design). He only had about ten minutes before he had to be on the fourth floor of Nelson Hall, and he didn't want to go all the way back to the apartment or even to the coffee house across campus. He walked out into the open and thought about the fact that tomorrow he would not be surrounded by brownish grass and boring buildings. By tomorrow, he'd be in the car with

19

Andrew, Mike and Rob and on his way to Breckenridge, and in two days' time, he'd be up to his knees in snow and girls in ski suits. That had him waking up just enough to make it through his last class. After that, all that awaited him was freedom.

The boys left campus at six on Thursday morning, having elected to skip Friday's classes in favor of getting to the lodge by that morning. According to Google Maps, the whole trip, nonstop should take about twenty-six-and-a-half hours. So Andrew and Logan figured that if they left at six, that'd put them in Colorado by nine a.m. on Friday at the latest, even allowing for food and bathroom breaks, as long as someone was driving straight through the night.

None of the other three trusted Rob with their lives in the wee hours of the morning after they had been on the road all day, so he got the first three-and-a-quarter hour shift by general consensus, meaning that it wouldn't be his turn at the wheel again until sometime after sunup Friday morning, and by then they'd be too stoked to sleep, since they'd almost be there. In typical Rob fashion, however, he was unhappy with the arrangement.

"Dude, this sucks," he yawned as they turned out of the parking lot and onto the street. They'd opted not to take his H2, despite the fact that it would fit the four of them and all their stuff comfortably, on the grounds that it would suck down too much gas and because taking it would have given him an edge on decision-making that the others weren't about to concede. Instead, they settled on Mark's light blue, hand-me-down minivan, even though it sported wood paneling because it was better on mpg's and wasn't a compromise on space, but the fact that they were four single collegiates spring breaking in Colorado and had chosen such a "lame" ride was yet another cause for Rob's discontent. "We're gonna roll into the resort, and all the chicks'll ski the other direction when they see this mom-mobile."

"At least we'll have money left over from what we'll save on gas to pay them to come back," Logan grinned.

"Who says we'll have to pay 'em?" Andrew raised a brow. "*I* won't. In fact, by tomorrow night, I'll bet you I can have a girl paying *me* to hang around!"

"Didn't take him long to go gigolo, did it?" Mark quipped.

"Long? Naw, dude, Stevenson's been a player since he winked at the nurse two seconds after he popped outta his mom!" Rob smiled and surprised all of his passengers with the appearance of a personality.

To cover the silence, Logan wondered, "How much you willing to wager there, Don Juan?"

"Fifty?" Andrew offered. "I mean, I wouldn't wanna take advantage of friends or be accused of highway robbery," he chuckled.

"An even hundred says you're wrong," Logan challenged.

"You're on, bro!" Andrew's face lit with the challenge. "Just remember that you're dealing with 'The Italian Stallion,' baby!"

The pot was too rich for Mark's tastes, but it seemed that Rob had no qualms with spending every dime he could get out of his old man and was happy to ante up on the side of Andrew. "Nothing against you, man," he told Logan, "I've just seen the way The Stallion operates."

"Makes no difference to me," Logan shrugged and cast a glance at Mark, who was proof positive of how persuasive Logan could be.

Chapter 2

Logan pocketed a cool two hundred while he watched Andrew and Rob start trying to forget their humiliation in shots of Jäger. Mark took the opportunity and snuck a finger or two of Rob's scotch. "Never thought I'd see the day that Stevenson would be outdone by anybody other than Johnny Freaking Depp," he bellowed after he'd set the bottle back down.

"Shuttup, Malone! Everybody knows the only reason Michaels is as smooth as he is is all that practice he gets seducing your women for you," Andrew retorted as he downed another swallow.

"And even *he's* not good enough to seal the deal for you," Rob added, laughing, but realized soon enough that the others weren't.

"Cold, man," Logan told him and passed Mark the bottle. "But this'll warm you up."

It was one thirty when Logan reluctantly stepped out of the warm cabin and onto the cold porch. It was his crappy luck that he'd been the only one man enough to down that much hard liquor and still have the ability to stand. And it was too dang bad that he didn't think to grab his parka or at least a toboggan before he went outside. *Why the crap couldn't they store the firewood next to the hearth? That was the logical place for firewood, wasn't it?* He took a few more steps to look for the kindling that was supposed to be stacked up somewhere around there, but found that it was too dark to see much more than the feet in front of him. Still, the fire was getting low, and he didn't plan to freeze his butt off all night long when he needed to be sleeping off the booze and on his A-game by the next day. *Happy birthday to me*, he thought as he resigned himself to the fact that he'd have to get some branches from the tree line that was about twenty yards away.

He trudged through the snow a few feet and cursed himself as the cold seeped into his feet. A couple more steps and he was wondering what had possessed him and his roommates to go to the *frozen north* for Spring Break instead of Cali. And how was it that he'd won the stupid bet, but was out here in the cold while the losers were warm and toasty in the cabin, snoring their heads off and dreaming of little blonde bunnies? He'd blame it on the Jäger, he decided. It was the Jäger's fault that he was a freaking human popsicle on his freaking twenty-first birthday. Yeah, the Jäger and his stupid pride. What made him think he had to keep up with Andrew and Rob anyway? They were only knocking it back like fish because they'd lost the stupid bet. *He* was the freaking winner for Pete's sakes, and here he was acting like he needed a consolation prize. Well, his head would be pounding like the base at a Lacuna Coil concert in a few hours—*that* would be his consolation prize. He'd be too wasted to even see daylight before one or two. So much for making the most of his vacation time. Waste half his birthday with a pillow over his eyes, and by the time he dragged himself out of bed, Stevenson would have made off with *both* the girls. *What were their names? Jessie and . . .* Well, who gave a crap? They weren't here now, were they? And they dang sure weren't any help gathering this freaking firewood.

Logan stopped and watched the puff of his breath escape his lips. He'd walked farther into the trees than he'd meant to, but at least he could tell by the dim glow of the lodge's lights that there were plenty of sticks lying around. He bent over to grab some and nearly lost his balance. *Just what you need Michaels. A face full of snow. How's that for a birthday present? A face full of snow ice cream.* He may have been drunk, but he hadn't lost his sense of humor. He laughed at his own wit, and the volume of the sound seemed to vibrate off the trees. He decided laughing wasn't the best plan when you were trying not to land in snow and drop all the dang wood you'd just collected. He was more careful as he picked up a few more branches, and when the load in his arms felt large enough to fuel the fire until morning, he turned to go.

The snap of a twig had him jerking his head back to see where the sound came from. But there was nothing in the darkness but trees. He chalked it up to his inebriated gait and headed for the lodge. He was almost out of the cover of trees, he knew, because the light from their cabin was getting brighter and the outline of the porch more defined. Logan occupied himself by thinking about how nice it would be when he put all this wood on the fire, and it was blazing in front of his face and hands, and once he was warm again, he'd crawl into the bed that he'd claimed and sleep until those morons woke him up. *Well, it better be after nine o'clock, or they'll be losing more than a hundred a piece!*

He got a great deal of satisfaction from picturing himself bloodying Rob's nose. *He deserves it after what he said to Mark tonight.* It still angered him to think of it.

25

They all knew it was pathetic that Mark was a grown man and couldn't get a girl on his own, but that didn't mean they had to go and talk about it. That was just cold, like he'd told Rob. But that *was* Rob. He was one cold SOB. Yeah, Logan would get an awful lot of pleasure out of popping him a good one. Why he didn't ev—

There was another crack, louder this time, and Logan turned around. He was sure that it wasn't his elephant-feet now. He stared hard into the pitch in front of him, but there was no movement. He had to be hallucinating. He made to head for the cabin again when he felt the hair rise on the nape of his neck. There was only a second to drop the armload of wood and protect his face before the force of the thing had him crashing into the snow, slamming his head onto something solid and searing into the skin of his forearm.

He just *thought* he was cold before. Now he was cold and wet as a seal. *Freaking snow.* He didn't remember snow being so cold as to burn, but then he'd never been covered in it and having to walk back to the house, sopping wet, in the middle of the night with a throbbing head. And now he'd dropped the firewood, he realized. *Great!* He managed to gather the wood back into his arms, though his right one was too sore to cooperate very well. *I must've landed on it.* At least it wasn't broken. But he winced as he touched it with the fingers of his left hand. It was wet, like the whole of his body, and probably bruised and scraped to pieces, but it wasn't broken.

Logan picked up his pace once he'd situated his load and dashed to the porch. There was no way he was gonna spend any more time outside than he had to.

Not now that he was wet. He made it to the porch and stumbled onto it, shifting the wood again so that he had a free hand to open the door. He burst through and into the relative warmth. He took all the kindling over to the hearth where the flame was beginning to dwindle and added it a stick or two at a time. But instead of blazing up, the fire dimmed. *Crap!* It had never occurred to him that the branches he was gathering were sitting on snow and probably just as waterlogged as he was.

"Forget this!" he hissed, and dropped the rest of the pile where he stood. Now that there was no warm hearth to sit by, he realized he was shivering and stripped off his shirt, pants and socks, then padded up to his bedroom to find a towel.

He flipped the light on and strode across the room to the bath that adjoined Mark and Rob's rooms to his and Andrew's. Knowing how much Andrew had had, he wasn't too concerned about waking him as he slept like a stone on the other side of the wall. He reached for a towel before noticing a flash of red in the mirror. Logan looked down and found a horizontal gash ripping down the back of his right forearm. *There won't be any bruises. There isn't anything left to bruise*, he thought and was amazed that it was so deep.

There was a first aid kit in the common room, so he grabbed it and some liquor, just in case. He was able to locate gauze and tape, but the antiseptic he found was more suited for a paper cut than this jagged tear. Resigned, he uncapped the bottle, took a large gulp, and doused his wound, all the while cursing and blaming the Jäger.

"What did you *do* last night, dude? Kill somebody?" Rob roused him at ten. "There's blood *all* over the place, and the trail leads right up here to you."

"No. I didn't kill anybody. And stop yelling. My head feels like a grand piano fell on it," Logan said from under his pillow.

"Spoken like a man who can't hold his Jäger. But where'd you put the body? I need to dispose of it before the cops pin us all."

"Norton, I *told* you. I didn't kill anybody. That's all my blood. I fell and cut the crap outta my arm when I was getting wood for the fire."

"As long as I don't end up in Sing Sing," Rob replied and then was gone. But it was too late. Logan was conscious, and with his head in its current condition, there was no way he was getting any more sleep. Plus, his mouth was like the Sahara, and he was cold again. He needed some aspirin, a hot shower, and a soft woman to cure what ailed him, so he clawed out of the sheets and willed himself back to reality.

When he got downstairs, he had to admit that Rob was right. There were little drips of blood everywhere in the cabin. Well, he couldn't blame *that* on the Jäger, so he poured a glass of water and got to work. No girl he'd ever met would have any desire to hang around a place that could pass as a crime scene. It was still his twenty-first birthday, after all, and as lame as it had been so far, he wanted to be sure he ended his first day of legal adulthood on a major high.

Logan and Andrew lucked out when they hit the slopes. Andrew found two bunnies on the ski lift, and Logan found one of his own on the slalom. He wasn't so much in it for the competition as the girls who competitive glory could get him. The fact that he'd beaten Andrew on the downhill three times made up for the slight advantage Andrew's genes gave him over Logan. And when it was getting too dusky to see the trails, Logan brought Mark something to snuggle with too. Much to Mark's delight, she was a redhead.

They were in the common area, shedding the extra layers of their clothing since they didn't need them to insulate against the snow any longer. Rob was disgruntled by being the odd-man-out and because Andrew wouldn't share the spoils, but that didn't mean the rest of them couldn't have a good time while Rob sulked in his scotch.

"*I'll* get the wood this time," Mark volunteered with a nudge at Logan. "Wouldn't want you to hurt yourself again, man! I still don't see why you went out in the woods when the pile is right here," he called from his position just to the right outside the door.

"I told you I was plastered. And it made sense at the time," Logan shrugged and sent a wink to Jenny who'd been hanging on him since he won his second race with Andrew several hours earlier. She was small and had dark, glossy hair and brown eyes that reminded Logan of a good brandy.

"What did he mean, 'hurt yourself again?'" she wondered as she filled a small pot with water for hot chocolate.

"Oh, nothing. Michaels just had so much to drink last night that he couldn't find the wood pile three feet from him and decided to trek into the forest to get some. And while he was stumbling around in the brush, he lost some skin, that's all," Andrew laughed.

"Do we have any marshmallows?" Tara, one of Andrew's girls, wanted to know as she stood on her toes to see into the upper shelf of the cabinet. "Ah, here they are," she answered herself and pulled the bag down. "Speaking of accidents in the woods, did you guys hear about what happened here about two weeks ago?"

"No. What?" Logan saw an opportunity for a subject change and went for it.

"Well, I wasn't here when it happened, but I read an article about it in the local paper," Tara said. "Jenny, Megan, were y'all here then?" When the other girls shook their heads, she grinned and slid onto the counter to tell her story. "Two weeks ago, there was a youth group that had come here for a long weekend. They checked in on Friday, just like they were supposed to, but they never showed up on the slopes the next morning. So some of the lodge employees went to check on them about noon. When they knocked, there was no answer, and when they went in, the whole group was dead. Seven bodies all torn to pieces."

"Uh-huh," Rob's tone wiped the excitement of the story off her face.

"It's true," Katie, the other of Andrew's girls, agreed. "The only person's body that wasn't found was this one little girl's. Her clothes were all shredded, but there was no body and not a speck of her blood to be found anywhere."

"Well, who do they think killed 'em?" Mark asked.

"Not *who*, but *what*." Tara was glad to continue. "The paper said it looked like a wolf had done it."

"Really. Could a wolf kill *that* many people?" Rob was skeptical again.

"I wouldn't be asking whether a wolf could actually kill all those people, bro," Andrew interrupted. "Wolves are wild animals, so if they were unarmed, then, yeah, I'd say a wolf could kill 'em. What I *would* be asking is *how* the wolf got into the cabin in the first place. It isn't like wolves have opposable thumbs."

"That's true," Logan accepted a cup of cocoa from Jenny and patted the place next to him on the couch. When Jenny snuggled into him with her own cup, he looked down at her with a hint of humor in his face. "The big, bad wolf sure couldn't knock on the door and come right in."

"That's what they can't figure out," Tara shook her head. "They've searched all over the woods and can't find a body or a wolf that's acting crazy enough to have done it."

"It's kinda creepy to me," Megan shivered as she sat next to Mark. On cue, he slid an arm around her shoulders. Logan barely covered his snicker of surprise that Mark'd actually made some sort of move on his own. He did glance at Logan a little too obviously, seeking his approval, which lost Mark the one and only point he'd scored thus far less than five seconds after he'd earned it.

Logan almost laughed again when Jenny squeezed a bit closer, but he caught himself. "*You're* not scared too, are you?" he breathed in her ear.

"Not if *you're* here," she whispered back.

"Kill me now," Rob groaned in disgust and downed another glass.

It was decided that they were eating chili for dinner since there were eight people, and one pot would still be plenty, even with Mark eating. Because he was the only one who was dateless, Rob was chosen to go to the store for supplies.

"I'll go," he finally groused, "but I'm getting a little something extra for me for my troubles, and I'm putting another bottle of scotch on your tab." When the other three began to protest, he held up a hand. "I've gotta entertain myself somehow tonight."

When Rob returned with groceries in tow, the guys stoked the fire in the hearth, and the girls set out to make the chili. Since stoking didn't take as long as cooking, Rob suggested they play a few hands of five-card while they waited on the girls and grub. Logan figured Rob was trying to win back the hundred he'd lost the night before, but that didn't mean Logan wasn't willing to take him up on it and try to get even more of Rob's cash. As this was his only form of retaliation against Rob's caustic attitude, he felt no remorse about bleeding him dry. It was just too bad that his trust-fund padding wouldn't let him feel a thing.

Five rounds later, Rob and Mark were the last men standing. The chili was ready, and the others had crowded around to watch how the last cards fell. It was clear that the group was pulling for Mark, but Rob was all ice, like Val Kilmer in *Top Gun*. That was how he'd systematically eliminated Logan and Andrew. It was Mark's sheer ignorance of the game and subsequent unpredictability that had saved him until now.

Rob had checked, and now it was up to Mark to call or fold. Mark looked nervously at Logan and Andrew as he tried to decide what to do. Logan saw that all the boy had was an ace-10. The problem was the odds of Rob having the higher hand, and there was no way that Mark could bluff Rob into folding at this stage. His ever-present aviator shades didn't help the situation at all. If it was Logan, he would have called; then again, he would have been more likely to be able to bluff Rob, but Mark couldn't poker up the way Logan could, and the appearance of Rob's smirk after a minute or two's deliberation seemed to say that he was smelling death. Rob cleared his throat. "Since we're all hungry, let's make this a little easier. The only way you can beat me is with an ace-10, so why don't you just fold, and we can all go eat some chili?"

To Mark's credit, he didn't throw his cards down on the table and reach for the $400. He stacked his cards neatly and laid them face down. "Call," he said flatly.

"I tried to be nice, man," Rob shook his head and turned his cards over, then reached for the pot.

"Don't you wanna see my hand, Norton?" the tone of Mark's voice had Rob's hand stopping inches over the chips.

"Fine. Show me," Rob seemed unconcerned as Mark spread out his cards face-up, revealing a winning hand.

"Sorry, bro. Sucks to be you," Mark grinned at last and swept up the chips, then started stacking them into their rows in the case. Rob had been silent since Mark's reveal, and now he tossed his cards in Mark's direction, grabbed his bottle off the counter, and went upstairs.

The minute Rob's footsteps faded from the stairs, the girls brought in glasses, and they toasted Mark's victory with Jäger and Raspberry Sparkletini. When the table was cleared of poker chips and everyone had a bowl, they served and ate the chili. If their laughter or the smell of food floated up to Rob, he made no concessions, and once they'd all eaten their fill, they were too busy with each other to be concerned about him.

After roasting marshmallows in the fireplace and cuddling on the couches for a while, it became clear that the girls were planning to spend the night. Logan got up to refill the girls' glasses and found that Mark had followed him into the kitchen.

"Pretty smooth in there, Card Shark," Logan gave him a punch as he reached for the bottle of wine.

"Yeah. I think it was beginner's luck," he shook his head.

"There's no such thing, man. You just played the odds and won because they were in your favor. Eighty percent of the game is bluffing, and 100 percent of bluffing is reading other people."

When Logan would have headed for the common room again, Mark's hand on his shoulder stopped him. "I-I was just wondering . . . how, how much did you get for me?"

Logan read the desperation Mark was trying to hide and sent him a smile. "Only got you dinner, Malone. The rest you got for yourself."

"You mean I-I, she didn't promise she'd stay over?" he couldn't hide the hope now.

"The deal I cut with Jen was that she could bring a friend along and that they'd stay at least for dinner. They've held up their end, and it doesn't look like they have any plans to leave tonight," Logan tilted his head in the direction of the doorway where they could see Megan curled up with her feet tucked under the couch cushion. "Looks like her feet are getting cool. Don't you think you oughta go in there and get them warm again?" he raised a brow before grabbing the glasses and moving out of the kitchen. He chuckled when he heard Mark coming right behind. "Everyone's got a tell, bro. You just have to know what it is. Find the tell, and you can call anybody's bluff," Logan slapped Mark's back when his eyes popped at the suggestion.

"Thanks," Mark grinned once he'd recovered. "And by the way, happy birthday, man."

"Oh it will be," Logan grinned back and then went to snuggle with his bunny, hoping his friend could find an ace in the hole.

Chapter 3

Logan came down the stairs the next morning and felt like a rock star. His birthday had gotten off to a pretty pathetic start, but he had to admit that the ending couldn't have been any better. Mark was in the kitchen trying to scrape what seemed to be hopelessly charred egg from a frying pan, so he guessed that Mark had fared the same.

"What were you trying to do, fry all the flavor out of it?"Logan asked as he reached in the cabinet for some cocoa mix.

"Shuttup. Do you know when the last time I made breakfast for a chick was?" Mark waved the spatula as he talked. When Logan shook his head, he continued. "That's because neither do I! If I didn't already owe you a lifetime of gratitude for last night alone, I'd ask you to help me out here, but I'm not sure I like the sound of eternal servitude."

"Tell you what. Why don't you do the dishes for me while we're here, and I'll see what I can do about throwing together a few more omelettes," Logan laughed.

"You're on," Mark agreed.

"But that doesn't cover the lifetime of gratitude," Logan warned as Mark passed him the pan and spatula. "Heard anything from Andrew or Rob?"

"Norton's probably still swimming in his scotch, and I haven't heard a peep from the Italian Stallion, but I figure they've gotta be coming up for air pretty soon. I know he's a legend, but, I mean, it's two against one. How long can one man last?"

Logan shook his head. "I'm not sure. I think he's going for some sort of record."

"I think it's the same with Megan. She's been in the shower for half my life anyway."

"No, dude, that's just girls. Jen woke me up singing Bon Jovi, and I listened to her for a good fifteen minutes before I got up and came down here."

"Maybe they'll get out before the eggs get cold," Mark sighed.

"Oh, they'll be out before I'm done making breakfast, since they're both using up the hot water at the same time," Logan predicted.

He and Mark had a private chuckle when they heard the water shut off upstairs about ten minutes later, and then again when both the girls came downstairs nearly simultaneously twenty or so minutes after that. Logan only grinned when Mark watched the last omelette that Logan deftly scooped out of the pan and onto a plate while the girls leaned on the counter and waited for good morning kisses.

The rest of the week sped past them faster than Andrew went through women. Then it was Friday and their last day at the lodge. They headed out to the slopes to get in as many runs as they could, and even though they had to start loading all their crap that night, Andrew still had a girl in tow, which meant he wasn't going to be doing much packing.

37

"I have a theory," he'd told Logan when they'd gone out for some provisions for the return trip. "Why do it yourself when you can get a chick to do it for you?"

"Because one of these days, Stevenson, you're gonna lose that mojo of yours and be SOL when it comes to the ladies," Logan smirked.

"Lose the mojo? The Italian Stallion? Not possible," he shook his head and reached for his cell, which had just received another text.

"Then why are you flying solo now, bro?"

"Because I was waiting on a text from Katie," he grinned and tapped his phone.

"Dang, dude! You gave her your number? You're never gonna lose her now. I thought you were smarter than that," Logan was surprised that Andrew had made such a rookie mistake, with his godlike skills with the women.

"Of *course* I gave her my phone number. How else was I supposed to ensure she'd be at my beck and call all week otherwise? I just told her that it was a disposable cell I'd gotten for the trip, since my personal one's on roaming up here. And when we leave town, I'll block her number, so she'll never know any different. What's your deal, Michaels? You know this ain't my first rodeo."

"I was just checking. Everything's kinda outta whack up here, you know. I mean, Mark's getting lucky in cards and love . . . it's entirely possible that you could've lost your touch."

"Like I said, Logan, not possible. What about you, Mr. Thirty-one Flavors? Why is it that you've been tasting the same sample all week? You becoming monogamous?" Andrew eyed him with suspicion. "In the immortal words of *Friends'* Joey Tribbiani, 'Grab a spoon!'"

"You're one to talk. Haven't you been with Katie all week, and you're texting her now?" Logan raised a brow. "I've kept Jen around as long as I have because we have a good time together. I didn't see the need in ditching her, just to have to find someone else. I've got no intentions of confining myself to one chick for the rest of my life, but being exclusive for a week's no problem at all. She's got a nice body and a good personality. Plus she's friends with Megan, and that makes things a little easier for Mark."

"So what if I've been with Katie all week? I've been with four other girls besides her. And how often does a guy come across a girl who's willing to share him?"

"Apparently it happens quite often, since you've managed to find five of them," Logan answered.

By the time that they got back to 317 on Sunday morning, all four of the boys were ready for bed. There was nothing like a week of vacation and twenty-six-and-a-half hours on the road to wear a guy out, especially with the way the snow bunnies seemed to multiply, at least for Andrew. So when Mark pulled into the closest parking space to the apartment, they did little more than empty the van of their luggage before crashing until their respective classes the next day.

Logan got out of the shower at a quarter after nine. *Man, I hate Mondays after a break!* he thought as he dried himself and stepped to the sink to shave. As he brought the razor to his cream-covered cheek, he saw the reflection of the cut on his right arm that was beginning to develop a scab. It was deep and wasn't too pretty with its jagged red-brown lines tearing through the lighter flesh. He hadn't really thought much about it since Jen's exclamation the first time she'd pulled back the gauze. He'd let her be the nursemaid a little when they woke up in the mornings and again when they were getting ready to go to bed, though, since he didn't want to get tetanus or gangrene or some other infection that could cause his skin to rot away or his jaw to lock. That would *not* be good for business, since he was pretty sure it would be clinically impossible to make out with lockjaw.

And it seemed to be healing fairly quickly, mostly thanks to Jen's insistence that he pick up some Neosporin and actually use it, which he had to admit, was a much better plan than the one he had that involved dousing it with Jäger every time he changed the bandage. At least hers was a lot less painful. Still, he was betting it would leave a wicked scar, which meant he'd have to come up with a better story than "I got plastered and fell on a log," but he was resourceful; he would think of something.

"Got shoved through a window during a fight," Logan told Amy, a girl from his Marketing class, a few nights later. "The glass doesn't shatter as easy in real life as it does in the movies."

"How many stitches?" she asked with sympathy.

"Didn't go to the hospital," he waved away her flittering hands. "Figured I was gonna be paying out the nose for the Destruction of Private Property fine, so I might as well save several hundred in the ER by fixing it up on my own." He shot Rob a silencing glare when he heard a derisive snort come from that direction.

"Does it hurt much?" she wondered, looking like she wanted to put him to bed and play Florence

Nightingale. Normally Logan wasn't adverse to any woman wanting to put him to bed, but the look in her eyes told him that if he let her, she wouldn't be coming in with him.

"Nope," he grinned and flexed the tendons to prove it.

"Well, I hope the girl was worth it," she said in a brisker tone.

"What girl?"

"The one you went through a window for. But I guess she wasn't, if I'm here with you right now, huh?" her voice shifted again, and now she was almost purring.

"Let's just say there were irreconcilable differences," he grinned and pressed his lips to the soft skin just beneath her ear.

Logan was playing *Call of Duty 3* on the Xbox 360 that Thursday night with Andrew, while Rob was holed up in his room doing who knew what, and Mark was passed out on his bed. It was a rare occurrence that Andrew had a free night, so they hadn't wasted any time getting an Xbox Live game going. They'd elected to go with ranked matches so that they could rack up more player points. Their team was surrounded by a swarm of Axis soldiers and was trying not to get decimated, when there was a knock on the door.

"I didn't think you were expecting any company tonight," Logan told Andrew through his teeth, as his player narrowly missed another bullet.

"I wasn't. It's probably for you," Andrew cut his eyes in Logan's direction and then back to the screen where he watched as his player took a hit.

"I doubt it." Logan pressed pause, since the knocking didn't appear to be going away. He hadn't picked up any girls for the night, and Amy had some sort of report due the next day, so he wasn't expecting anyone until tomorrow night.

As he crossed the room, the knocking became pounding, and a voice called, "UPD! Anybody home?"

"Dang!" Andrew said, as they exchanged looks of alarm.

"COMING!" Logan answered, as he grabbed the knob and opened the door to find two campus police officers on the other side.

"Mark Malone?" the taller of the officers asked.

"No, sir. But he's here. I'll go get him," Logan told them and dashed to Rob and Mark's side of the apartment.

After Logan had banged on Mark's door a couple times, Rob opened his. "What the crap's with all this noise, dude?"

"Cops are—"

"I *knew* it! I *knew* you'd killed somebody up at the lodge," Rob exclaimed with more emotion than Logan had ever heard him use.

"Shuttup. They're looking for Mark," Logan said, as he gave up waiting and went in to drag Mark out of bed.

Five minutes later, Mark was at the door in boxers and a T-shirt, listening as the cops told him that some drunk driver had hit the parked car that was next to his minivan and sent both vehicles crashing into his.

"STELLA!" he screamed, as he ran out to survey the damage.

"He named it Stella?" Andrew questioned. "That sounds like a grandmother! No *wonder* he can't get girls on his own!"

"It's 'Stella the Minivan of Desire.' He thought he was being clever," Logan explained.

"Why is it we couldn't have stayed in Colorado forever?" Mark demanded, after having given his statement and signed all the necessary forms. "I was actually lucky there. I had money and a woman there. We come back home, and I've got no money, no woman, and somehow I'm involved in a traffic accident without even being in a car. This *sucks!*"

"I told you. There's no such thing as luck," Logan told him. "It's all about perspective. When you look at it the way you are now, things do seem pretty rough, but look at it this way: you're not at fault, so there's no ticket on your part, and it sounds like your parents have uninsured motorists coverage, so you're pretty 'lucky' from where I'm standing."

"You wouldn't be saying that if you saw what Stella looks like now. The bumper's barely attached, and the right front fender's probably kissing the engine, as far as it's pushed in!"

"Look, if you've gotta go somewhere between now and the time Stella gets fixed, you can borrow the Camaro or Andrew'll probably let you use his Grand Am. You're good, dude," Logan slapped him on the back. "You just gotta change your perspective a little."

There was absolutely nothing good about Mondays, Logan decided, when he woke up a week after that first Monday back. It wasn't just Mondays after a break, but Mondays altogether. *They should be outlawed for causing cruel and unusual punishment, or violating the Geneva*

Convention, or whatever. He groaned and rolled over.
There was a terrible taste in his mouth, and his back
was killing him. He felt . . . filthy. Like he'd run a
fever during the night and then sweat it off or, God
help him, peed in his bed and slept in it as it dried.
Horrified at the thought, he sat up and found himself
on the floor of his bedroom in 317.

"What the crap?" he hissed as he stood, surveying
the room. The floor and himself were both covered in
mud, leaves, sticks and . . . *Is that grass?* He was
completely naked. *Why the freak am I naked?* He began
to run his fingers through his hair and found that it was
a veritable bird's nest. It was hard too, probably
because it was filled with mud that had hardened as it
dried. He felt what he thought were more sticks and
leaves, but it was like they'd been cemented in. He
tugged, but that crap wasn't coming out. He just hoped
he wouldn't have to resort to a jackhammer to get rid
of it.

He had to think. What the mess had he done last
night? Because trying to remember anything felt like he
was making a hole in his head with a drill bit, he sat on
his bed. That was when he noticed that his sheets, as
well as his mattress, had been slit several times with
what could have been a box cutter. *What the—* and
then he saw that the screen in his window had been
ripped too, and the window was standing three-fourths
of the way open.

Logan couldn't remember whether he'd left it open
the night before or not. Of course, it would help if he
could remember *anything* about the night before. He
wished that he could blame it on the Jäger again, but
this time, he couldn't remember if he'd even had any.
All right, man. This is getting a bit ridiculous, don't you think?

he thought, as he looked around for an empty bottle. *Losing a couple hours is one thing, but a whole night? That's a good way to die of alcohol poisoning.*

He checked the digital clock on his night stand. It was six in the morning on April second. *Talk about an April Fool's joke.* After realizing that he wasn't going to figure anything out by sitting on his ruined bed, butt-naked and covered in dirt, he went to take a shower. He'd deal with his jackass roommates after that.

Chapter 4

He was lying on the couch, flipping through the channels, waiting for those slackers to get up so he could vacuum his room. He'd already thrown his sheets away and found his spare set in the front closet. Once the others got up, he could get the floor clean, flip his mattress over and get back in bed. The problem was, by the time all that happened, his alarm would be going off anyway. Disgusted with the entire situation as well as the fact that even with nearly a hundred channels, there wasn't a single thing to watch at six thirty in the morning, Logan turned the TV off and rolled onto his side, facing the back of the couch and tried to calm down enough to sleep.

That was where Mark found him an hour later. "Dude. What're you doing in here this early in the morning? I didn't think you had class until ten on Monday, Wednesday, Friday."

"I don't. That's why I'm trying to sleep, you moron," Logan said into the couch.

"Wouldn't that work better if you tried it in your own bed?"

"You'd think so, wouldn't you?" Logan turned his face to Mark with the question. "Why don't you take a peek in my room and see why that might not be such a good idea?"

Mark shrugged and disappeared. "*What* happened in here, bro?" Logan heard him ask a few seconds later and knew that he'd done it.

"I dunno, man. I was kinda hoping that maybe you could give me a clue," Logan nearly shouted.

"How the heck am I supposed to know? I don't even live on this side of the apartment!" Mark retorted.

"All I know is I woke up at six this morning on the floor, and covered in mud. My bedroom looked just like it does right now, except I've already thrown away what was left of my sheets."

"Well, don't look at me. I haven't been to your side in days," Mark turned his hands up in a gesture of confusion. "I dunno what to tell you."

"It looks to me like somebody thought it would be funny to play a prank on me, and seeing as how I don't think anybody could get in and out of the window, even if it was wide open, and the living room doesn't seem to have been broken into, I have to guess that it was one of you three. Why you, in particular, would find this situation even remotely funny escapes me, but you never know," Logan sat up and crossed his arms.

"I've told you before: I owe you a lifetime of gratitude. Why would I go and screw you and risk the great gig I've got goin' over some teenage prank?"

"Beats me, but somebody did it," Logan repeated.

"Well, that somebody sure wasn't me," Mark went to grab some milk and Cap'n Crunch.

When Logan asked Andrew about it just before he left for class, he felt like an even bigger jerk than when he'd talked to Mark. Andrew had been curious about why Logan, who always had a girl willing to do his chores for him, would be vacuuming his bedroom floor on a Monday morning, and like the proverbial cat, he'd soon come to regret that curiosity.

"WHAT DO YOU THINK I'M DOING?" Logan didn't bother checking his tone. The noise of the vacuum was already loud, and he didn't happen to find the prank amusing in the least. "I'm running the vacuum for the fun of it!"

"Jeez, man! It's just a question. Don't go all PMS on me here!" Logan ignored Andrew's insult and cleaned a particularly dirty patch of the carpet instead of punching him in the face. "What in the world happened here?" So Andrew had finally gotten a good look at the mess.

"You," Logan spat.

"Me? Just how do you figure I made that big of a mess in here, if I spent most of last night with Lucy and the rest of it with Steph?" his voice hardened with Logan's accusation.

"You are a god. You've probably got magical powers and can be in two places at once," there was no humor in Logan's tone.

"I'm a legend, not a supernatural being. And besides that, I only use my powers for—well, bad example. Anyway, why would I wanna waste the night doing some juvenile crap like this when I could be spending it like a man? Think about it, Logan."

So he did, and he knew that Andrew was right. That only left Rob, and Logan didn't plan on confronting him, thereby giving him a chance to deny he'd done it. He would find a way to get even with Rob for this and all the other annoying crap he'd put Logan through since the beginning of the semester. This was going to be sweet.

For the second night in a row, Logan woke up on his bedroom floor, and this time it wasn't any better. He still couldn't remember what he had done the night before, but he knew good and well that he hadn't touched a drop of alcohol. He wasn't going to let himself be vulnerable to any more of Rob's mischief until he'd had a chance to retaliate.

But something wasn't right. He was stone sober as far as he knew, and he was still on the floor. The room wasn't as trashed as it had been the night before, and neither was his bed, which was good, since the mattress only had two sides he could lie on, but there was still mud caked on the floor and all over him. He wondered for a second if the déjà vu he was feeling was only part of a dream, but then he remembered that people don't usually have blinding headaches in the middle of their dreams about their lives repeating themselves.

He got up and headed for the shower, all the while trying to recall what he had done the night before. But he couldn't remember anything after about seven thirty. He'd eaten a burrito from a build-your-own place not too far from campus and then gone back to 317 to study for a test he had in Advanced Database Management, which he'd done for about an hour or so and then everything went blank.

He obviously hadn't had a girl over, since there was no one screaming her head off anywhere in the apartment, and that was a plus, but it was still annoying that he'd lost two nights running. As he rinsed his hair, he felt his scalp to see if there were any bumps that might be the cause of all this amnesia. There was nothing.

It wasn't as if he'd had some sort of superhuman computer-like memory in the past, and it wasn't like he hadn't ever blacked out after a drinking binge, but he usually remembered *something* about the experience. Like his birthday. He knew he was wasted, and there were parts of the night that were a little hazy or even missing altogether, but he vividly remembered the feeling of being soaked with snow and the freezing walk back to the cabin. Yet when Logan tried to bring back any memories from the last two nights, he was at a loss.

By Wednesday morning, Logan was getting extremely frustrated. It was the third night this had happened, and no matter how he asked Rob, the creep consistently claimed to be just as ignorant about it as his other roommates. For reasons that he couldn't explain, or didn't care to figure out, he was willing to accept Mark's and Andrew's stories, but couldn't exonerate Rob in his mind. There was no way it could be anyone *but* Rob, with the other two eliminated. The only part he couldn't figure out was: how Rob was doing it. Logan had purposefully avoided liquor since Monday morning, so he couldn't be spiking the booze. Logan also wasn't taking any cold or allergy meds, so that was out too. It looked like it was coming down to food, and Logan worked to remember what he had eaten or drunk at the apartment that he hadn't seen the other guys eat or drink.

It had to be the Gatorade! Logan kept a canister of orange Gatorade in powder form in 317 at all times. It was cheaper to mix it yourself than to buy it bottled, and he also thought the flavor was better when it was homemade. *Why didn't I think of it before?* Logan mentally smacked himself. Rob was probably spiking his Gatorade with GHB or roofies or some other drug, and how was he going to know the difference? He wasn't. He had to admit that it was a pretty clever trick, as he picked up his razor and grinned at his own reflection. Rob may have won these past three rounds, but that didn't mean Logan couldn't make a comeback, and there was nothing better than an unexpected rally to bring about some sweet, sweet revenge.

Logan purposefully drank only water all day on Wednesday, except when he walked over to the coffee house and bought a couple cans of double shots just to ensure that he could stay awake. He definitely didn't touch the contaminated Gatorade. When seven thirty was approaching, Logan popped the top on the first of his double shots and chugged like he was a freshman during rush. He'd also called Lindsey, a girl he'd met at one of the Greek formals last fall. He needed company to ensure he didn't get blitzed when Rob found out that he was onto him, besides, it had been way too long since he'd had a girl over . . . he thought.

Logan awoke triumphantly at seven thirty on Thursday to the pleasing sensation of lying on a bed and being wrapped in sheets and the arms of a girl and with the memory of the entire night playing through his head. *Who's the man now???* he laughed to himself before leaning over and kissing Lindsey awake.

When he took a shower that morning, the water that pooled at his feet was not brown with mud. It felt extremely good not to have to work at getting the dirt off himself and out of his hair after three days of doing it, just like it also felt good when he walked across his floor after his shower and didn't have to avoid piles of leaves and whatever else he'd had to vacuum up every morning since Sunday. Instead of having to clean a pigsty, he was free to make eggs-in-a-window. He was so happy about his victory that when Mark got up about an hour after Lindsey had gone, Logan offered to make him breakfast too, at no obligation.

"Wow, man. Maybe you should give Lindsey a call more often," Mark told him around a bite of toast. "You're in a pretty awesome mood."

"Yeah, I guess I am," Logan agreed. "But it doesn't a have much to do with Lindsey."

"Sure," Mark grinned. "You just happened to get up on the right side of the bed this morning, since the other side was taken."

"Don't get me wrong. Lindsey's great, but that's not the reason," Logan said again.

"Then what is it? 'Cause you've been walking around here like you were the victim of a conspiracy theory or something."

"Well, dude, I was beginning to think I was, but I've got it under control now," he smiled slowly, and the menace in his expression had Mark pulling back fractionally.

"Remind me never to get on your bad side, bro," Mark shook his head.

When Logan went to the library for his required hour later that afternoon, he had an eye out for any new chicks he might be able to snag. Since he'd been preoccupied by Rob's evil scheme, he hadn't really done much socializing, and he thought it was time to bring in some more girls to party with. He'd invited Lindsey, of course, but they both knew she'd only come last night because she was bored, and he was looking for a good time. She had other plans by the time she'd walked out his door, and that was the good thing about her. With

Lindsey, you got what you saw; there were no messy strings to get tangled in or hang yourself with.

He texted Andrew and Mark, and they were both up for a little fun, especially since they hadn't gotten together with a group since before Spring Break. Some people were probably wondering if they were still alive. Well, he'd prove that he was tonight. All he had to do now was find a few girls to invite and make sure they brought along a few of their hottest friends.

He passed a couple chicks as he went inside, but they were the typical brainy girls who tended to live in the stacks, like the books were their source of life or something. Not that there was anything wrong with a smart girl. There wasn't. Logan just preferred that the girl he was with looked at him when she was talking instead of walking around with her eyes glued to some printed page. Plus, smart chicks were just intimidating, the way they stared at you over their glasses like you were some kind of alien intruder who was incapable of forming logical statements. They had this way of pinning you, the way some high school teachers did, their eyes boring holes into you and filling you with embarrassment, while simultaneously robbing you of all intelligent thought. It gave him the creeps, which was why he jumped as he felt that particular stare on him at that very moment.

He willed the redness from his cheeks as he turned to face her. She was sitting behind the circulation counter, pretending to look at a clipboard she was holding in front of her, but Logan knew that it was just a prop. He was well versed in the art of watching women, and he knew fake disinterest when he saw it. Besides, she was the only one behind the counter, so it had to be her eyes that he'd felt.

She had stick straight hair that was a river of ink falling past her shoulders, but it was uneven on the ends, as if odd pieces of the puzzle were missing. He couldn't see the color of her eyes, as she seemed to be reading, but he bet they were as sharp as her chin. She was small and thin, but the set of her mouth told him that she could hold her own when the need arose. If he had found her in any other setting, he would have approached her, but he knew how intense the studious ones were and decided to back off. Yet, even as the thought formed in his mind, it rang of weakness, and he hated that.

He'd just have to pretend to be the Italian Stallion for a few minutes. Stevenson had never met a woman who intimidated him. If he liked her looks, he would make a move, and 98 percent of the time, he scored. According to him, the other two percent was not his fault, since it was comprised of those who were taken and monogamous or those who weren't attracted to guys.

Logan took a minute and then walked up to the girl behind the desk. When his shadow fell over the page she was looking at, she met him with a professional smile and forest green eyes. "Can I help you?"

"Yeah. I don't mean to bother you, but I had to come over and introduce myself. Otherwise, I'll be kicking myself for days."

"I know who you are," she answered as that practiced smile of hers disappeared. "Logan Michaels. Since I've saved you the trouble, you can leave now."

It took him a moment to process the situation. Rejection wasn't a common reaction; still, it happened to him a little more often than two percent of the time.

"Thanks. I owe you one," he nodded politely as he headed for the study room without turning back.

That evening 317 was packed to capacity. Andrew had made a couple calls, and Logan had found a few friends while he was doing his time in the library. Mark had left his touch back in Breckenridge; thus, he was no help getting girls, and Rob wasn't even consulted, seeing as the chances of him getting a girl were slimmer than the chances of him getting a personality. The scene was a familiar one, as Logan searched for a place to sit and was once again forced out onto the hammock on the balcony, but he hadn't minded then, and he didn't mind now. It was April, and the weather was nice as he swung slightly with the wind.

The sun was setting, and he watched as it went. It was a great end to a good day, and he couldn't see how anything would spoil it. He'd gotten hold of Renée, and a night with her was always a pleasure. And to top it off, some of the girls were cooking, and it smelled like fajitas, but he wasn't sure and didn't care to venture into the kitchen to find out. It would be good, whatever it was because someone else had made it. Cleaning up 317 tomorrow would be a small price that he would definitely be willing to pay.

When Renée came to find him a little later, he had dozed off. Her lips grazed his cheek, and he awoke with a start, nearly rolling out of the hammock and knocking her over, but he caught himself and her before disaster struck.

"A little jumpy aren't you?" she asked as he got his balance again and took his hand from her torso.

"Roommates," he shook his head. "Can't live with 'em. Not supposed to shoot 'em."

She laughed as he'd expected, and then he let her coax him out of the hammock and back into the apartment.

Chapter 5

The next few weeks seemed to pass overnight, since Logan had assignments and projects due in all four of the classes he was taking. When he'd signed up for twelve hours, it had seemed like a light load. But now that the end of the semester was approaching, he began to regret his decision, even though going below twelve meant that he no longer would have had enough hours to live on campus. As long as he could make it a few more days and survive finals, he would be good.

Everyone teased him about how easy it was to be a business major and how that was the one people chose when they couldn't hack it with anything else. Sometimes Logan conceded that those people had a point, but not at the moment. It was times like these, too, when he fancied he might see a glimmer of wisdom in requiring Greeks to log all those hours in the library studying, if they actually spent that time studying instead of texting, Facebooking or surfing the net on their phones. If he'd actually done that, maybe he wouldn't be in the library right now, looking for last minute sources for his final project in Marketing. But here he was, in the stacks on a Thursday, long after his compulsory hour was over, and unless four more sources magically materialized in front of him, he didn't see himself leaving anytime soon.

He sighed as he sat down at the nearest computer and accessed the electronic card catalogue, hoping that if he typed in a few key words, it might give him some useful call numbers. Obviously reference books were not a going to help. The computer listed three books under the criteria he entered, so he shuffled through his bag for some scratch paper and a pen.

A few minutes later, he was scanning the shelves, praying that those titles hadn't been taken off the shelf and were sitting somewhere, waiting to be put away; but after finding his section and scouring it three or four times, he was beginning to think that that was exactly what happened, and if it was, he was screwed because this project (including all ten academic references) had to be turned in in less than twenty-four hours. He wanted to pace, but checked the reflex and continued to read the numbers, methodically checking to make sure he hadn't overlooked anything.

"Can I help you?" the voice behind Logan would have startled him had he not felt her stare seconds before she spoke.

"I think I've got it covered, thanks," he answered without turning. If she wanted to play it cool, he'd show her cool.

"All right." Logan waited at least two minutes after she'd spoken before turning around, just to make sure the girl was gone, and when he did and saw that she had indeed disappeared, he felt a twinge of disappointment, or was that regret? Regret. That's what it was. He regretted the fact that he'd sent her away, even though she could help him find the stupid books tons faster than he could alone, since he obviously had no idea how to use the library's reference system. But what was he supposed to do? The chick had been so cold to him that time at the circulation desk that he couldn't just ignore it. *But are you even sure that it was the same girl? Dangit!* He shook his head and went after her, taking a chance that she might only be a few shelves over.

He only had to backtrack once to find her. As he'd hoped, she hadn't gotten very far. He approached her and had no idea what he would say that could improve the situation at all. Still, he was a man, and he could swallow his pride if need be. He might choke on it, but it could be done.

"I changed my mind," he shrugged when she looked at him with those sharp eyes of hers. "Is the offer still good?"

"It shouldn't be," she told him tonelessly, "but since it's part of my job, I guess it can be. What books are you looking for?"

"These," he handed her the list he'd jotted down. She gave it a cursory glance and moved to a different section than he'd been searching.

She quickly selected the ones he needed and handed them to him. "Anything else I can help you with?"

"There is one thing. . ." he made himself say before he could stop himself.

"And that is?"

"The only thing your eyes haven't told me. Your name," he replied, hoping she would be a little more receptive than she had been before.

"Persistent aren't you, Michaels?" she cocked a brow. "Unfortunately, helping you find that information *isn't* part of my job," she gave him a cruel smile and walked away.

Dead Day. It was the perfect time for revenge. He held his breath as he tugged on the edge of Rob's mattress. It scooted a bit, and Rob never stirred. "Okay, Mark," Logan whispered, as Mark moved over to Rob's feet and lifted that end of Rob's sheet at the same time that he lifted his end of it. They crept out of Rob's room and into the corridor, with Logan walking backwards and Mark going forwards. He was taking no chances that Mark's uncoordinated feet might find something to fall over and ruin the entire scheme. Next, they carried him across the living room and to the door that Logan had already opened all the way. All they had to do now was get him down two flights of stairs and into Stella, and they were good to go.

Mark had already folded down the back rows of seats to create a flat surface that they could put Rob on, and Stella was running, so all they had to do was put him inside, get in, and go. The situation inside the van was tense. Mark was petrified that Rob would wake up, so the entire time he was driving, he was giggling hysterically. Logan wanted to slap Mark, but he didn't want to get into a wreck and have to explain their comatose cargo to the cops. Instead, he kept an eye on Rob and Mark's driving so that they didn't get lost and wind up taking the long way around to University Plaza. Of course, keeping an eye on Rob was sort of superfluous since he'd had three times as much Jäger that night as he normally drank (because he didn't normally drink *anything* but scotch) due to Logan challenging him to a drinking contest which Logan subsequently threw. With that much Jäger in his system, Rob would be lucky if he saw the sun at all the next day.

Rob was snoring like a pig lying out in the sunshine when they parked on the side of the library and hauled him to the grassy lawn in front of it and the food court. Logan had purposefully planned ahead and brought an inflated twin air mattress so that Rob would be up off the ground and thus more likely to sleep there longer. He hoped that Rob wouldn't wake up until sometime tomorrow morning, when an unsuspecting girl was on her way to the food court for breakfast and started screaming her head off when she saw a dude passed out in his boxers.

It would be ten times sweeter if he could figure out how to tape it so that he could see Rob's reaction when he woke up and realized what happened, but he didn't want to leave any evidence like a camera lying around that could eventually be used against him by the cops. That was also one of the reasons that he wasn't going to stick around to see the show himself. That and the fact that he had himself a little blonde alibi sleeping in his bed who he was anxious to get back to. So he'd just have to settle for seeing Rob's reaction once he finally made it home from the other side of campus.

He was enjoying a leisurely post-pancake cuddle with Allison when he heard the apartment door open. He had sent Mark to the store with a ridiculously long list of crap that they would need for the next few weeks and knew that he couldn't have returned so quickly. Especially since he'd made sure that some of the items required Mark to make multiple stops, since they all couldn't be found in the same store. Logan was famous for being very finicky about things, and he made sure to reiterate to Mark just how crucial it was for him to get the exact item Logan had put on the list.

Andrew had his own company, and they hadn't even emerged when Logan had knocked on his door and announced that he was making pancakes, and they were invited to breakfast. Logan hadn't expected otherwise, but he invited them anyway to cover his bases and shore up his alibi. So when he heard the door open, he told Allison to get in the shower, as that would be the safest place for her until he could gauge exactly how angry Rob was. He didn't need casualties to screw up his brilliant plan. But Allison was reluctant to leave the bed, and he ended up tossing her into the bathroom and turning the water on with the promise that he'd be back in a few minutes. He could tell by the look on her face that she wasn't too happy about being slung over his shoulder, but if she'd had any idea of what he was protecting her from, he knew she would feel different.

Just as he was shutting the door on her, Logan heard Rob slam the front door, and it was accompanied by a string of expletives that he was sure Allison would be glad she missed. He pretended to have been on his way to the bathroom when Rob's entrance distracted him. "Hey, man. Where've you been? And, dude . . . what happened to your clothes?"

"I have absolutely no freakin' clue, Michaels, but I'm pretty sure you do!"

"What are you talking about, Rob? The last I remember, you dominated with the Jäger, and I let Allison console me after I lost a hundred and fifty bucks," Logan turned his hands up.

"Yeah. You have absolutely no idea how I ended up on an air bed in my boxers in the middle of University Plaza?" Rob was so livid that his face was actually red.

"None whatsoever. I was here all night. You can ask Allison as soon as she gets out of the shower.

Which reminds me . . ." he headed for the bathroom where he could shut the door and laugh all he wanted over the cover of the water. *Revenge is so sweet!*

Logan walked out of his last final on May first and was confident that if he hadn't aced his exams, he'd definitely passed them all, and that was the ultimate goal. Sure, a high GPA was great and looked good on a transcript, but there were other things in life, and he didn't plan on spending any more time hitting the books than was absolutely necessary. He had just over a month of free time between now and the time first summer term started, but as far as his dad knew, there was no such overlap. Which meant that Logan didn't have to go back there until at least Thanksgiving. He would have to make some obligatory calls, but he could deal with those, as long as they staved off actual face-to-face interaction.

Life was good. Rob was going back to his parents' place in a couple days, which meant that he didn't have to worry about any retaliation until the fall, and there would be no one there to kill the buzzes that he and Andrew got, unless the university gave them some totally annoying Asian roomie for the summer who wanted nothing more out of life than to write computer programs all day. And honestly, what were the odds of that?

Mark was going to stay on campus since he was still trying to catch up from a year-and-a-half of slacking, and that would be fun. Logan had to give him props for keeping his cool over the past week. Mark had given some near Oscar-worthy performances in front of both Andrew and Rob, and his good-guy image had him nowhere near the suspect pool. Conversely, Logan was up to his neck in suspicion, but neither Andrew, who totally appreciated his genius, nor Rob, who likely wanted to kill him, could quite figure out how he'd done it. *Life is definitely good*, he smiled as he plopped on the couch to watch *The Bourne Identity* on Fox and begin his Summer Break.

This sucks! was his first conscious thought when Logan recognized the hardness of his bedroom floor beneath the roughness of the cheap carpet the next morning. He opened his eyes and discovered that he was, once again, mud-caked and naked on the floor, despite the fact that he'd thrown out the spiked can of Gatorade and hidden the new one in the back of his closet behind the suits he only wore to Greek formals. And since he hadn't told anybody about the Gatorade in the first place, he didn't understand how Rob knew to look for a new can yet, unless he'd noticed its absence in the cabinet. He mentally smacked himself for that stupid move. *Of course Rob checked the cabinet! He wanted to make sure his plan was still in operation!* Well, Logan couldn't blame anybody but himself for getting punked again, and he couldn't exactly get too upset, since he'd just retaliated in a major way.

He got up and checked his stash of orange powder; it was exactly where it had been, so he left it where it was and went to shower. Then he was going to buy some of the bottled stuff. There was no way Rob could tamper with that and not leave evidence behind.

When Logan got back from the store, Rob had commandeered the TV and was watching *SportsCenter*, so Mark had resorted to reading *The Technician*, NCSU's daily newspaper. Logan read it occasionally in the bathroom, but in situations other than that, he wasn't interested. He didn't even bother with *The News and Observer.* If he couldn't get it on Google News or Facebook, then he didn't waste his time.

He sat in the chair opposite Mark, since the other end of the couch from Rob seemed too dangerous a place to be. He listened to the sports talk pouring from the TV but didn't bother to interpret the sounds into anything meaningful. After several minutes of quiet, Mark let out a huge cackle. "What some people do, I'll never understand!"

"What do you mean?" Logan asked, more out of boredom than interest.

"Well, there's this feature article here that claims that the full moon makes people do crazy crap. And it says that during last month's full moon, some cracker put Kool-Aid in the fountain, another one called 911 just to talk, and somebody else stole the Chancellor's cat. Then they've got this poll they've conducted, seeing as how tomorrow's the full moon for this month, and the top three oddities predicted were: 'Everyone *will* believe it's not butter,' with 12% of the vote; 'The couch on the Kappa Sig porch will actually be moved inside,' with 18%; and an overwhelming 57% of students believe that 'Mr. Fuzzwhiskers (the Chancellor's lost cat) will come back as a zombie.'"

"Well, we know that couch'll be inside if Chet has anything to do with it!" Logan smirked.

"Yeah," Mark laughed. "He's always wanting to move that thing in, and everybody keeps telling him how bad it'll smell after being wet and stuff." He was silent again for a few more minutes and then exclaimed, "Hey! Rob's briefs made the news briefs: 'Last week Rob Norton, junior, was found by campus police, asleep on an air mattress in University Plaza at approximately 9:30 a.m., wearing nothing but boxer shorts. Consumption of large quantities of alcohol is the suspected cause.'"

"Awwww! We should laminate that and put it on the fridge," Logan grinned. Rob's only response was to turn up the volume on the TV.

When Rob packed his Hummer a few hours later and drove away, Logan couldn't say he was sad about it. This way he knew for sure he wouldn't have anymore blackout episodes. To celebrate the occasion, Logan sprung for pizza for the three of them before popping open another bottle of Jäger.

"No!" but his protest was moot because when Logan sat up on Thursday morning with his back aching and his mouth full of grit, he was not in his bed. Rob was gone. How the crap did this keep happening? He stalked off to the shower, determined that he was going to get to the bottom of whatever it was that buttwipe was doing, even if it killed him in the process.

"It would be seriously helpful if you could remember what you did last night, man," Mark yawned from his seat on the couch.

When Logan had gotten out of the shower, he was still so aggravated that he couldn't sleep, and to his way of thinking, since it was about the fifth time this had happened to him, if his roommates really were his friends, they shouldn't be sleeping either. That was how Andrew and Mark had come to be in the living room in their underwear at six thirty in the morning on a day that they didn't have class.

"I *know* that! But knowing that and actually being able to remember what happened are two different things!"

"Stop yelling, Michaels. My head is pounding as it is. The least you could do, since you've dragged us out of bed at such a heinous hour, is to give us a little time to think and a couple swallows of coffee! Jeez!" Andrew retaliated as he took a sip of his dark roast.

"Sorry, but I've had about enough of waking up on the floor and looking like I've been skinny dipping in a mud hole," Logan purposefully made his tone softer.

"I feel you, man. I really do, but if you can't remember anything that happened in the past eleven hours, I don't know how in the crap we're supposed to help you figure this out," Andrew shook his head. "I mean, a heck of a lot of stuff can go down in that span of time."

"What is the absolute last thing you remember doing last night?" Mark wondered.

"I took what was left of my Jäger and went to my room to pass out," Logan replied.

"Ok. Do you remember getting undressed?" Andrew sounded a bit more awake since he'd had several drinks of coffee.

"Yeah. . ."

"Did you normally sleep nude, or in your boxers?" Mark asked.

"Ever since that fire drill Freshman year, I wear boxers if I'm sleeping alone; you *know* that, Mark!"

"I was just checking, dude, dang!" Mark grumbled.

"So, do you remember taking off your boxers?" Andrew ventured.

"No. I took off my shirt and shorts and . . . and . . . that's where it goes blank," he sighed.

"Now we're getting somewhere," Andrew grinned. "I feel kinda like Sherlock Holmes or something!"

"Oh, Lord," Logan covered his face with his hands.

"No, but seriously, man, we've gotta find those boxers. I bet we'll find some sort of clue when we do," Andrew sobered.

"Yeah. Stevenson's got a point, bro," Mark perked up.

"Okay, but I'm beating the crap out of anybody who says anything about it being 'elementary my dear Watson!'" Logan glared at them to make sure they knew he was serious before he led the way to his room.

After thirty minutes of searching, Andrew had the bright idea to look underneath Logan's bed. What he found was a lot of dirt clods and leaves and sticks, and five pairs of boxers, all ripped or torn in someplace or another. "Aha!" he shouted when he'd laid them all out on the floor (as Logan looked murderous at the suggestion that they be put on his bed) and dodged a punch. "There were no previous stipulations made about the exclamation 'aha,'" Andrew reminded Logan. Then the three of them squatted down to get a closer look at the underwear.

"Okay. So they were all torn, which tells me that you weren't consciously removing them because if you were, then you could just slip them off, no harm; no foul," Mark said. "But they weren't all torn at the same place, which doesn't make sense because if one person was responsible for it, you'd think they'd get them off him the same way every time."

"That's a good point," Logan nodded and wondered just how many episodes of *CSI* Mark had watched.

"What do you make of all the mud and crap?" Andrew asked, holding his nose, having evidently gotten too close to the stench for his nostrils to tolerate it.

"At first, I thought maybe Rob was slipping me some roofies or whatever and then trashing me and my room while I was passed out. But Rob's gone now, and I got rid of all the Gatorade I thought he was spiking, so unless he somehow got into my alcohol or something, I've got no idea how he did it. And besides, he left yesterday afternoon, *before* I blacked out." Logan shrugged.

"I dunno either, dude," Andrew shook his head. "Unless maybe you sleepwalk or something."

"If that was it, wouldn't he sleepwalk every night, though?" Mark pointed out.

"Well, maybe there's some sort of trigger. Like every time a certain thing happens, you sleepwalk," Andrew added.

"So, what did you do last night that you also did the night before?"

"Uh, all I know is, I ate pizza, drank Jäger and passed out." Logan sighed.

"Did you eat pizza and/or drink Jäger the night before?" Mark pressed.

"No. I watched *The Bourne Identity*, ate some taco Hamburger Helper and drank orange Gatorade, and passed out," Logan shook his head. For a second there, it had looked promising, but even Mark, who seemed to be Grissom's protégée, had failed him.

Logan was not any happier when he woke up on Friday morning, and neither were Mark and Andrew who consequently got woken up.

"We gotta figure this out," Andrew mumbled. "I'm getting sick of losing sleep just because Michaels didn't get any."

"Uh-huh," Mark agreed while rubbing his eyes.

"Will the two of you stop whining and help me think? The faster we figure this mess out, the faster you can go back to sleep," Logan reminded them.

"It's too late, man. I'm awake *now*," Andrew told him. "So, the only incentive I have is to figure it out before this time tomorrow."

"Actually, your incentive should be to figure it out before I bust in on you and some chick one morning because it's happened again," Logan corrected.

"That might not be good for your rep," Mark grinned as Andrew's face became serious. You didn't mess with Andrew's mojo. It would be like taunting a Doberman.

"But it's hard to think when you haven't eaten," Andrew complained.

"Fine. I'll pop some Eggos in the toaster," Logan headed to the kitchen.

The three of them were fighting for their lives in the middle of Germany, a few hours later, when Mark threw down his controller without pausing their game. Amid cries of annoyance, he announced, "What if it has something to do with the phases of the moon?"

"What the crap are you talking about, Malone? We're trying to play here!" Andrew seemed incensed.

"Man, forget *COD* for a sec and listen. What if Logan's blackouts are related to the moon?"

"What? Like I'm a crazy person now?" Logan demanded.

"Not crazy exactly, just somehow or other affected by the lunar cycle. Like the tides or whatever," Mark explained. "Think about it. If we rule Rob out as a suspect, then you have to look for some other trigger, which could either be internal or external. I happen to think that since you haven't eaten or drunk anything that could have caused blackouts (other than the Jäger, which usually doesn't affect you like that), the said trigger is likely to be external. And what more obvious external trigger is there besides the moon?"

"Who says we're ruling out Rob?" Andrew threw his hands up. "If we rule him out, then that leaves us, and I don't like to say it, but *I* sure wouldn't keep doing crap to Logan for kicks if it was going to deprive me of sleep. So that just leaves you," he pointed at Mark. "Are you sure you wanna rule out Rob?"

"I don't think we have a choice, bro. I mean he's not even in town! How could he be responsible for this, if he's miles away at his parents' place? Granted, he *was* here Tuesday night, so he *could* be responsible for that time, except that it kept happening after he left. So how do you explain yesterday and today?"

"Maybe he paid somebody?" Logan suggested. "I'm with Andrew. I don't buy the moon theory at all. If the moon was making me black out, I'd have been blacking out my whole life. So that can't be it."

"Yeah, he paid somebody to use his key to sneak in here and drag Logan outta bed, then strip him down and cover him with dirt; all the while, the three of us slept like statues and didn't hear a sound. That's *waaay* more logical than blaming it on the moon, which people have done for centuries, I might add. I mean, where do you think we get the word 'lunacy', for Pete's sakes?"

"Okay. Let's say, hypothetically, that I buy your 'Moon Unit' theory," Andrew began to crawfish when he saw how heated Mark was getting. "Why now? And why not every single night? And why did the blackouts stop the last time when Logan caught on to Rob's trick with his Gatorade?"

"Well, I'm not positive, but I'm pretty sure that Logan's reaction has something to do with a certain stage in the cycle, and that's why the blackouts don't happen every night."

"So, if we figure out what cycle the moon's in right now, then maybe we've found the trigger," Logan finished. "But that still doesn't explain why they've only been happening in the past several weeks. I mean, if it really is connected to the cycles of the moon, then I should have been reacting this way to whatever part of the cycle for my whole life, and I obviously haven't."

"I didn't say the theory was perfect. I just said it made more sense than Stevenson's." Mark picked up his controller, and they resumed their Xbox game.

When he woke up in his bed on Saturday morning, Logan relished the feel of the mattress beneath him. There were those days when he first came to NCSU when he really hated them, but now he gladly accepted the firmness and the odd spring that poked at him when he laid a certain way and went back to sleep.

The second time he woke up that morning, the sun was sneaking through the slits in his blinds, and he decided that to stay in bed any longer was criminally negligent, seeing as how it was officially Summer Break. He wandered to the kitchen to find a bowl of Cap'n Crunch and found that Mark and Andrew were up, and had been for a while, since neither of them was yawning or using their coffee mug as a lifeline.

"'S up?" he asked as he opened the cabinet and reached for the cereal box.

"Since I didn't hear otherwise, I take it you woke up in your bed all nice and clean," Andrew stopped flipping channels and looked at Logan momentarily.

"Sure did," he answered as he poured milk on top of his cereal and put the jug back in the door of the fridge.

"Does that mean we're in the clear?" Andrew raised a brow, "Because I'd really like to keep sleeping in until Summer I starts."

"I really hope so," Logan answered as he crunched.

But Logan hadn't put the ordeal out of his mind that quickly. He'd done that last time, and he didn't plan on making the same mistake twice. This time, he was going to do a little recon and be prepared for whatever it was, whenever it decided to resurface.

Step one of his plan was to figure out the dates of all the blackouts he'd had so far, and that wasn't too hard because he already knew the dates for the past three days, and he remembered that the last time it had happened, it had been around April Fool's, which is what he'd attributed it to in the first place. *Was it before or after? Or was April Fool's smack in the middle?*

Why hadn't he thought of writing the dates down? Probably because all he was thinking about at the time was how to get back at Rob or getting clean and back in the bed. Anyhow, he knew that there were three days close to the beginning of April and now three days at the beginning of May. Maybe Mark was onto something, not that he thought Mark was right about the moon thing, but maybe it was all about timing and that timing had something to do with the beginning of the month for the past two.

Now that he had something to go on, Logan headed to the library to do research, something he abhorred and normally put off until the very last second. But in this case, the last second was the second before he blacked out again, and he did not want it coming down to that. He settled at a table in the reference section and started looking at any information he could find about body changes that might cause blackouts and/or sleepwalking. He'd done some preliminaries on the Internet, but there was always the issue of site credibility, and he didn't have time to waste with misinformation. Logan had a rather large and growing pile of books on the table he'd settled at and was reading one of them intently.

"So you've decided to retaliate by making me shelve tons of books?" her question had Logan jumping before he turned to find the dark-haired girl who refused to tell him her name.

"And if I have? There's nothing you can do about it. I'm a student, and I pay the library fee same as everyone else. I could pull down every book on this floor if I wanted to, and you'd have to put them all back up because *that's* your job," he gave her a cocky grin and returned to his book on hormonal changes.

"Maybe I could help you find whatever it is you're looking for without having to scour all these tomes," she spoke again, and when he looked up, she met his eyes with a warmer smile than he'd ever seen her wear.

"And let you make your life easier? Why would I be interested in an arrangement like that?"

"Let's just say it would be a mutually beneficial arrangement. I could save you lots of time and eye-strain finding what you want, and then you could get back to your keg." Her smile was still appealing, even as he felt the acid drip off her words.

"What makes you think I've got a keg to get home to?" he heard the appalled tone he used and thought,

74

Dang, that was good! "You think just because I'm a Greek, I drink myself to oblivion?"

"You're right. I shouldn't have made that comment. It was stereotyping," her voice was soft and apologetic. "Except, is it really stereotyping if I've heard multiple eye-witness statements to support that theory?" It wasn't soft anymore, but as sharp as a stiletto. She turned to go, and he acted before he knew what he was doing. He grabbed her arm. "*Excuse* you?" she sliced with every syllable.

"Maybe you're right. Maybe I do like to drink more than I should. That doesn't mean you can look down that pretty little nose at me because of it," his words burned like frostbite.

"I look down my nose at you because I know what you think of women, and that makes you unworthy of my time," she snarled.

"Another assumption. That's two in, what? Two minutes? Don't you know what assuming gets you?" his hand was still on her arm, and he wondered if she was aware of it, since she hadn't jerked away yet.

"I call 'em as I see 'em. Maybe those things are assumed because they're, I don't know, um . . . *true*!"

"Look, I know you seem to think you know all about me just because you see my face and hear my name all over campus, and that's a nasty little side effect of going Greek, but the fact is, you don't actually know anything about me at all. And if all you're going to do is annoy me, you can go now. Mission accomplished," he deliberately let go of her and went back to his book.

"Believe it or not, I came over to help you, which I did offer to do. You could disprove my assumptions and let me," she stood in the same spot, hands at her sides, waiting.

75

"One condition," he countered. "Your name," he told her when she continued to wait.

"When you prove me wrong," she grinned and leaned over to read the notes he had written.

Chapter 6

With the chick from the library helping him do research, Logan quickly decided it would be a good idea to go to the doctor and make sure he didn't have some sort of brain aneurysm or something, since it was the scariest of the possible causes of the symptoms he was "researching for a paper." Of course, it was also possible that he had Type 2 diabetes or meningitis, which he did *not* like the sound of, or none of those conditions at all. None of them explained why it had only happened six times in two months or why every time it happened he woke up covered in dirt. Lucky for Logan, he was signed up to take summer classes and had already paid the summer health fee, so his dad didn't have to know a thing, unless he did have something seriously wrong with him, but he doubted it would come to that.

When he got back to 317, Mark was on the couch watching *Gone in Sixty Seconds*, and Andrew's door was closed. He had no need of socks. He just shut his door. Logan grinned and went to watch Nicholas Cage destroy some sweet cars.

"I'm thinking of going to Student Health and seeing a doctor," he told Mark when a commercial came on.

"Why? You sick or somethin', Michaels?"

"Maybe. Maybe that's why I'm blacking out and sleepwalking and crap," he shrugged. "I was in the library a while ago, and some of the causes are serious, dude. I'm talkin' brain aneurysm serious."

"Calm down, bro. You're starting to sound like a girl. Just because your head hurts and you can't remember what you did doesn't mean you're dying, you hypochondriac!"

"Well, it fits the symptoms," he reminded Mark.

"Since when were *you* pre-med? Or does being a business major qualify you to make diagnoses now?"

"I'm not. It doesn't. That's why I'm making an appointment with a real MD who *is* qualified to make diagnoses." Logan rolled his eyes.

"Man, if I didn't know any better, I'd think you'd been watching some stupid deadly-disease-movie marathon on Lifetime," Mark laughed.

"Shuttup." Logan dialed the number for Student Health Services that he'd just found on the fridge and made an appointment for the upcoming Friday, which was the soonest they could schedule him, and tried not to think about the fact that, if it was an aneurysm, he could be dead before he made it to the end of the week.

The good thing about using Student Health Services instead of using his own doctor was that this way, Logan's dad would have no idea what was going on, as long as it wasn't something totally serious that his summer health fee wouldn't cover. *Boy, would he be ticked if he found out there was something wrong. "You can't be sick! Did I **say** you could be sick? You don't have time to fake illness! You have to finish school and learn the company. You've got to start at the bottom and work your way to the top. That's the only way to make it in the real world, son. You can't inherit the business until you make your own way."* His father's voice came to him as clearly while Logan was sitting there in the waiting room as if he was standing right next to Logan instead of shacking up with some gold-digger while pretending to be at a business meeting, but Logan shut it out as fast as he could. He could tell it had been too long since he'd had a woman or a drink. Well, he could remedy one, perhaps both of the two tonight.

When Logan answered Anna's knock that evening, he had the apartment to himself. He'd arranged for Mark to have a date with Sara, which meant that he also had plans with her the next night. Andrew was wherever Andrew was, and Logan would have bet all the money he had in the world that he wasn't alone, since this was Friday night. His doctor visit had confirmed that he drank too much and needed to eat a little better than he was, and the doctor assured him that he didn't have insufficient insulin levels, and said that he couldn't be positive without a CAT scan and spinal tap (which were not covered under summer health fees), but he was also fairly certain that Logan didn't have any brain bleeds or infected spinal fluid.

Although he was glad he wasn't dying, he was a bit disappointed at being back at square one. However, since he really wasn't dying, he could at least celebrate the fact. So he'd given Anna a call and told her that he'd cook, if she'd bring the wine. She brought a white zinfandel, and he made salad, tilapia and baked potatoes. It wasn't steak, but he wasn't looking for a relationship. When they were finished with dinner, they decided to make dessert a joint effort.

"You're in a good mood this morning," Anna smiled sleepily at him after he'd woken her.

"I guess I am. Aren't you?" he smiled back at her.

"I think I'm in just about the most perfect mood of all time," she giggled as he pressed kisses along the side of her neck.

"What do you say to French toast for breakfast?"

"In a minute . . . " she whispered.

"He shoots; he scores," Mark cried as soon as Anna had left the apartment.

"And how'd you do last night, Malone?" Logan grinned as he started the water for dishes.

"Let's just say, I ain't in Colorado anymore," Mark laughed as his own ineptitude and got out a towel to let the dishes dry on.

Logan had finished washing, and Mark was almost done drying when Andrew came back.

"What'd I miss?" he wanted to know.

"Breakfast and half of the morning. Was it worth it?" Logan flipped past another commercial.

"Totally," Andrew yawned. "Wake me up when it's time for lunch," he muttered on his way to bed. He had only been asleep about thirty minutes when someone knocked on the door.

Mark got up to answer, though neither he nor Logan was expecting anyone. It was Ryan from Res Life, and he had brought their new roommate for the summer, Batukhan, a guy from Mongolia. He had a single suitcase with him and seemed to have a severe case of culture shock. He looked a bit panicked when Ryan left him and his suitcase alone in 317 with Logan and Mark.

"Hey, man. I'm Mark Malone," Mark offered his hand, and thankfully, the guy took it and shook. "I've got the room right next door to yours, and we'll share a bathroom. This is Logan."

"Hello," was all Batukhan could mange.

"Good to meet you," Logan told him. "I live on the other side of the apartment, and so does Andrew. He's your other roommate.

"Yes. Very nice to meet you," he smiled, apparently no longer worried that he was going to be eaten alive by the strange Americans.

They gave Batukhan a tour of the apartment and woke Andrew up so that they could meet each other.

"You can't sit there and tell me that you've got everything you need for the summer in that suitcase, dude. Where are your sheets and pillows?" Andrew asked after Batukhan had begun to unpack.

"I only brought blankets," he shrugged.

"That's it! We're takin' you to Wal-Mart," Andrew announced, and he did so a little too vehemently for Batukhan's tastes since he cringed when it happened.

"Good plan. I need Pop-Tarts anyway," Mark agreed. "And we can take my car, since Stella got her groove back! I swear her paint-job is better than ever!"

"I'm driving, though," Logan snatched Mark's keys from the top of the TV.

"Who is Stella?" Batukhan wondered as he followed the others out to the parking lot.

"That's the name of Mark's minivan," Andrew answered as he slid into the backseat next to Batukhan, since Logan and Mark were already climbing into the front. "By the way, there's no freakin' way I'm gonna be able to remember how to pronounce your name, so I'm just gonna call you Batu.Okay?"

"Yes. You can call me that if you wish, Andrew."

"Awesome. Now let's go show you the wonders of being an American."

Batu almost had a heart attack when they got to the food aisles in Wal-Mart. As a result, they came back with more than just Mark's brown sugar and cinnamon Pop-Tarts and Batu's sheets and pillows. Batu also insisted on buying a toothbrush holder, a star fruit and eleven boxes of fudge rounds, though none of the others were exactly sure why.

Despite his strange food preferences, by the end of the night, Batu had become one of them. He might not have been able to catch all of Andrew and Logan's snide comments, but he knew enough to laugh at the appropriate times, and he didn't look as confused or frightened as he had when he'd first been dropped off at their door.

Logan was on his way to the library. He had a plan. He was going to prove to that infuriating girl that he wasn't the jerk-off she had him pegged for. He was going to find out her name on his own and then call her by it, and then she'd answer out of habit. Then, the fact that he could accomplish this task without her would prove that he wasn't as self-absorbed as she thought he was.

He walked up to the circulation desk and grinned at the blonde who was reading *The Devil Wears Prada*. She smiled back at him and lowered the book to the counter top. "May I help you?" she drew out the question in a way that the brunette probably would have thought of as cheap, but he knew she didn't see it that way, and that was the difference between her and his Jane Doe. It was why he generally preferred to approach the blonde's type. She played by the same rules as he did, and that made things easier all the way around.

It was only when you stepped out of your box and found a new type of opponent that you ran into trouble. New opponents brought their own rules to the table, and then there was the matter of discovering what those rules were and just how many of them you could bend or break without losing entirely. He usually didn't feel like working that hard, but there was something about this mystery girl that made him *want* to do the research, *want* to learn the rules of play, *want* to work on his strategy so that he could come out on top. But that didn't mean he had to quit the game he was already a master of. "As a matter of fact, there are *several* ways," he winked. "But for right now, let's just stick with business."

The light in her eyes changed at that statement, but the position of her mouth stayed as it was. "Okay. So, businesswise, is there anything I can help you with?"

"I'm looking for a girl that works here. About five-two; thin, straight black hair . . ." he described her as objectively as he could so that he'd have a better chance of keeping on the blonde's good side. He knew from experience that it wouldn't do him any good if she thought he was more interested in the other girl than her. "She's kinda sarcastic. I was in here a couple days back, and she helped me find a book, which I didn't write down the name of because I'm an idiot, and so I was hoping she was around and remembered what it was called."

"It sounds like you're looking for Lillie Thackery," she rolled her eyes. "But the fact that you found her helpful is sorta surprising."

"Really?"

"Yeah, she's not exactly what you'd call a social butterfly, you know?"

83

"Well, she's certainly not as *friendly* as you are," he gave her a sly smile that Rob would have envied. "That's why it's so unfortunate that *she* was here the other day and not you." He paused to make sure she understood his veiled compliment. "So . . . do you know when she'll be back at work?"

"Well, we aren't exactly girlfriends," she began, but saw that she was losing his interest and added hastily, "but I can check."

"I would be *very* grateful," he made sure to restore the former grin.

She typed a few sequences into the nearest computer and added several clicks of her mouse. A couple more clicks and she had evidently pulled up the work schedule. "It looks like she took Summer I off . . ." she frowned as she rolled a finger over the scroll button. "I don't see her name again until August. But I'm sure that *I* could help you find whatever book it is you need," she had cheapened her voice again, once her professional tone wasn't needed. "I'm Amanda, by the way," she gave him her hand, and he saw nails that were Malibu Barbie Pink if they were anything, before he wrapped her fingers in his.

"Malone. Mark Malone," he winked again. "And I don't want to bother you. I can't even remember what color the cover was, much less the author's name, so I guess I'll just have to sift through the trash compactor that is my backpack and hope I get lucky." Then he pulled her hand a little closer to him and opened it so that her palm was up. He grabbed the pen that was chained to the desk and scrawled Mark's number across her lifelines.

Just because he had missed his chance with Lillie until fall didn't mean that Mark couldn't get something out of the deal. Who knew, Amanda might be thanking him when this was all over. Logan pictured Mark's surprise when Amanda called him and then Amanda's when they eventually met up, and she found Mark to be somewhat different from what she remembered. Either way, he got a good laugh out of it as he made his way back to 317.

When he got back to his room, he booted up his laptop, opened Firefox and went immediately to Facebook. He hadn't anticipated that Lillie would leave campus for the summer, but he was determined to prove to her that he had taken enough interest in her to learn her name. He typed her name in the search box and got nil, so he tried an alternate spelling of her first name and using the network filter to search only the NCSU students, and there she was.

Her security settings were tighter than the Pentagon's, almost. He could only see her name and network without being her friend, so he did the only thing he could, which was coincidently a thing he rarely ever did (though he seemed to be doing things he rarely did quite a bit when he was around her)– he friend-requested her and added a personal message to it: PROVED YOU WRONG.

He clicked "Send" and was wondering what he was going to do for the next million years while he waited for her to check her profile, when he smelled something strange coming from the vicinity of the kitchen. Logan was about to ask the others what the crap they were doing in there, when a terrifying thought struck him. Batu was attempting to cook.

"So, Batu, can you make Mongolian beef?" Mark was asking him and watching warily as his chopsticks clicked, and he tossed some ingredients around in his wok when Logan came to investigate.

"Absolutely . . . Can you make American cheese?" he asked without even cracking a smile.

It took Mark a second to realize that he'd just been burned by a guy who'd been in the country less than forty-eight hours, but when it happened, he laughed and whacked Batu in the back, probably harder than he had ever been whacked before because he almost fell onto the hot stove and wok full of food, but his agility was as competent as his English, and he prevented disaster from happening, at least for the moment. Still, Logan could already see that there was no way that he was ever going to leave those two alone in the apartment. He valued his $500 room deposit way too much for that kind of carelessness.

The next few days were awesome ones for Logan. For one thing, there was no Rob moping on the couch in his scotch to bring Logan down. He gleefully clicked past ESPN, and there was no one to protest the fact that an episode of *SportsCenter* was being neglected. Besides that riddance, Logan was also fairly excited about the fact that he could sleep in as long as he wanted for at least two more weeks. There was pizza waiting for him only a speed dial away, and there was plenty of beer and Jäger if he wanted it, and there were loads and loads of days that were as empty as Mark's top night stand drawer, and for that very reason, Logan's own top drawer was very, very full.

On Wednesday, Mark stopped in the middle of their *Halo* game when his phone said an unfamiliar number was calling him. This was not a common occurrence for Mark because the only people who usually called or texted him were in the same apartment with him or were family, and they all held their own space in his address book.

He tried to hide his curiosity when he answered, "Malone." He looked even more concerned and wondered, ". . .*Who?* Amanda Who?"

Logan nearly strangled on his Gatorade. *What I wouldn't give to hear both sides of this conversation.*

"What do you mean, 'Amanda from the library?' I haven't been to the library since before Spring Break! I dunno how you got my number. All I know is, I wasn't in the library three days ago. I wasn't even in there three *weeks* ago! I think you have the wrong number. Yeah. How the crap do you know my name? . . ."

Logan could see that if left to himself, Mark was going to choke, so he motioned to Mark and got his attention. "*Just go with it, man.* **Trust** *me*," he whispered. Then he held up a finger when Mark started to ask questions. "*Go with it.*"

"Well, now that you say that, I think I do remember a pretty blonde. . ." Mark changed course, and Logan gave him a thumbs up before turning in the other direction to grin, since Logan couldn't belly-laugh like he was inclined to. Mark was the most hopeless dude he had ever met. Since there was nothing more he could do without compromising Mark's meager chance of success, Logan picked up the controller he'd abandoned and restarted the game for a single player. He had the free world to defend. He only hoped that Mark could hold his own.

It was another two days before Logan saw any change in his Facebook message inbox. He had begun to think that he'd requested the wrong Lillie Thackery and was wishing for an undo button. But when he checked his profile on Friday morning to see if he had any prospects in that area, there was a new message: JUST BECAUSE YOU WENT TO THE LIBRARY AND SEDUCED MY NAME OUT OF THE FIRST BLONDE YOU CAME ACROSS DOESN'T MEAN YOU'RE NOT SHALLOW AND SUPERFICIAL, ALONG WITH BEING RESOURCEFUL. LAST I CHECKED, THE TERMS WEREN'T MUTUALLY EXCLUSIVE.

Logan grinned. He had won this round, and the scent of total capitulation was getting stronger. He clicked her name, only to find that she still hadn't accepted him as a Facebook friend. *Two can play at that*, he opened her reply and composed his own: ACTUALLY, MY BEING RESOURCEFUL PROVES THAT I'M INTERESTED IN MORE PEOPLE THAN JUST MYSELF. HENCE, I CAN'T TECHNICALLY BE CALLED SHALLOW, AND THE FACT THAT I APPROACHED YOU (WHO ARE NOT BLONDE, BUT, IN FACT, BRUNETTE) PROVES THAT I AM ALSO NOT SUPERFICIAL. YOU WERE WRONG. ADD ME AS A FRIEND, AND WE'LL CALL IT EVEN.

Now that she was taken care of, Logan decided to see if any of the Chi O girls were interested in grilling out. It was summer, and that meant time for barbeque, babes and bikinis. Not that it would be real barbeque with pork and vinegar sauce, but it would still be fun.

He got hold of Melissa, whom he hadn't seen since returning the favor just before Spring Break. She was sure that Rosie and a few others would be up for a party, as long as the boys agreed to be the ones buying the steaks and getting smoky. Once he'd made those arrangements, Logan went to find Mark, Andrew and Batu.

Batu was stoked at the notion of anything that necessitated a trip to a grocery store, though his favorite by far was still Wal-Mart. To his dismay, their destination was to be Kroger. It would be quicker, the boys figured, to shop there on a Friday instead of Wal-Mart.

"I cannot believe there are so many McDonald's here," he exclaimed from the back seat as Mark passed another pair of golden arches. "I have lost count of the number!"

"Don't worry, man. I've lost count too! There are tons all over the place," Logan shrugged.

"And they are all the same?"

"Pretty much," Mark told him. "Except that some have kids' areas, and some don't."

"But the food's exactly the same," Logan assured him. "That's the beauty of it. No matter where you are, you always know that Mickey D's will taste just like it does at home."

"Which isn't the best, if you ask me," Mark told him. "The only thing worse than McDonald's is Wendy's."

"I like American food," Batu argued.

"No. You like American *fast* food. There's a difference. Just wait until tonight. We're cooking steaks and baked potatoes on the grill. *That's* real American food," Logan explained. "And since the girls will be coming, I'm sure we'll have to have salad, even if it is only for show."

"Girls?" Batu looked spooked.

"Yeah, girls. Don't worry. You're gonna love 'em even more than those Little Debbies you're so attached to!"

89

Andrew claimed that the smoke got to his "asthma"–the ailment only appearing when he was asked to do something that might involve him having to do something unpleasant–and so he was nestled on the couch with Claire while Mark and Logan ate the smoke from the grill. Melissa was good as promised, and she had brought Claire along with Lori, Kristen, Brittni, and Geena to the party. Because Logan had been the one to procure the chicks, by rights he had the first pick of them, but with the Italian Stallion around, normal rules of play were out. As soon as Andrew had opened the door to the giggles of six girls, Lori attached herself to his right side, and Melissa clung to his left.

Normally, Andrew's rate of conquest didn't bother Logan much, but the fact that he already had sort of a prior claim on Melissa from before did get him a bit annoyed. "Gonna try *all* the flavors 317 has to offer?" he asked her as she and Andrew and Lori took over the couch.

"Why not? What's the use in making 31 flavors if people don't try them out?" she arched a brow before turning all her attention to "Andy."

Logan scanned the four faces he had left to choose from. There was no doubt that Andrew had taken the pick of the bunch, but he couldn't be blamed for that . . . entirely. He settled for the brunette, Geena, leaving Mark his preference of a redhead in Claire (since he was sure to get her eventually), and Batu to choose between the blonde Brittni, or blonder Kristen. Whichever one was leftover, he'd be willing to take.

The more he thought about it, the better he liked that arrangement. This way, he'd essentially be getting three girls, which was better than Stevenson was going to get, as long as Mark and Batu could keep their girls entertained. He flipped the steaks over one at a time, turning them exactly 45 degrees, so that they'd have the diamond grill marks he liked. There was something to be said for precision, after all.

Lori was cleaning the counter tops while Claire and Melissa washed the dishes. Andrew and Mark were chatting with Brittni and Kristin, and Geena was trying to get Batu to talk to her.

"I'm telling you, doll, it doesn't matter what you say. It just sounds so *sexy* . . ."

At this Batu blushed. Logan would have been aggravated with losing Geena's attention, but he was too amused by Batu to mind.

"Yeah, dude. Haven't you ever heard that girls love foreign accents?" Logan smirked as Batu stared at his lap while Geena did her best to make him look at her again.

"Hey, Andy. D'y'all hear about all the cats that've gone missing on campus?" Lori called as she finished the task and hung the towel on the oven.

"Cats?" Batu glanced gratefully at her.

"Yeah. There are something like fifteen or twenty cats that are missing from faculty and staff housing. It started with just the Chancellor's cat, but now they think some frat is doing it as a prank," Lori explained.

Batu missed the looks that she traded with Logan, Mark and Andrew. "I thought Americans were opposed to eating cats," came his confused reply.

Chapter 7

Several grill-outs and girls later, Logan became startlingly aware of how cold he was. He tried to remember where he was or what he had done. It hit him fast, like one too many shots of vodka. He was naked. *It's happening again! How can it be happening again?*

He checked his clock. It was shortly after six in the a.m. He tried to remember what day it was, and his head answered with a ferocious throb that had him nearly puking. He got up and tried not to think of anything while he showered. If he could just get all the crap off him and get rid of this nausea, he could probably figure out what was going on.

When he got out of the bathroom, it was six forty-five. And entirely too dang early to be up and awake, even if it was a week day he had class at eight. Now that he could form thoughts without giving himself a migraine, he tried to remember what he had been doing before he fell asleep.

Predictably there was nothing, which sucked a mother, but what good did it do to complain about it? *Not a crapping thing.* All that was left now was for him to figure out *why* this kept happening and how in the world to stop it. He grabbed his phone and checked the date. Thursday, May 31. He didn't have to be in class until 9:30, and he was up at the butt-crack. *Great.*

He knew from past experience with this that there was no use in going back to the filthy remains of his bed, so he started his sheets for what felt like the millionth time and stretched out on the couch to think.

He'd written the dates of all the blackouts on the inside cover of a notebook so he wouldn't accidentally drop them or tear them out. *That would suck.* He'd brought it with him to the living room, and so he opened the book now and looked at them: 04/01/07, 04/02/07, 04/03/07, and a little further down: 05/01/07, 05/02/07, 05/03/07. The pattern that emerged was immediate. But that couldn't be right, because if it was, that meant that his next set of blackouts shouldn't have happened for two more nights. He got up and checked the date on his computer. It agreed with his cell. It was definitely the morning of the 31st. He wrote the new set of digits a couple centimeters lower than the last and debated whether to go ahead and log the next two nights beneath it since the blackouts always seemed to come in threes, but the precisionist inside him wouldn't let his pen form the necessary strokes, so he clicked the nib back inside the shaft and sighed.

There must be some sort of logic to it. Part of his mind insisted that even as another part shouted that none of this made any freaking sense at all. Too much of it was unexplainable, irrational. There was no way Rob was responsible for this from more than two hours away. According to the doctor, there was no chemical imbalance or other physical reason that his body would be reacting to. Andrew and Mark had no reason to screw with him, and Batu wasn't even living with them when all this crap started. There was no rational explanation for what was happening. Hell, he couldn't

93

even remember what *was* happening to him. How could he even attempt to find an explanation?

Still he stared at the numbers and the almost perfect pattern that seemed to have no formula. Or if it did, it didn't have to do with the sequence. *So what do all the numbers have in common? They're all three sets of two digits. And?. . .They're all dates. And? . . . Maybe it **isn't** the numbers at all, but the days of the week that they fall on!*

Logan accessed the calendar on his phone and tested his theory. The first three dates fell on Sunday, Monday and Tuesday; the second on Tuesday, Wednesday and Thursday; and it appeared that the third would be falling on Wednesday, Thursday and Friday.

*What **is** it with last night? It's throwing off every stupid pattern I can possibly find!* If the day of the week had been the key, the next sequence would have been: Thursday, Friday, Saturday, instead he had rewound to Wednesday, which made absolutely no sense. That left only one rational conclusion–he was losing it.

That's it! I'm not going to think about it anymore. I'm not crazy. Can't be. If I was, wouldn't I be crazy all the time and not just three days at a time every so often? And since when does having memory loss make a person nuts? People forget crap all the time, and it doesn't make them crazy. Then again, those non-crazy people don't usually wake up filthy and naked on the floor of their bedrooms.

For the thousandth time, Logan wished he could remember anything about what he did on those nights before he found himself on the floor. If he really was crazy, would he ever come out of that haze enough to realize it had even happened? He couldn't answer any of the questions he was asking. Come to think of it, every time he asked a question, he came up with several more instead of the answer. It was as if he was in an episode of *LOST* or something and was stuck on The Island with Jack and Hurley wondering just who "The Others" were and how the heck to get back home. Except he hadn't crash-landed anywhere, and he didn't know of any smoke monsters, polar bears, or tribal groups that were after him, so maybe it wasn't that similar after all, save a certain set of foreboding numbers. He only knew that it was as if he stopped existing sometime after dark on those nights and didn't start again until right before six the next morning.

A terrible inkling seeped into his thoughts on the heels of that realization. There was only one way Logan knew of that he could stop existing totally for a period of time and then start existing again later. It was the only logical explanation for his mysterious behavior and the unaccounted blocks of time. Multiple personalities. *I wonder if the student health fee covers psychiatrists.*

When the guys got up a while later, they were surprised to see him up, dressed, coherent, and on his third cup of coffee. But coming to the conclusion that he was a mental case had taken some thought, and thought required coherence, and coherence required coffee if it happened before ten in the morning.

"Did you even sleep at all last night, bro?" Mark wondered as he scarfed a raw brown sugar cinnamon Pop-Tart.

"That's a good question. Wish I had the answer."

"Don't tell me you're blacking out again, Michaels," Andrew said around a slice of cold pizza, which he swallowed and washed down with a swig of Milwaukee's Best.

95

"Don't tell me you're drinking beer again before class," Logan countered and a cocked brow.

"It's just one beer, and—Don't change the subject! I thought you were over that crap."

"Apparently not. And it's *you* who's changing the subject!"

"Dudes. Chill. Andrew is gonna stop with just the one, and Logan is gonna tell us what happened, right?" Mark broke in.

"I'd love to tell you what happened, but seeing as I *blacked out*, it's kinda hard for me to do that," Logan reminded them.

"Well, at least we know you're not dying," Mark slapped him on the back.

"Yeah, but how much of an improvement on that is being insane?" Logan frowned.

"Dude. You can't be insane if you actually *think* you're insane. Not knowing you're nuts is what makes you certifiable," Andrew threw up his hands.

"Well, it's not a prank, and I'm not sick, so I must be crazy, 'cause it's gotta be something!" Logan covered his face with his hands and then slid them into his hair and wondered how he was going to make it through the next two days.

Just like he knew he would, Logan woke up on the floor Thursday night and Friday as well. There was nothing he could do to stop it, so he just resigned himself to the certainty that it was going to happen, and he found that when it inevitably did so, he was not as confused as he might have been. Angry, yes, but somehow also comforted by knowing it was coming, even if he didn't know why or how or what was coming. And despite what Andrew and Mark seemed to believe, Logan was sure that finding comfort in anything like unexplained blackouts was another sign that he was teetering on the edge of insanity.

And just as Logan knew it would, his life went back to normal on Friday night. He even went out for seafood with Jodie before bringing her back to 317. When Andrew and Mark found out that he'd made plans with her, they worried about the consequences of him passing out while in bed and scaring the crap out of her when he returned from his sleep-rock-climbing or -mud-rolling or whatever the heck it was that he always did to get so dirty. But as sure as he was that the blackouts would come more than once, he was also sure that they would only come in threes. Thus, he knew exactly what was happening when the press of Jodie's lips woke him on Saturday morning. The only problem was that the blackouts came in threes was the only thing he *was* sure of. There was no telling when they might return.

From the first two sets, he would have predicted that they happened on the first three days of each month. But then, the latest one had to happen partially in one month and partially in the other. Which meant that calendar days and days of the week were of no consequence, and that left him with no way of knowing how long he had before all this mess started again.

His gut told him that he should go see a shrink. That was the last recourse that he had. Yet he couldn't help wondering what would happen when he did. He could find out that he was perfectly sane. But then what? How could he explain the blackouts then? And if the shrink did think he was crazy, would he spend the rest of his life on Xanax?

The thought of becoming co-dependant disgusted him enough that he almost talked himself out of going. Almost. But the thought of the blackouts continuing for the rest of his life disgusted him even more. He called the Counseling Center and set up an appointment. Apparently you couldn't just ask for a shrink. You had to see a counselor first, and if they thought you really were crazy, then you got on the shrink's schedule. At least his student health fee did cover three appointments with a psychiatrist, and if he was that bad off, there would be no keeping it from his father anyhow.

He went with his gut. He walked into his Tuesday afternoon appointment ten minutes early. It wasn't like he couldn't wait to hear that he was a lunatic. It was just that he had a thing about being on-time, and since he had never gone to the Counseling Center, he wanted to make sure he had time to find the place without being late.

He was seeing a Dr. Miller, which confused him since he thought he had to go through somebody else before actually seeing a doctor, but whatever. The sooner he could figure out how to get rid of the stupid blackouts, the better. The receptionist got to him after he'd waited another fifteen, which Logan figured was a calculated move to put him on-edge so that he wouldn't be able to fake the doc out. And he had to admit, as he was sitting there, staring at the second hand on the clock, he did get a little antsy. But he worked to calm himself as he walked to the office where he was led. It was important that he was taken seriously. He knew he was crazy, which he also knew *sounded* crazy coming out of his mouth, and that was going to make it hard to convince the doctor that it was the truth. So, it was imperative that he at least appeared to be calm and logical, if there was any way he was going to get help. He stepped inside and sat in a chair facing the doctor's desk. Directly across from him was the doctor's black leather desk chair, and behind it was a bookcase that stretched almost all the way across the slate gray wall it was against. The desk was large and made of polished amber colored wood. It held a nameplate which told him that the doctor's name was Douglass Miller, which made him sound like he would fit in with Logan's father's crowd.

*God. What if he **is** in Dad's crowd?* But that line of thinking wasn't exactly promoting a calm and collected exterior, so he tried not to think of it. Besides the nameplate, there was also what looked to be a leather-covered legal pad, a desk lamp, a cup of pens, a dish of paper clips, a stack of blue sticky notes, a Rolodex, and a desk calendar. It was as clean a desk as Logan had ever seen, and he had to wonder if the guy really used it.

He had begun to scan the titles on the shelves and was observing that there were a lot that included the word "Freud," which made him think of a past professor telling his class that he once went to a Halloween party wearing a woman's slip, when the door opened, and a blonde woman appeared and was pulling it to.

"Hello, Mr. Michaels. How are you?" she gave him a broad smile.

"Um . . . good," he lifted his shoulders and dropped them again. He was set to ask who she was when she settled into the chair facing him and scooted up to the desk. She was a small woman, almost petite, and she looked no more than thirty. Her lips were pink, and her eyes were a deep brown. If she wasn't a shrink, he would probably think she was hot. "You're Dr. Miller."

"Yes, quite." What he had first taken to be a Bostonian accent was suddenly revealed to be a very refined British one. *Aren't you full of surprises?* "The secretary tells me that you wanted to see a psychiatrist, Mr. Michaels. May I ask why you felt that was necessary?"

She smiled again, and Logan was sure that the action was meant to put him at ease, but it annoyed him. What annoyed him more was that it seemed genuine.

"Call me Logan. It's necessary because I'm blacking out and waking up covered in dirt on my bedroom floor," he sighed. "The MD I saw said there was nothing wrong with me physically, and my roommates aren't *that* good at pulling pranks, so I've gotta have multiple personalities."

"I see." Dr. I'm-a-Walking-Contradiction said as she scribbled his answer onto the legal pad she had opened. He noticed that the polish on her nails and the color of her lips were almost the same shade.

When she looked up, he asked, "Does that make sense?"

"Yes. Which leads me to believe that you've come to a misdiagnosis," she answered.

"You're saying it's something worse." He was proud of the fact that he didn't flinch as he said it.

"Not necessarily. I just don't believe you actually have dissociative identity disorder, which is the new name for the condition of multiple personalities," she explained when he started to argue that he hadn't said anything about disassociation. "You see, Logan, the problem with your self-diagnosis is that you didn't take into account the fact that the vast majority of patients

100

who have this particular disorder are unaware of their condition. This is because only one of their personalities is cognizant of the others' existence. Have your roommates ever accused you of lying about not remembering something that you did or were responsible for?"

"No." They hadn't even thought he was crazy.

"Then how did you come to believe that you have more than one personality?"

"Process of elimination. The cause wasn't anything external, so it had to be internal, and when it wasn't physical, then it had to be mental."

"But what made you think you have DID, specifically?" she pressed.

"The blackouts. I wake up filthy and naked on my bedroom floor. So obviously I'm out for a while, and while I'm incapacitated, I do *something* that I'm not aware of. How else could I end up coated in mud, with my hair full of leaves and sticks and have absolutely no memory of how it happened?"

"How frequently do you experience the loss of time?" was her only reply. He watched the motion of her hand as his words filled her page.

When the stream stopped he said, "Nine times over a two-month range. The first time was on April 1st, and then it happened again the second and third. Then it was the first three days of May. And then again Wednesday, Thursday and Friday."

"I see." This seemed to be her standard response when she needed more time to write, in between asking questions.

Logan wasn't sure how things were supposed to work when you saw a shrink, since this was his first time, but he knew from movies and TV that the patient was supposed to do the majority of the talking. It still aggravated him that for all his talking, he hadn't gotten any answers. "What does that mean?"

"It means that I understood what you said. Do they always occur in groups of three?"

"Always," he answered, wishing she would do the same when he asked her a question.

"And you said the first two times happened on the first, second, and third days of April and May? And that the most recent occurrence took place on the thirtieth and the thirty-first of May, as well as June first?" She looked up as he nodded and then flipped back a few pages on her calendar.

"There's no connection between calendar days or days of the week," he told her before she could make the observation she was bound to. "There's no formula. I've tried to find one. It's completely random. That's why I don't care what you say. I don't know who this other dude is or why he likes to mud-wrestle nude or whatever, but he's not me! So I'm not asking you *if* I have another personality. I'm asking you *how* to get rid of him."

Chapter 8

Logan had been keeping a log of everything he ate
and drank, the time it was consumed, and the amount
of consumption at Dr. Miller's request for about three
days when he noticed that he was finally able to see a
bit more of Lillie's Facebook profile. From there, he
learned that Lillie Thackery was born on June 10, 1987,
that she was "looking for friendship," that she was
from Manteo, and that she was Catholic. He wasn't
surprised by the fact that she liked reading, but he was
rather intrigued by her love of "researching ancient
cultures, photography, anthropology, intelligence,
puzzles, mysteries, accents, six-packs, and John of
Gaunt." *Who the crap is John of Gaunt?* She surprised
him with her music choices too: "European folk songs
and 'Whiskey in the Jar,'" *whatever song that was.* For
movies, she listed: "foreign films, black and white
movies, *Lord of the Rings* trilogy, and *North By Northwest.*"
There was only one book listed besides the *Bible*, and it
was one called *Katherine*. Apparently, she didn't believe
in watching TV.

He was riding high when he realized that he couldn't
see her wall or her photos. She had him on her limited
profile list. She was still playing the game. He scrolled
down to get her phone number and found that her
contact info was missing too. *Clever, Thackery. Very*

clever. But there was more than one way to find a phone number.

He opened a reply message and typed: YOU CALL LIMITED PROFILE FRIENDSHIP? NO WONDER YOU DON'T KNOW THE DEFINITION OF WORDS LIKE SHALLOW AND SUPERFICIAL. He hit "Send" and couldn't wait for her to log-on again.

On Wednesday, Logan came back to 317 after his classes and found Mark and Batu watching *Happy Days* in the living room. It seemed that pop culture was a little slow in filtering all the way from the U.S. to Mongolia because Batu was amazed that the other guys in the apartment had grown up with the show and had subsequently lost interest in watching Richie and Potsie before puberty. "But what about Fonzie? Is he not still very popular?"

"Not really," Mark shrugged. "Once you've seen all the episodes, he sorta ceases to be cool."

"Wow," was Batu's only response.

"Don't look so sad, dude," Logan told Batu. "There are other TV shows that're cool. *The Office* is pretty funny, and then there's *Family Guy*."

But Batu would not be cheered. "I do not understand how people do not like The Fonz."

"We *do* like The Fonz, or at least we did. It's just that compared to modern TV, those shows from the '70s are sorta primitive," Logan tried again.

"Primitive?" Batu wondered.

"Lame," Mark corrected.

"Is Andrew lame?" Batu retorted.

"No. Andrew's all right," Mark looked confused by Batu's line of thinking.

"Then how is The Fonz not 'all right?' Andrew is just as cool as The Fonz. After all, he is the only one of you who can get two girls to spend the night with him at the same time. The Fonz is the only other person I can think of who could do such a thing."

"He's got a point, man," Logan grinned at Mark, who had once more been bested by Batu.

"I just can't understand it."

"What can't you understand, Mother?" Logan frowned. He had been hoping to avoid this conversation, but there came a point when he just couldn't live with himself if he shady-buttoned her one more time, no matter what it might cost him to pick up the phone. *He* couldn't be that callous.

"I can't understand why you won't make time for us anymore! You didn't come home for your birthday; you didn't come home for Mother's Day; you're missing the family vacation, and it's Fathers' Day on Sunday!"

"Mom, we've been through this before. It wouldn't be a good idea for me to come," he closed his eyes. He'd lost count of the times they'd had this exact same discussion. *How many more times will we rehash this before she accepts reality?*

"Of course it would! You're part of the family, and we miss you." She spoke brightly.

"No. *You* miss me. There's a difference." He refused to whitewash it. She did enough covering up for both of them.

"Logan, you know that isn't true! Your father and Preston miss you too."

"Please. Dad doesn't care about anyone or anything but himself, and Preston's stepping right into his shoes." *It's not a coincidence that they look so much alike.* There were thirteen years between Logan and his brother. There might as well have been a hundred.

"Why do you *always* do this? Why do you always have to be so stubborn?" The pitch of her voice rose with each word.

"And why do you always have to be so passive?" He was deliberately calm.

"Don't take that tone with me, Logan." And sadly, hers still worked on him.

"Yes, ma'am," he spoke as tonelessly as he could.

"Now, I want you to drive on down after your last class on Thursday, since summer school doesn't meet on Fridays. That'll give us plenty of time out on the boat." That false happiness she spread over everything was back.

"Mom, you're not listening to me. I'm not coming home this weekend." He closed his eyes.

"We just agreed that you would!" Her words had become shrill again.

"No. You *told* me to. I'm not five anymore. I make my own decisions." It hurt her, he knew, but there was no way around that.

"You weren't raised to act this way, Logan," She had gone cold now. It was about time.

"Right, pretending's the polite thing to do. Living a lie's much better than acknowledging the ugly truth." The ice froze, like he hoped.

"If you're going to treat me this way, I'm going to hang this phone up. . ." She couldn't cover the tears, and he regretted causing them, though he knew it was necessary.

"I love you, Mom," he softened his tone.

"I love you too, Logan," she sighed as he clicked to end the call.

He walked to the cabinet and grabbed the Jäger. He usually wasn't one to drink in the middle of the day, but considering what he'd just endured, he figured he'd earned it. When Ginnie Michaels decided she wanted something to happen, it was almost unthinkable that the thing would not come to pass. To that way of thinking, he'd just done the impossible, and accomplishing such a feat deserved a celebratory sip.

He was sitting with Batu that Sunday, watching *The Dukes of Hazzard* on TV Land, when a commercial came on the screen, and they were able to look away after losing sight of Daisy and her infamous shorts. "Logan, why is it that you are not with your father on Fathers' Day? Is that not where Andrew and Mark have gone?" Batu inquired.

"Yeah. They've gone home for the weekend like good sons are supposed to, but I'm not exactly what most people would refer to as a good son," Logan passed Batu the bag of Nacho Cheese Doritos he'd just grabbed a handful of chips from.

"Why would you think that? You seem to be a good person." Batu took a few of the orange tinted chips and crunched on them, one at a time.

"If you ask my parents, they may not agree with you. I guess it just depends on what you consider 'good.' Take Andrew. He's home for every holiday and on the fast track to becoming a gastroenterologist just like his old man. He's the best of the good sons. I, on the other hand, avoid going home as long as possible, and only went into business as my major because it happened to be something I was good at, but definitely not because it was what my dad wanted, even though it was. If I had my druthers, I'd rather not have to see or talk to my dad ever again. What about you?"

"I love my father very much. He has worked hard for many years to help give me the opportunity to come to the United States. It has been his dream for me my whole life."

"But what about *you*, man? What's *your* dream?"

"I want what all children want: for their parents to be proud of them," came Batu's simple answer. "I don't know why anyone would want anything else in life."

"Well, that's not what *I* want for *my* life. I want to become nothing like either one of my parents." Logan continued when he saw the look of confusion on his roommate's face. "Don't get me wrong. I want success too, of course. I just don't want to have anything to do with them when I get it." Batu's expression didn't appear any clearer. "Speaking of which, I'm going to go study for finals." He tossed the remote in Batu's general direction and went to his room, though the exams were still a week away.

By the time finals were finished, cultural expectations were the farthest thing from Logan's mind. It had been a tough two days. All he wanted was a woman and something to drink, and he preferred them in that order so that he could appreciate each one equally.

He called Lani, who was more than happy to agree to some stress relieving activities. She was a tall, dishwater blonde who was known for her flexibility. He'd seen her before at some of the joint parties that the Kappa Sigs and the Chi Os sometimes threw. He

108

couldn't remember much about her, but when he hung up, he knew he liked the whiskey-timbre of her voice. It was like she opened her mouth and Jack Daniels came pouring out, and he'd be more than happy to drown himself in that river.

Mark answered the door when she knocked. "You here for Logan?"

"Unless you can think of a reason I should stand him up for you," Lani smiled, and he saw two deep dimples.

"Logan!" he called.

"Right here," he answered with a chuckle. Logan could only imagine what had been going through Mark's mind when a girl was blatantly flirting with him. He stepped out of his doorway, and in two more strides, he was out of the corridor that housed his and Andrew's rooms and in the living room.

"Lani, this is Mark Malone," Logan watched the color creep over Mark's cheeks.

"Really?" she raised a brow. "My friend Amanda was talking about you the other night."

"She was?" Mark finally found his voice. *Jeez, man! Do you have to sound so eager? Have I taught you nothing?*

"She was," Lani repeated.

Mark looked like he'd just been declared MVP of the Super Bowl.

Logan suppressed the urge to laugh. "Stop flirting with my roommate," he winked at Lani. "I'm hungry. You want some Chinese?"

"As long as that invitation includes crab rangoon, I'm all about it." She didn't flutter her lashes. She didn't have to. He had been wrong earlier. It wasn't just her voice that was intoxicating. He could drown in the depths of her smoky eyes too.

"Well, I might be persuaded to part with a rangoon or two . . . maybe more," he shrugged as he grabbed his keys. "If you give Mark his heart back, I may even let you have a fortune cookie."

"It's not me that's the thief, Logan. To hear Amanda talk, Mark's the one who stole *her* heart," she retorted before Logan shut the door.

The only bad thing about Chinese food was the fact that it never kept Logan full very long, no matter how much of it he was able to consume at the restaurant. The rumble in his and Lani's stomachs (and her pleading) had him out of bed and searching for his boxers so he could raid the freezer. He kept a tub of Cookies & Cream for these kinds of situations. Getting up wasn't his first choice, and neither was getting into the cold to grab the ice cream, but one look at her face, and he knew that it would be well worth the momentary inconvenience of letting Lani go. This theory was tested when he came back to her with the carton and two spoons, and proved to be true shortly thereafter.

The sunlight sliding through the slits in his blinds met him the next morning, along with a slightly sticky Lani who wasn't averse to them conserving water, since he found himself in a similar situation. By the time they were done with the shower, Batu, and Mark had surfaced from their rooms, and surprisingly, so had Andrew.

"You hungry, Lani?" Logan inquired when she came into the living room after she finished doing whatever females did to their hair and faces. He didn't feel right sending her off without showing her a bit more courtesy than half a tub of Cookies & Cream in the middle of the night.

"I could have a little something," her voice of liquid smoke surrounded him, and he wished that he'd thought to pay more attention when his parents' cook tried to show him things. As it was, he knew the basics: eggs fried, scrambled, or in an omelette; pancakes from a mix; waffles from a box; and doughnuts from a sack. Not that he thought she was anything out of the ordinary, she just seemed to be the type of girl who might prefer crepes to some of the more domestic options; and after the treat she'd just given him, she deserved a little more than the breakfast equivalent of Hot Pockets.

"I've got the makings for French toast, omelettes or pancakes, or we can go pick something up," he stood and took a step toward the kitchen so she'd know that he was serious about the offer to cook. His repertoire was not vast, but he was confident in what he had mastered.

"It's been awhile since we've had any o' your omelettes, man," Mark announced.

"Yeah, it has," Andrew agreed. "And since he isn't American, I bet Batu hasn't *ever* had 'em . . ."

Logan looked at Batu, who, sure enough, was just baffled enough to prove Andrew's point for him. "It sounds like the guys have invited themselves to breakfast," he sighed. "Are you okay with omelettes?"

"Well, who could deny a man his first experience with omelettes?" Lani grinned at the looks of gratitude that came from all three of Logan's roommates. "I'll get the eggs!"

"I am very excited to be trying these omelettes of yours, Logan," Batu called over the sizzle of the yolks

Logan had dropped into his pan, "but how can you make them, if you are not French?"

"Shuttup, Batu," Mark stuck an elbow into Batu's ribs, as Logan rolled his eyes. "We really have to work on your English."

Three nights later was the first Friday in a while that Logan was alone in 317, and perversely, he didn't feel like company. He didn't know why. It wasn't like he'd had class all week. He'd finished that on Tuesday and worked out all the residual stress with Lani. And Becca. And Taylar. He was in a bad mood and had absolutely no reason to be. But there was pizza and Jäger, and he managed to find *Pulp Fiction*. There could definitely be some possibilities with that combination.

Tarantino was always entertaining with his artful combination of murder, mayhem, and humor that no one else could make believable. Logan figured he had to have some sort of Jedi powers or something, seeing as how he'd done it again with the *Kill Bill*s. However it was that Tarantino managed to pull it off didn't matter so much to Logan after a few swigs from his bottle and a couple minutes watching Honey Bunny and Pumpkin. *This movie is cinematic gold! Who am I to question the man? It's like asking whether this pizza would be better off covered in anchovies.*

There was nothing better than a large sausage and pepperoni from Domino's. That pizza was perfect as is, and to mess with something that delicious was a crime against nature. He ate a bite, just to confirm what he already knew, and his taste buds pronounced the flavors' flawlessness. Satisfied, he turned back to the screen just as Jules and Vincent started talking about a "Royale with Cheese."

For a second Logan wondered if he had become a victim of Jules and Vincent and they'd stuffed him into the trunk of a car to die, but he opened his eyes and saw that it was worse than that. At least if he had been their target, he wouldn't have to clean up the mess. That would be The Wolf's job. But there were no hit men responsible for the mud that was covering his floor and his body. If they were behind it, the only mess they'd leave would be the blood spatter left from their bullets in his face.

How many freaking times am I gonna have to do this before somebody can tell me what the crap is going on??? he wondered as he stood up and went to shower. *No split personalities huh, doc?* he thought as he stepped under the steaming spray.

By the time he'd gotten himself dry and his room cleaned up, he was raging. *How ridiculous is it that no one can tell me what's wrong with me?* He opened the cover of the notebook he was using to record his blackout dates and wrote: 06/29/07. Though he still hadn't figured out the pattern, it looked like they were coming sooner and sooner with each occurrence. The first two sets had started on the first of the month, the last one started on the 30th, and today was a day earlier than that. *Maybe the blackouts are getting closer together over time.*

He accessed his phone's calendar and counted 27 days between the last day of the first set and the first day of the second. When he discovered that there were 26 days between the last day of the second set and the first day of the third, it looked like he'd finally stumbled upon a pattern. His excitement was extinguished shortly when his tally revealed the 27 days between the last day of the third set and today. *Of course! It would be asking too much if one single part of this whole mess made any sense, wouldn't it?* he threw his hands up and began to wonder if he shouldn't just let it happen, whatever it was.

All his postulating hadn't gotten him anywhere closer to an answer than he had been the first morning after. There seemed to be nothing in the world that he could do to stop the blackouts, since there was no known trigger, and he had no way of predicting when they were coming. According to his latest figures, the best he could do was get ready for it to happen 26 days from Sunday. Then again, he was working with a limited amount of data, and that figure could just be a fluke like every other possible pattern he'd proposed.

He was still keeping Dr. Miller's food journal, but he didn't know how much good that would do. Logan hadn't kept a record from the onset of the blackouts, but he was sure that during the second set, he'd been sober. That knocked alcohol out of the running, along with the Gatorade that he had managed to abstain from. He was also pretty sure that he hadn't had pizza every time it happened, and he knew for a fact that it didn't happen every time he ate pizza. Aside from that, he couldn't think of anything he'd ingested last night that was also ingested during any or all of the previous incidents. And because this was the first time he'd blacked out while keeping the journal, he knew that he'd have to black out again before that technique would yield any useful information.

The thought that he'd be losing tonight and tomorrow night and three more nights in the near future before any change could take place didn't do much to help the mood he'd woken up with. That and the headache he remembered so fondly from all the other mornings made it even worse. He wasn't sure that he couldn't give The Hulk a run for his money in the rage department. Logan brewed a cup of coffee and waited for the others to wake up. Since it was just past six (why couldn't he come back to himself at a more humane time of day?), he knew he had at least two hours to kill. He turned on the TV and began to flip, hoping that there was an action movie playing on at least one of the channels.

Chapter 9

Logan's third blackout night was the night before the first day of the second summer term, which sucked, but the up side was that he knew it wasn't going to happen again until right before the end of class, and if he was lucky, not that he thought he would be, he might even escape it until after he was done with exams. It was also good that his next appointment with Dr. I'm-a-Woman-Who-Thinks-it's-Cool-to-Have-a-Male-Name was only a few days away. And even though he was only supposed to log food related information in the journal, Logan also wrote down any detail he thought might have been important, not that he knew what his criteria for "important" were, but it was something.

He went to his first class with a massive headache that he knew would dissipate only when it wanted to. Tylenol, Advil, and any other over-the-counter pain relievers he had tried had no effect on them. He thought that the caffeine in his coffee helped a little, but that was probably all in his mind. Still, he downed three cups black before leaving 317. There had to be some way to make surviving Marketing Research a little easier.

Logan walked back to the apartment after he finished Logistics, his afternoon class, and decided that surviving those classes could not be made any less

painful. His only hope was to power through them the
same way Mark powered through sub sandwiches. If
he went quickly enough, maybe he wouldn't feel too
much of the agony.

The appointment with Dr. Miller on Friday came,
and Logan wondered how it could be productive. Still,
he went to the Counseling Center and took his food
journal with him. When she'd told him to start keeping
it, he figured that keeping track of everything he ate and
drank would go out the window after about two days.
He surprised himself, though, because once he got in
the habit of writing down the time, type of food or
drink, and amount consumed, it was more like keeping
books than he had imagined. Now that he'd been
doing it for over a month, it wasn't even a habit
anymore. It was more like a compulsion, like his need
to be on time, which explained why he was there ten
minutes early, despite the fact that he knew where he
was going this time.

As expected, Dr. Miller wasn't as prompt, and he
was waiting another fifteen before he was called to her
office, which was vacant when he got there, and took
his seat. His eyes returned to the spines on her shelves
in front of him. *Has she really read all these books? Or are
they just for looks?* If he knew his father's type, and he
still wasn't sure that she wasn't one of them, then the
books and leather and polished wood were part of the
pomp they continually surrounded themselves with.
That faux prestige only fooled those who weren't part
of their world; therefore, it was useless. The pretense
disgusted him. Underneath all his suits and finery,
Philip Michaels was nothing more than a greedy, lying
piece of filth who didn't deserve all the respect his

money and the morons who were blinded by it gave him. In reality, though, Philip was lower than his lackeys. *If only they knew how filthy his pristine hands were . . . * But money was good for more than buying respect. You could also cover up any multitude of sins you felt like committing if you were wealthy enough. If there was one thing his father taught him, it was that—

"Hello, Logan. How are you today?" Dr. Miller had taken a seat and was now watching him carefully, her pen poised and ready to record his every reaction.

"Fine. How are you?" he smiled as naturally as he could and hoped she didn't see anything significant in the action.

"I'm doing well." Apparently she didn't, since her pen had yet to stain the paper. "Have you had any blackouts since our last visit?"

"Yeah. Saturday, Sunday and Monday."

"And have you been keeping up with your food journal?" she raised a brow and her pen.

"Yeah," he handed it to her and watched as she leafed through it.

"Did you notice any changes in your diet that coincide with the losses of time?" she had set his notebook aside and was writing on her legal pad again.

"Not really, but then again, I've only got one set of blackouts to look at, since I didn't think of writing down what I ate the first three times. That's not really going to give us an accurate picture," he shook his head. *I can't **believe** I'm going to have to go through this again before we figure anything out!*

"And you noticed nothing different about your habits or behavior during those three days?" she seemed to be looking for a tell that he was lying, the way she watched him as she posed her question.

118

"Nothing. Anything that I thought might be important, I wrote down in that journal," he sighed.

"You're sure?" Her question had him losing the calm he'd tried to maintain since she walked in.

"Look, Dr. Miller, *I* came to *you*, not the other way around. So why would I try to hide anything from you that might help you diagnose my problem?"

"I have no idea, Logan. Why *would* you try to hide anything from me?" When he tried to protest, she held up her hand. "Your reaction to my innocuous question shows me that you're agitated about something. So tell me what it is that's bothering you."

"Agitated? *Of course* I'm agitated! I'm blacking out, and I have no idea why! I come to you for help, and all I seem to be getting is more questions than answers! You're not the only one who thinks scientifically. If I didn't, I wouldn't have been able to figure out that I have another personality. All I need to know now is how to get rid of him. So tell me what scientific method we can use to solve my problem." His voice was low, and his hands were clenched into fists at his sides. He was still sitting, but it was taking all of his strength not to shove to his feet and loom over the small figure behind the desk.

"First of all, Logan, let me remind you that I'm not certain that you have dissociative identity disorder. On the contrary, I'm fairly positive that you *don't* have that particular problem. Second, I'd like for you to refrain from getting so upset. No one is accusing you of anything. I'm just trying to understand how you're feeling by collecting the most accurate information possible." She paused and eyed him until he let out a breath and relaxed enough for it to become visible. "Is there something you'd like to ask?" *What are you, a mind reader?*

"Yeah. If I don't have DID, then what *is* wrong with me?" He dared her to try to say there wasn't anything wrong with him. *If one more person tells me that, I'll jump off the library roof!*

"Logan, how would you feel about testing out a working theory I have?" she smiled.

"Depends on what the theory is and how you plan on testing it exactly," he smiled too.

"I believe that we're dealing with a mild case of posttraumatic stress disorder." She said it as if she'd just unveiled the answer to the universe. *I got news for you, lady, PTSD is **not** 42!*

"How the crap could I have PTSD? I haven't had to overcome any stressful situations that might have traumatized me!" Now *he* was beginning to think *she* was crazy.

"You haven't had any traumatic experiences that you can *remember*," she disagreed. "I believe that the losses of time that you've been experiencing are manifestations of PTSD, which is stemming from a childhood experience."

"And how are we supposed to figure out what that childhood experience is, if I can't remember it?" All her technical terms didn't do anything to make the idea more believable to him.

"Are you agreeable to hypnotherapy?" she raised a brow again, as if daring him to accept her challenge.

"As long as I don't end up clucking like a chicken every time someone snaps their fingers, I'll try anything once," he shrugged.

It was dark. The air was cool as he moved. He could hear the wind around him and the crunch of leaves with every step he took. He was running. Striding with a purpose past trees and other shadows that did no more than blend into the darkness. There was an overwhelming drive inside him. A need to press on, to get to where he was going. He knew *where* that was, just as he knew *how* to get there. It was obvious to him in that moment, but not now. Not looking back in his memory as he was. He breathed in, and no familiar scents came to him, just the trees and the dirt and leaves and some animals near enough that he could hear them even if he couldn't see them. He tried to concentrate on how he felt and realized that he was hungry. Dreadfully so. At first, his only thought had been to go, but now the deep rumble from his belly sounded louder in his head than the snap of a twig or the call to move forward. He wanted food, the taste of it in his mouth, the feel of it in his stomach, so badly he was shaking.

"Logan. It's Dr. Miller. Can you hear me?" When he came back to himself, he was shaking still.

"Yeah," he opened his eyes and he was sitting in front of her desk in her office at the Counseling Center. "What *was* that?"

"*That* was a repressed memory," she told him without looking up from what she was writing.

"Ok. So what does it *mean*?" He was getting annoyed at her simplistic interpretation. She was the one with the PhD.

"I believe it indicates that you were once lost in the woods as a child. Because you were unfamiliar with the area and unable to locate any landmarks, you were

121

probably a child who was too young to know to look for things like that or to have developed the skills to do so instinctively. That you had no concerns other than the need to find a certain place–probably your home–and your extreme hunger, also supports the thought that you were very young. An older child might worry about other people and their reactions when he or she returned. Still, there seemed to be no fear, which suggests that you weren't too young to play on your own, at least for short periods of time. Did your parents ever take you camping? Or to a lake for the weekend?" Her sudden question startled him.

"Sure they did. We went all the time before my brother Preston was born. But Mom never let me out of her sight . . ." *Don't all families go camping once in a while?*

"And why did you stop going? Do you remember?" She was caught up in her letters again.

"Right after Preston, my dad stopped coming home for dinner. It was later and later every night, and sometimes he didn't bother to come home at all. Mom was really upset about it at first, but then it was like she just decided to pretend it wasn't happening." He seethed at the thought of how different his mother had been before his father had become bored with her and looked elsewhere for entertainment.

"Do you know why was he missing dinner and coming in so late?" She made eye contact now, and Logan wondered why his reaction to this question was more important than his reactions to the questions before it.

"He was seeing his call girls," Logan heard the flat tone that he used and was proud that there was no emotion to be heard.

"And when did you understand that it was your father's extramarital affairs that kept him out and not business obligations?" She was watching, he knew, though he was staring at his lap. He could feel her keen gaze on the top of his head.

"When I heard my parents fighting about it one night after they thought I was asleep."

"How old were you?" her voice was soft.

"Preston was still a baby, so I was probably thirteen-and-a-half or fourteen," he guessed.

"And you understood enough of their conversation to come to the conclusion that your father was unfaithful to your mother on your own?" He heard the skepticism in her voice.

"I was thirteen, Doc. Not five!" his voice was louder in response.

"Did your father ever take you with him when he went to meet these girls?" She'd returned to that clinical tone.

"No. And as far as I know, he never went to meet them. They always came to his office. What does this have to do with that repressed memory?" It seemed like she was trying to get into his head more than she was trying to figure out the scene he'd just remembered.

"I'm not certain. Our time is almost up for today," she gave him a friendly smile, "but I'd like you to continue with your food journal, in case you have any other blackouts, and I'd like to see you again next month."

"Hold on a second, Dr. Miller. I've only got three free visits with you before I have to start paying out of pocket, and doing that without alerting my dad's gonna be a bit tricky. So I need you to tell me if we're any closer to figuring this thing out, because if we're not, I'd

123

just as soon not waste your time and mine, and my money." She was shooing him away, and he would have none of it.

"Logan, I think we've made considerable progress. I may not have arrived at a suitable course of treatment yet, but I am confident in my diagnosis of PTSD." It was as if he was a small child, and she was patting his hand.

"But there are treatment options? That can get rid of the blackouts?" *Lord, Logan! You're beginning to sound as desperate as Mark!*

"Yes," she nodded.

"What are they?" *And apparently, I don't care, as long as I get an answer.*

"Though I'm reluctant to suggest a particular method of treatment to you at this time, I can tell you that we have several options; among them are continuing hypnotherapy, trying cognitive therapy and/or exposure therapy, and in the event that your periods of time loss have persisted, I could prescribe an antidepressant such as Paxil." To her credit, she didn't seem any fonder of the idea than he was.

"Great. Thanks." He shoved out of his seat. She stood as well and extended her hand.

"Don't forget to make an appointment for four weeks from now," she smiled when they'd shaken.

"Right," he nodded.

"And Logan? Don't worry. We'll figure this out. I give you my word." *That's comforting.*

The month of July passed quickly for Logan, perhaps because he was kept busy with the two classes he was struggling through and the girls he spent his nights with. He and Andrew managed to carve out a little Xbox time, and if he was around, Mark was always happy to join in, but Batu was not as amused by American video games as he was with TV shows, so he stuck with what he knew and somehow became addicted to watching *Law & Order* reruns on USA. He would occasionally stop when he found *Law & Order: SVU*, but it wasn't as good in his opinion. The whole idea that Batu had switched from one totally outdated show to another that had been running as long as Logan could remember was sort of funny. If he had his pick of crime dramas, Logan would've chosen *Criminal Minds* over Jack McCoy and Lennie Briscoe, but he had spent quite a few hours watching McCoy prosecute the scum that Lennie and his partners hauled in.

Logan was in his room, checking his school email to make sure he had no more surprise assignment changes, and when he found that there was nothing waiting for him, he decided to check Facebook and get it over with, so he could get the rest of his studying done before Kammi came over later. When he logged in, he saw that Lillie had finally decided to respond to his last message:

I HIGHLY DOUBT THAT YOU EVEN KNOW THE CORRECT DEFINITION OF THE WORD YOURSELF, SINCE YOU SEEM TO THINK THAT "FRIENDSHIP" ENCOMPASSES MORE THAN SHOWING COURTESY TOWARD AND HAVING SURFACE KNOWLEDGE OF ANOTHER PERSON. NEVERTHELESS, I SUPPOSE I COULD SHOW YOU A GESTURE OF GOOD FAITH, AS LONG AS YOU DON'T ABUSE IT, AS YOU ARE LIKELY WONT TO DO.

He clicked out of the message and checked. Sure enough, he now had access to her photos and wall. *It took you long enough!* He scrolled down a little and discovered that she had made connections with people from all over the world. She had friends from China, Indonesia, Australia, Germany, Brazil, Spain, and even Slovakia. *The girl gets around!* He grinned and looked at a few of the posts on her wall. Evidently she'd had a birthday last month because her wall was nothing but birthday well-wishes except for a few indecipherable messages from a chick named Paige, and judging from the frequency of her posts, he would have to say that Lillie and Paige were BFFs. Who else would write crazy messages like "In our world, it's ALWAYS Tuesday!"? He couldn't see their wall-to-wall but was sure that even if he could, Lillie's reply wouldn't make any more sense than the initial post. Logan chuckled as he opened a reply:

GLAD TO SEE THAT YOU'VE FINALLY DECIDED TO TREAT ME LIKE A HUMAN BEING. BY THE WAY, I LIKE LOOKING AT PICTURES OF YOUR FACE. WHEN DO YOU THINK I MIGHT BE ABLE TO SEE THE REAL THING AGAIN? I KEEP GOING TO THE LIBRARY BUT CAN'T SEEM TO FIND ANY HOSTILE BRUNETTES WHO WANT TO CUT ME TO PIECES WITH THEIR WORDS.

Logan awoke cold and naked on his floor again on Sunday morning before Summer II finals began on Monday, which meant he wasn't going to be getting any real sleep until after his exams were over. *This sucks a mother!* He squinted as he made his way to the bathroom for the shower he knew would be necessary to get rid of the mud he could feel caked all over him. He tried not to think too much as he stepped in and pulled the curtain as quietly as he could across the rod. By this time, he knew better than that. He had come to a tacit agreement with the pounding in his head: as long as he didn't attempt to recall what he'd been doing before or during the "time loss," as Dr. Miller called it, his head wouldn't throb so much that he hurled. *This is way worse than a hangover.* At least if it was a hangover, he could have taken some aspirin and slept it off. But this monster was not a result of dehydration and couldn't be cured by anything other than time.

Since it was almost six thirty, it was a pretty safe wager that he'd be rid of the headache before he would have usually been up. On the bright side, it meant that he wouldn't lose any time that he would have been studying. The crappy part was that he was losing two-and-a-half hours of prime sleeping time, not to mention the time he spent doing whatever got him so dirty instead of snoozing in his sheets. *There's no way I'm going to be awake for finals after two nights of this mess!* He shook his head at the terrible timing of the blackouts and dried off, then went to get his notebook and write the dates inside the cover: 7/28/07, 7/29/07, 7/30/07. He no longer cared that the other two nights hadn't happened yet. It had been 26 days. They were inevitable.

By the time Logan was done with tests on Tuesday, all he wanted was to actually get some sleep and to wake up Wednesday morning without feeling like he'd drunk two gallons of Jäger. He came back to 317 fully intent on crashing for the next twelve to twenty-four hours, but when he got there, it became obvious that passing out was not going to be an option.

Batu and Mark were clearly agitated about something, and true to his usual MO, Andrew was nowhere in sight. "What's wrong?" Logan yawned and threw his backpack on the opposite end of the couch that they had just plopped on.

"I must move," Batu sent him a wild-eyed look.

"Move where?" Logan calmly inquired. *Somebody in this room has to be.*

"Who the crap knows!" Mark threw up his hands. "Res Life sent him this stupid letter saying that he has to be out of the apartment by noon on Friday, but it doesn't say a dang thing about where the mess he's supposed to go from there!"

"I have no idea what to do," Batu shook his head. "I must move out by Friday, but my class begins on the 22nd, and I have no place to stay until that time, or even afterwards . . ." He covered his face with his hands.

"This ain't right, man!" Mark yelled, as if his incensed tone would do any good.

"Chill, okay? Just chill. I know a girl who works in Res Life. Maybe she can help us out." Logan stared hard at Mark until he knew Mark had gotten ahold of himself. "Batu, try not to freak out. The University screws up stuff like this all the time. I'm sure we can get this all worked out. And if worse comes to worst, you can always sleep on our couch until we find you another apartment."

"I hope you are right, Logan," Batu sighed.

Logan dialed Residence Life and asked to talk to Beth (who he knew from freshman year). He couldn't remember what class they'd had together, but she'd never made it to his bed, so he was fairly sure that even though they hadn't seen or spoken to each other in nearly two years, she wouldn't hold it against him. "Hello," came a female voice from the other end.

"Hi, Beth. This is Logan Michaels. We met during freshman year."

"Hey, Logan." He imagined that she smiled as she said it. "I see your face all over campus. I was wondering when I'd actually get to talk to you again."

"Yeah, sorry about that. I guess I misplaced your number, but I'd be really relieved if you could help me find it again." *It would be so much easier to do this in person.*

"I think that could be arranged . . ." He heard her tone change and knew that his plan would work.

"That's great!" He waited until she gave him her number, which he wrote on his hand so that he could put in his cell when they hung up. If she was as helpful as he thought she'd be, he had a feeling he was going to be calling it soon. "Listen, Beth. I have a friend who's got a housing problem, and I was wondering if there was any way you could help us out."

Half an hour later, Beth had found Batu a room in 217, the apartment just below theirs, and he would be allowed to move into it as soon as he moved out of 317. Coincidentally, Logan suddenly had plans for Friday night, and so did Beth. *Now I can get some sleep.*

Friday morning Logan, Mark and Andrew managed to help Batu get all his stuff shifted downstairs in about two trips. There really wasn't much to move, but it was the gesture, not the actual workload that was important. Of the three of them, Andrew took the most offense at Batu's being kicked out. "This sucks!"

"That's about the five millionth time you've said that," Logan reminded Andrew when they'd gotten Batu situated and left him downstairs to meet his new roommates.

"That doesn't make it any less sucky. Why did they have to go and kick him out like that anyway?" Andrew scowled. Logan had to hold his breath to keep from laughing at the way Andrew looked like he was a five-year-old with that face.

"They kicked him out because Rob has dibs on the room when class starts in August. You know that." Logan couldn't banish the flash of a grin on his lips.

"I'd rather live with Batu for a year than with Norton and his everlasting PMS. Are we even sure he really is a dude?"

"Oh, trust me. He's got all the right equipment, if that's what you're asking. I *know*. I share a bathroom with him," Mark grinned.

"Better you than me," Andrew scowled again. "If I'd been living on that side of the apartment, good ole Rob would've woken up dead a long time ago."

"I'm sayin'," Logan agreed.

He went to see Dr. Miller that afternoon and wasn't confident that he knew anything more to tell her than he had at his last appointment. Still, he had come, and that was the best he could do. She flipped through the pages of his journal, giving his entries a cursory glance.

"There still seems to be no evidence of an obvious trigger. Have you blacked out since we last talked?" Her pen was ready for his answer.

"Saturday, Sunday and Monday." he nodded.

"I see. And was there anything about this particular set of blackouts that was different than the others?" She must have thought she was on to something, since she was looking at her paper and not him.

"Besides the fact that it fell during final exams? No." He didn't bother to hide his annoyance.

"Perhaps the timing wasn't a coincidence. Did you become stressed over taking your final exams?" *What the crap sort of question is that? Has she been living on Mars since leaving England?*

"Sure. Doesn't everyone?" He looked at her to see if she was even able to sympathize. Surely, out of all the tests she had to take for her PhD, a few of them had stressed her out.

"Stressful situations could be the trigger for your episodes, Logan." She used that clinical tone again, and he figured that she must be some sort of android.

"That doesn't explain what triggered them the other four times they happened," he pointed out, glad that there was a hole in her theory. *At least now I'm not the only one who's at a loss.*

"Well, did the fourth set happen during anything stressful? Such as other final exams?" Her brow was arched to punctuate the question. *Superior, much.*

"That one happened a couple days after I'd finished the finals for Summer I." He took delight in proving her wrong.

"Perhaps the episodes have nothing to do with food and everything to do with whatever is happening in your life at the moment." She made eye contact now, and her smile seemed triumphant.

"So I've been keeping this journal for nothing?" *This is just awesome!*

"Of course not. Without the journal, we'd have no way of eliminating food as a trigger," she continued to smile, proud of the fact that she'd finally been able to solve the problem.

"Okay. So now we know what's causing the blackouts, and possibly how to stop them, given some time, but what the crap am I doing for all that time?" It was the one question that bothered him the most.

"I have a working theory on that, Logan. I believe that the reason you wake up covered in filth is because you are reliving the initial trauma every time you black out. You wander about outside, probably tripping and falling, and even crawling at times." *Wow. I guess that **is** a possibility . . .*

"But why do I do it naked?" he posed another of the questions that had been eating at him.

"I'm not sure. The removal of your clothes may be a result of your activities. Maybe you feel restricted by your clothes and remove them in an attempt to reach your destination quickly. Or it may have to do with the fact that the trauma you're reliving happened when you were much younger. Lots of children go through phases in which they dislike or even refuse to wear clothing. Perhaps your getting lost took place during a similar phase in your childhood. Or it could be caused by any number of other factors. As with your treatment, when given more time and data to work with, I'll be able to give you a more concrete answer." Her words made him realize that that was all he was to her. He wasn't a human being with a weird problem that was starting to ruin his life. He was a set of facts that she used to solve a problem. Little more than a pastime or other form of entertainment. A case. A bill. A means to an end.

"So what am I supposed to do until then?" *Just sit around and hope it doesn't happen again?*

"Avoid stressful situations as much as possible. Find something that relaxes you, and do it as often as you can. Continue the journal, but this time focus on events and day-to-day activities as well, just to make sure we're on the right track." She smiled, and for the first time, she actually looked human. That gleam he

132

saw let him know that she knew she'd just given him license to slide in class and drink and sleep around as much as he wanted. *It's every college guy's dream come true. Too bad it comes at such a heavy price.*

"So there's no way you can give me anything by way of treatment before next month?" *Heavy price is right.* He'd be paying for the next appointment, which meant there was no way of keeping it from his father.

"I suppose we could try hypnotherapy again, as long as we don't go too long past the sixty minute mark. My schedule has very little room for deviation today." She'd lost her humanity again. It was no wonder he didn't see a ring or evidence of one on her left hand. She was way too cold for that.

"Let's do it," he sighed and tried to clear his mind.

Since Dr. Miller's hypnosis yielded nothing that they hadn't known before, Logan left her office wondering exactly how it was that he was going to go about paying $40 per hour he spent with her without telling his father. Then he remembered that he was supposed to be *avoiding* stress and decided that he would worry about where that money would come from when the time came. *If it comes down to it, I could cut back on the booze.* The thought did make him get a little panicky, so he pushed it away as he drove back to Wolf Village.

When he got to 317, Mark was playing *Halo* solo, and Logan managed to talk Mark into restarting and letting him in on the action. Besides sex and alcohol, playing Xbox was one of the most relaxing things he could think of. The boys played until the game was interrupted by front door flying open and Rob striding through it.

"Honies, I'm home!" he announced as he walked right in front of the screen, blocking both their views, and, thereby, causing their untimely deaths at the hand of the Covenant.

"We can hear *and* see that, Norton," Logan made sure he heard even though he was already in his room.

"I can see I was desperately missed," Rob answered as he came back towards the living area and deposited some bottles of scotch on a shelf in the section of the cabinet that was his. Then he headed back out to his Hummer to grab some more of his stuff.

Logan's player had come back to life after it had been a motionless corpse for the appropriate amount of seconds, and they were waiting for Mark's to do the same when he pressed pause and turned to Logan. "You wanna finish this later? I'm betting Rob comes back and forth through here at least two more times before he pours himself a few fingers and starts complaining that he can't watch ESPN if we're playing Xbox."

"Just like old times," Logan nodded with a sour smile and turned the system off as Mark stowed the controllers.

"Ain't life grand?" he asked as Logan headed for his room and the Jäger that was waiting there.

By Monday, Logan wished that Rob could have stayed home with his parents, or at least transferred to another college. After a near three month break from him, Logan had actually forgotten how insanely annoying the guy could be. The way he slunk around, making snarky comments and sipping his scotch like he was better than the rest of them, it was no shocker that the guy couldn't get laid, and that was his chief complaint. Logan never had understood how it could be his and Andrew's fault that they could get women and Rob couldn't. But the discrepancy had to be somebody's mistake other than his, so there you go. It had to be Logan and Andrew. Not even Rob could pass the buck onto Mark in that department. It had only been three days, but Logan was nearly ready to commit the murder Rob liked to accuse him of, stash Rob's body, and beg Batu to move back upstairs. For a quiet little dude, it surprised Logan how much he missed having Batu around. Now there was no one to ask questions about the dialogue on some rerun. There was only Rob with his aviator shades on, watching another never-ending stream of *SportsCenter*.

Being alone in 317 with Rob was not a good idea, so Logan kept to himself as much as he could and stayed in his room. This was the safest option until Mark or Andrew got back from wherever they'd each gone, but that didn't mean it was very entertaining. Thus, he did the only thing he could do until it was late enough in the day to make plans with whomever he decided on today (right now that was looking like Nikki, but who could tell what would happen to change his mind before then): he got on Facebook.

After logging in, he saw that he had a new message, and found that he wasn't quite as bored as he thought he was. It was Lillie's reply to his last message.

STILL WANT TO PROVE ME WRONG? IF YOU COME TO THE LIBRARY AROUND 2:00 ON MONDAY, YOU MIGHT BE ABLE TO LOOK AT MY FACE AND SEE IF THE PICTURES DO IT JUSTICE. NO PROMISES THAT I WON'T TRY TO EVISCERATE YOU WITH RHETORIC.

He debated on sending his own response, but saw that the message was dated a few days ago. Chances were, she wouldn't even see the message until after they met up at the library today, so he opted out of that. Instead, he decided to investigate her profile page a bit more and see if he could figure out what kind of coffee she liked. When it became clear that the search was a bust, he decided that taking coffee into the library was a bad idea anyway, and not doing that would only give him the chance to ask her out for coffee later, which could possibly lead to inviting her into his bed that night. Logan was thankful, not for the first time, that he liked approaching things logically.

He went to the library at 1:30. He knew he was giving himself plenty of time, which might make him look too eager, but he also acknowledged that she hadn't told him where in the library to meet her, and finding her might take some work, seeing as how she hadn't made anything easy for him since the day they met.

Logan didn't find her at the circulation desk or near the stacks, where he had encountered her before. He was sure that she didn't plan on making finding her easy for him, but he hoped she wasn't sadistic enough to pick a place (like the upper floors) that only library staff had access too. *That would be rich.* And it would be just like her. She liked to tantalize her victims. Play with their minds a bit before she sucked their insides out. He wondered why he'd even decided to come here. He should have known from past experience with her that she was just screwing with him. He looked around for any sign of a surly brunette who was dying with laughter, but didn't see one. *You idiot! Haven't you lived through enough prank wars and rushes to know a trap when you see one?*

136

He was cursing himself when he remembered that he hadn't replied to her message. *Sweet! I can cut my losses and get the freak out of here before she even knows I was here!* It was not the first time he would be grateful for his need to be on-time. Without the padding the extra thirty minutes gave him, escaping unseen wouldn't be possible. He was heading back down to the lobby with a sneer of triumph on his face when he collided with someone hidden behind a towering stack of books.

"Watch it, man!" he cried as he dodged the toppling volumes.

"I could say the same to you," came a feminine voice from behind what remained of the pile of paper and ink. That it was a female surprised him, but he was quick to recover and bent to retrieve the books that had clattered to the carpet. She had set the stack on the floor and was attempting to get them faster than he could, but his hands were larger and gave him an edge. The six or so he'd managed to scoop up in the same amount of time she'd only collected half that were all the proof of his superiority needed. "You're early."

"You're hot. Are we done stating the obvious?" His lip quirked when she rolled her eyes.

"I'm *working*." She shuffled her pile into an orderly stack once again.

"Could you possibly be carrying anymore of those things?" he asked as he passed the books he'd gathered to her.

"Only if guys like you keep on making massive messes for me to clean up," her words had him looking at her. Really looking, and he liked.

"Lillie," he smiled.

"Logan," she spat. "Are you gonna crouch there and stare at me all day, or is it too much to ask for you to *get out of my way*?"

"It's nice to finally be able to put a name with that face of yours. It's been haunting me, by the way. . ."

"What? Your insatiable need for nookie?" She smiled as she dealt the blow.

"No. Your face. I can't get it out of my head." He smiled too as he deflected it.

"I don't see how you'd have any trouble losing it in the ocean of others that you've lusted over and forgotten about the second after you finished."

"There you go making *ass*umptions. . ."

"That's the pot calling the kettle, but I'll take it, as long as you're included too." Lillie stood and attempted to take the tower with her, but gravity had other ideas, and so did Logan.

He leaned on the stack like it was a pillar put there especially for him to use as a prop. What had previously been difficult was now inconceivable. "What do you want, Logan?" she sighed.

"You," he grinned. *If she only knew how much.*

"Besides the obvious," her eyes narrowed, and she crossed her arms. *How was it possible that she still looked so sexy and aggravated all at the same time?* He decided the physics of it didn't matter, as long as he was able to enjoy it.

"Is getting to know you too much to ask?" He tried desperately not to smile as her eyes became mere slits.

"That all depends on how *well* you want to know me," she cocked a brow.

"I'm only suggesting we go out for coffee. How much can happen in a public place?" Logan turned his palms up, thankful for the flash in her green eyes.

138

"With you, it's hard to say, but I wouldn't put *anything* past you." The hard line of her mouth remained.

"Is that a yes?" It was his turn to cock a brow.

"Is a Frappuccino on the table?" Her tone was indifferent, but he recognized a fold when he saw one in an opponent's eyes.

"If that's what it takes." He decided not only to call, but to go all in. Logan sent her a wink as he picked up three-fourths of the stack and stepped aside so she could take the lead.

Twenty minutes later, they were sitting at Hill of Beans, one of the on-campus coffee houses. Lillie was sipping her mocha Frappuccino from a bright blue straw, and Logan hadn't touched the brew he'd ordered black, though he stirred it occasionally with the wooden stick that was purely cosmetic. Something for his hands to do. He made three clockwise circles around the edge of the cup and watched the tornadic dip he'd just created in the center of the liquid until it was gone.

"You think if you stir it enough times, that'll turn into an Irish Coffee?"

When he looked up at her words, he found that the expression on her face could have sweetened a gallon of black. It was made all the more attractive by the sharp contrast of her tone.

"You think if you hold out long enough, I'll stop taking swings?"

"No. You got your three strikes a long time ago, slugger. You're just too stubborn to take the out." She took another sip.

"Who says they're not balls?" He watched as she waged a small war with her grin, and it won out after a moment.

"Well, you've obviously got more than your fair share of those, so I'd be glad to let you walk."

"To where?" He hoped she wasn't going to suggest anything as cliché as "hell."

"Anywhere but here," she sighed.

"You coming along? 'Cause I don't think I could get to second base without you." He could tell by her look that he'd gotten all over her with that one.

"I wasn't aware you'd made it to first, but maybe your definition's a little broader than mine is." She smiled again, all sugar over her fire.

"We're here, aren't we? Drinking over-priced, crappy tasting coffee," he reminded her.

"And your point is?" Her eyes were narrow again, and he sensed she was losing patience.

"The only reason we are is because *you* told me to meet you at the library. It was your pitch, Lillie. I can't help it if I got the hit." He tried to feel bad about smirking, but couldn't, especially when she wore her mad so plainly on her face. "So, the question is: Why did you ask me to meet you, if you seem to loathe me so much?"

"Don't you ever get tired of the banter?" It was a real question and not her usual clever quip.

"Who, me? I love the wordplay." He decided to be honest too.

"That's right. The chase is half the–no make that *all* the fun for you; isn't it, Mr. Lady Killer?" Her sarcasm was back.

"What are you so afraid of?" he retaliated.

140

"I could ask the same of you, but I digress," she stopped his protest before it was out of his mouth. "I don't want to be a casualty of yours, Logan. Don't you get that? Yes, you're hot. Yes, you're interesting and sexy. No, you're not worth it."

Logan had never understood women. He admitted that now as he drove back to 317. Sure, he could read them and know the right moves to make to get what he wanted from them. But he realized that he never knew what was going on inside their heads that made them do the things they did. He knew they were fond of flowers and chocolates, good wine, sappy movies, and expensive clothes; but why? For a seasoned player, he suddenly felt very ignorant of the game.

Since when does the why matter? It didn't, as long as he was able to persuade them into bed. And he always had been. Until now.

That *was why I had the policy against the smart ones.* Why hadn't he remembered it until now? What did he think he was doing with Lillie Thackery? She wasn't his usual type, and there was a reason for that. Her type of girl just didn't go for guys like Logan. Guys like Andrew, maybe, but not guys like Logan. *Why?* Why was it that they didn't? Unless they were practicing to be nuns, he was pretty sure that they wanted sex just as much as the other girls, the ones who slept with guys like him. *So what was it about him that they could resist and other girls couldn't?* There had to be an answer, since, in theory, Andrew was able to use it to avoid their rejection.

Logan was willing to concede that Andrew was better looking–but only slightly–than he was, and that could be a small part of the reason, but it couldn't be the reason entirely. *They just thought differently from the party girls.* He already knew they had different priorities. They lived in libraries, didn't they? Lillie was playing her own game, and the only way he could compete with her was by throwing out all the rules he thought he could play by and just winging it. Or maybe he should just cut his losses.

Summer break was winding down, and Logan didn't really want to think about what would happen in two weeks' time. It would be a long, long autumn, and at the end of it, were two holidays that meant he couldn't avoid going back to Asheville. Christmas and Thanksgiving were times he had come to dread ever since he left for college the first time. Just the thought of spending first a week and then nearly a month with his parents and his brother was enough to give Logan a tension headache.

And what good was the free license Dr. Miller had given him if he was going to ignore it? Like his grandmother had told him when he was little and worried about every little thing he could possibly think up: don't borrow trouble. It was good advice then, and it was just as good now. He had the space of a good three months before he had to go home, and maybe he could think of something between now and then. Maybe not. But there wasn't anything he could do about it now.

Right now there were fourteen days left of total freedom, and he was going to make the best of them. *Carpe diem*, he thought as he picked up the phone and dialed Tori's number. He hadn't seen her since the last formal he'd had to attend, and from what he remembered about that night, she was as sure a way to relax as any. He smiled as she picked up, and he heard the Georgian drawl that had earned her the name "Scarlett O'Hara" among the frats. She had long, dark hair, pale skin and blue eyes, and a way of making a man lose himself. "It's nice to hear your voice too, Tori."

"It's been entirely too long since I've seen you." Her vowels were drawn out longer than the line for coffee during finals.

"Well, that's why I'm calling. Do you have plans tonight?" He asked the question, though he already knew what her response would be.

"Not so far as I know . . . What did you have in mind, sugar?"

He told her and imagined that she was blushing as red as the lipstick she liked to wear.

Just like that he was back in the game, ready to do Dr. Miller proud.

The evening faired better than Logan had hoped, and they hadn't even made it to his bedroom yet. Tori was knocking on 317's door at precisely six o'clock, which was another of the many characteristics she possessed which appealed to him. He answered it and invited her into the living room while he finished folding the clothes he'd have been done with if Rob hadn't been born to complicate his life. He ducked back into his room after making sure that Tori was comfortable sitting on the couch and chatting with Mark, who was so overwhelmed by her looks and accent that he was doing dang good to nod or shake his head at the appropriate time, and hurried to finish before she realized that her current companion was incapable of speech.

He was halfway through the pile of socks when he heard a loud gasp and a splash and something shattering. It sounded too interesting to ignore, so he finished the pair in his hands and walked into the living room to find Mark doubled over laughing, Rob soaked in some liquid (which Logan assumed was scotch) with a pile of glass shards at his feet, and Tori standing in front of Rob, looking like she could gladly rip him to pieces and lick the blood from her lips with a smile.

"Logan, I'd like to go to dinner now, please," she said primly when she saw him from the corner of her eye. By the time she'd turned to face him, she was a pretty little debutante again, and all signs that she'd looked otherwise had disappeared.

"Good idea," he agreed and took her hand, just to make sure that the dark color on those shiny nails stayed the way it was painted.

"It was nice seeing you again, Mark," she called as Logan guided her out the door as quickly as he could. There was nothing he wanted to do more than to laugh hysterically, but he could tell by Rob's eyes, which were actually visible since he'd taken his shades off to dry them, that laughing out loud would not be a good idea.

Once they were in the Camaro and Logan was pulling out of his space, he couldn't hold it in any longer. After he'd belly-laughed until he couldn't breathe, and Tori was staring at him like he'd turned into an alien, he managed to pant, "Don't get me wrong. I'm glad you did it. Norton's had it coming for a long time, but what in the world did he say to you?"

"He said he'd be glad to pay me double your price, if I went with him instead," she seethed.

Logan hit the brakes. "He did *what*?"

144

"It's okay, Logan. Let's just go get some food," Tori touched his shoulder.

"No. It's not okay," he was talking through his teeth because he was afraid of what he might say if he didn't keep them clamped shut. He was pulling back into the parking space when she spoke again.

"Logan. Stop. You aren't my boyfriend. You aren't my brother. And you sure as heck aren't my daddy. It isn't your fight. I can take care of myself."

"Tori, I—"

"No. Don't say something you don't mean, just because you feel like you have to. What he called me isn't true. You know it, and I know it, and that's enough." She flipped the visor down and opened the mirror on the back of it, then fiddled with her face. He was politely looking out the windshield at a brick wall when she laughed, "Come on, sugar. I'm starving. If you keep sitting here in this parking lot much longer, I might make you buy me a steak."

"I might just do that anyway," he grinned, "just to watch you try to eat it!" He drove out of the lot and headed off campus. "I'm sorry, Tori."

"It wasn't your fault, Logan," she kissed his cheek.

"I'm sorry all the same."

Chapter 10

The situation with Rob got no better after the incident with Tori. Despite what she said, Logan still wanted to kill him for what he'd said to her. Wronging women was something that shouldn't ever be done, to Logan's way of thinking. His father had taught him that lesson early enough. And for some reason, hurting his mother seemed only to make his father feel stronger. Logan knew it actually made him weaker.

Since he couldn't trust himself not to sucker punch the little turd, Logan hadn't spoken to Rob since he came back from Tori's. If Mark or Andrew noticed the extra tension, neither said anything. It wasn't like they could defend Rob's actions or would want to anyway. There had been discord between Rob and the three of them from nearly the first moment they'd become roommates. Then his seniority had forced Batu out of 317 and downstairs, which was another, more serious strike against him. Now there was Tori. Logan was done. He felt like punching something, but didn't want to have to pay the $150 damage fee, so he settled for shooting the crap out of the Covenant on the Xbox.

Logan purposely played right through the time slot he knew belonged to *SportsCenter* so that Rob was relegated to his room if he wanted to catch the episode, and that did give him some satisfaction, but he could only kill his rage with surrogates for so long. Thus, he put on *The Fast and the Furious* and lost himself in the destruction of really fast, really sweet cars.

The credits were sliding up the screen when Andrew came in and sat next to Logan on the couch. "I think it's over," he observed.

"Yeah," Logan clicked off the set.

"Is FX the only channel we've got now? Or is there some sort of rule against watching TV for more than a few hours at a time that I didn't know about?"

"I'm just tired of watching it." Logan checked his watch and tossed him the remote. "Be my guest." He shoved off the couch and headed to his room.

"Dude!" Andrew called after him.

"Got a lot on my mind," Logan answered. He went to his room and opened a bottle of Jäger. If action movies and video games couldn't clear his mind, maybe alcohol could. It wasn't just Tori who wouldn't leave his thoughts. It was Lillie too. It was his mom and dad. Knocking Rob into next week would feel great, but it wouldn't solve any of the problems that were floating around in his head. Then there were the blackouts. Dr. Miller seemed to think they were caused by stress, but if that was the case, he'd never get any sleep at all. He'd been angrier in the past few days than he had been in a long time, and he knew that keeping that rage hidden had to be causing at least as much stress as he had during finals, and yet he awoke in his bed every morning. Seeing Miller wasn't helping. Seeing an MD hadn't helped. Pranking Rob hadn't helped. The Jäger sure the crap hadn't helped, yet he took another swig. He had to be missing something. He just had no clue what that something was.

Logan woke up the next morning fully expecting to be mud-covered and naked on his floor. Instead, he was wearing his boxers, lying in his bed. He had a slight headache from the empty bottle sitting on his night stand, but it wasn't anything a shower and an aspirin couldn't cure. He was done brooding. There was still some residual anger, but he had a plan now, and there was almost nothing Logan liked better than having a plan, except for using logic to form that plan. *All it took was a little Jäger and time*, he smiled as he got up and headed for the shower. What was it the real Scarlett O said? "Tomorrow is another day." *Tomorrow is **today**.*

He went to the library when he'd dressed and had his coffee. The fact that he was coherent and actually preparing to do some form of work during the last of Summer Break seemed sacrilegious to both Mark and Andrew, but they didn't have a lot of time to rag him, since they were just rolling out of bed as he was leaving. Plus, they weren't alert enough to think of trash to talk because they hadn't had any coffee, and he'd already downed two cups.

Logan tended to see things in the sharp contrast of black and white. He liked it best when there just wasn't any gray. That was his problem. He'd let too much gray into his life, and now he had to get rid of it. Doing that might take a while, but it was possible. All he had to do was balance the books in a way; make the amount of white the same as the black, and there would be no gray. Order would be restored. He sat at a table amongst the general collection, armed with a notebook, some pens and highlighters, a cup of coffee, and his student ID in case he needed to make copies. He

148

wasn't leaving until he was able to see a little less of the gray.

He had been sitting there about two hours when he heard her voice from behind him. "This must be *some* project if you're working on it before class even starts."

"You could say that," he answered Lillie without looking up. He wasn't here to flirt her into his bed. He knew by now it wouldn't work anyway.

"Are you going to tell me what you're working on, or am I going to have to guess?" she asked after a beat.

"I'm curious about some things," he shrugged.

She snatched a book he had open on the table and read from it. "Why are you interested in the hormone cycles of the human body? I thought you were a business major."

"Maybe I'm a biology minor." He made a note on the pad he was using and went back to the book he was pouring over.

"And maybe I'm Megan Fox," she scoffed. "The road goes both ways, you know. You want to know everything there is to know about me, but then you don't want me to know a thing about you that isn't common knowledge to the rest of the student body."

"Now who's the pot and who's the kettle?" he kept his eyes on the printed page. "You know how long it took me to find out your name?"

"Lillie Danielle Thackery. Happy now?"

"No. Too late. Knew it already. Don't you have a job to do? Like shelving books and helping people find stuff?" He had yet to make eye contact and planned to keep it that way. He didn't know what he would do if he met her eyes. What he would say.

149

"I guess I do. I just thought I'd give you another chance to objectify me." Her words had his chin coming up before he could do anything about it.

"What d'you mean by that?" Logan demanded and saw the flash in the lakes of her eyes. He wanted to dive into them and explore their depths. Discover what caused those little flecks of gold on green.

"Just what I said. I thought you might like another chance to try to seduce me," she smiled then, and those lakes looked chilly.

"I don't usually go for your type. You're too *studious*." He took aim and hoped for a well-placed shot. He could be just as cold.

"Oh. I thought most guys had school-girl fantasies now and again, but maybe you don't go for the sexy geek with glasses, a plaid skirt and matching tie. Maybe you're *different*, like you keep telling me." But she wasn't buying that now, anymore than she had in the past.

"Look. I know I deserve everything you seem to want to give me, and I'll take it, but I want you to know that I won't bother you anymore." His reply surprised her. It was the first time he'd seen her lose her footing.

"I thought the only thing you were looking for was a good time." That got him. And as much as he wanted to, there was no way he could deny that.

"I didn't look at it that way, but you're right. That was all I wanted," he met her eyes and hoped she could see it was true.

"Want*ed*? As in past tense?" She was skeptical, and he couldn't blame her.

"Yeah," he sighed. "It wasn't as painless as I thought."

"For who?" She hadn't bought it.

"The parties involved." He frowned. Had he really been reducing them to nothing more than a means to an end?

"It seemed pretty painless for you, Logan." Her disbelief echoed around him. He wanted to shake her.

"It takes two . . ." It felt strange for him to be making this argument with her.

"It can't be! Has Mr. One-Night-Stand actually developed a conscience?" Her eyes were slits of jade.

"Why is it so hard for you to understand? I'm *sorry*, okay!" He noticed that she was wide-eyed. Not only that, but so were several of the people in close proximity to him. Logan dropped his hands, and the tone of his voice, "I'm sorry. I thought as long as I treated her like a lady and made sure there were no strings, no one would get hurt at the end of the night. I was wrong. I know that now."

"What'd she do? Leave before you woke up? Give you a taste of your own medicine?" There was no empathy in her voice.

"You could say that. My roommate offered to double what I was paying if she went with him instead." He had to force his fingers to relax from the fist he'd made when he thought of it. "I never thought of it like that. The enjoyment was mutual, and I was always careful to make sure she had a good time before I had my fun. Always fed her dinner or breakfast or sometimes both. I had no idea."

"Now you do," Lillie laid a hand on his shoulder. When he turned at the touch, she offered him her hand and a genuine smile. "Hi, Logan. I'm Lillie. It's nice to finally meet you."

151

Logan left the library as he had hoped, with a little less gray than he had when he had come in. Unfortunately, that gray was not the gray he had planned to eliminate. He still had no explanation for his blackouts, and he had a feeling that making friends with Lillie was not going to keep them from returning and soon.

His prediction became reality a few days after the start of the fall term. He knew he was on the floor before he even opened his eyes. He could feel the layer of dried mud caked on his skin. Resigned, he opened his eyes, pulled himself off the floor and trudged to the shower. He didn't have to check the clock to know that it was only a few minutes past six.

When he got out of the shower and felt human again, he threw his sheets into the wash and put some coffee on. He had a little over an hour before he needed to go to class, and since he didn't think the guys would appreciate getting woken this early on a school day, he decided to send a text to Lillie's number, which he had recently been able to add to his phone book:

HEY YOU.

He was sitting on the couch, being disgusted with the lack of interesting programming at seven in the a.m. when he got her response:

UP PRETTY EARLY AREN'T YOU, SUNSHINE?

LOOKS LIKE. WANT COFFEE BEFORE CLASS? Logan wondered briefly how she would react to his invitation.

MEET YOU IN 20? Her response was in his inbox almost as soon as he'd send the message.

I'M THERE. He grinned as he got off the couch and went to grab his bag.

If Lillie had any fears that Logan would try to use the new phase of their relationship to get her into his bed, they were unfounded. It wasn't that he found her unattractive. He was a strong proponent of the long, dark waves that flowed down her back, the moss of her eyes, the smoke of her voice. He wanted the heady experience her entire being promised, but he knew that he'd never remember what happened during the next two nights, and when he did get to experience Lillie Thackery, he dang sure wanted to remember it. Besides that, he had no desire whatsoever to expose Lillie to a side of himself that he didn't even know.

Since Hill of Beans was convenient for Lillie, they met there the next morning. Logan had no problem planning such an early rendezvous, since he knew he'd be awake, and rising with the sun appeared habitual for her, but when he walked away from the café Wednesday morning after the second night of the blackouts, he wondered what he would do after tomorrow.

It was fun getting to know the girl behind the face that had hidden in his subconscious since the first time he'd encountered her. Originally he had been drawn to the fact that she'd rejected him, that and knowing nothing about her. He figured once they spent some time together, that pull would slack up like it always did when he sighted and subsequently wooed a woman whose looks he liked. But so far they'd had something like four dates, if you could call them that, and Logan learned more about her with each one, yet that pull hadn't lessened at all. Granted, the pull usually disappeared after a good lay with the girl. That was it. That was why he thought about her almost as much as he thought of the puzzle he never quite stopped trying

153

to solve. And maybe it was because of the shared frequency that Lillie and the blackouts had in his thoughts that he found himself wanting to talk about them with her.

And maybe he was just going soft. *See what a lack of sex and sleep can do to a man?* After class, he picked up some zinfandel and gave Danni a call. She was one of Andrew's old girls, and under normal circumstances, he wouldn't think of breaking that cardinal rule of dudedom, but it was Andrew he was dealing with, and who could even keep track of all the women he'd had and were thereby made off-limits? When the Stallion himself couldn't remember them all, Logan didn't feel bad about doing a little "forgetting" of his own. In fact, he felt pretty dang good about it.

Crap. Logan felt like crap. Not only was he on the floor again, but the sun was nowhere near rising. He knew because there was absolutely no difference when he opened his eyes from when they were closed. His room and the sky were both pitch. Something wasn't right. He crawled to his night stand and checked the clock. *4:52 in the freaking morning. What gives? It's more than an hour earlier than this mess usually wakes me up! This sucks!*

For a minute, he actually contemplated sliding into the mess that was his bed and sleeping until at least six. But at the last second, his scruples won out, and he plodded to the shower. *At least I don't have to deal with a screaming female.* He turned on the spray and let it hit him full-on, grateful that he'd had the foresight to send Danni packing right after supper. When he was clean, he saw that it was a quarter after five. He went to the

154

kitchen to turn on the brew, knowing he would be wide awake when he met up with Lillie in two hours.

Habit had Logan recording the new date, 08/29/07, just below the others on the cover of his notebook. It was the third in a row, thus completing another series. It was the sixth set of three nights he'd survived so far, and he felt a sick sense of accomplishment at that as he lay on the couch and tried to sleep.

"Who'd you spend the night with?" Lillie wanted to know as soon as he sat down at the table with her. The smile on her face wasn't exactly friendly.

"What?" Logan wasn't sure what the appropriate response was. He was never sure when it came to Lillie.

"Who'd you spend the night with?" she repeated, her expression unchanged.

"Who says I spent the night with anyone?" he countered, since he wasn't sure if she was annoyed or just feeling spunky.

"Your face is an open book, pal. You got absolutely no sleep whatsoever. And in Logan's world, that means he got laid."

"You want coffee? It's too early in the morning for arguing without coffee." He watched her face for a moment, still trying to test the water.

"Sure," she nodded, that mysterious smile still in place.

He escaped to the counter to order her latte and his black, but when he returned a few minutes later, her expression still hadn't changed.

She was quiet as he put her cup in front of her and then sat and took a few swallows of his own. "Now that you're awake enough to answer, who was she?"

155

Her eyes had found his somehow, and there was no breaking the contact.

There were hundreds of ways he could answer her, but at the moment, lying didn't seem like an option, though he wasn't sure why. "Her name's Danni, and I didn't spend the night with her. She left right after supper." He held his breath, hoping she wasn't feeling dramatic enough to slap him and storm off.

"So why do you look like a zombie right now? You spend the night tossing and turning as you pined for her company?" *Apparently she's just in a playful mood.* The smile was venomous again, but she didn't look violent . . . exactly.

"Actually I have no idea why I got no sleep last night. I can't remember a thing," he confessed, wondering why he felt so compelled to be truthful to her. *Lying would've been so much easier.*

"Empty your beloved keg?" Her eyes were slits again. *Yep, lying would've saved me a ton of trouble.*

"For the last time, I don't even own a keg. The Kappa Sigs might, but I, personally, do not," he threw up his hands.

"So what were you high on?" Her mouth was a firm line. *Great!*

"I don't do drugs. I may drink more than my share and sleep around too much, but I don't do drugs." He wondered if offering to pinky swear would help his case. *I'm thinking not.*

"So, for absolutely no reason at all, you lost an entire night of your life." He could hear her disbelief, actually hear it.

"Something like that," he sighed. She stood up. "Wait! Where are you going?" he reached for her arm, but stopped himself before he actually touched her. The look on her face said that was a wise decision.

"I like you, Logan. Despite the fact that every alarm bell in my head is going off, I like you. I can be your friend, but that's all. I'm not one of your dinner-and-a-show girls. And I don't like it when my friends do extremely stupid things and then try to cover them up. I'm not dumb. If you're not okay with that, I figure it's time we both cut our losses." She didn't show the disappointment in her face, but he could hear it in her voice.

"Lillie." This time he did put his hand on her arm. He felt her tense beneath it, but she didn't shrug him off. "Despite the fact that you're not my type at all," he had to hold up his other hand to keep from getting decked. "I like you too. I'm not very good at this guy-girl platonic relationship thing because, to be honest, I've never really tried it before. So I'd really appreciate it if you could cut me a little slack to begin with."

"I don't like lies. I'm not your girlfriend. If you're sleeping around, just tell me. Don't try to spare me with some lame story. All that'll do is tick me off," she sat back down and took a sip of her coffee.

"That's just it. I wasn't lying to you. I honestly have no idea what happens to me. I blackout, and the next thing I know, it's morning." He noticed she hadn't said anything about half-truths.

"How long has this been going on?" *Was that a note of concern in her voice?*

"Off and on since April." *No need to tell her about the pattern whose formula defied all logic. There was such a thing as being **too** honest.*

157

"Have you seen somebody about it?" She had taken his hand, and he wondered if she was aware of it. *Who the crap cared?*

"Had a couple bad moments a while ago. Thought it might be a brain tumor or something. But I saw a doc at Student Health Services who said I was fine except for my habit of drinking my liver into oblivion." He decided he would enjoy the feeling of her slim, slightly calloused hand in his for as long as she'd let him.

"And they haven't gone away. No wonder you're always reading medical books and journals. Have you found anything?" Her voice was the softest he'd ever heard it.

"Not yet. Went to a psychiatrist at the Counseling Center after I'd convinced myself that it was a mental problem, and I had some sort of multiple personality or something, but she said I didn't have that either. Now I'm hitting the medical books again because, if I'm not crazy, the MD had to have missed something."

It was quiet at their table for a while. Logan figured she was taking a moment to digest what he'd told her, and as long as he could keep her hand in his while she did, he was more than fine with that. When she was ready to speak, she took a deep breath. "Logan, I have an idea . . ."

The unsteady quality of her voice made him uneasy about hearing this idea of hers, but he nodded for her to continue. "Why don't you let me do some digging for you? After all, research is pretty much what I do. Maybe between the two of us, we can come up with something." She smiled at him, all warmth this time.

"Maybe we can," he agreed, knowing she wouldn't find anything he hadn't already seen, but wanting to keep that smile intact as long as he could.

Over the next few days, Lillie sent Logan several text messages which seemed random on first glance:

EXACTLY HOW MANY TIMES HAVE YOU BLACKED OUT?

DO YOU KNOW THE DATES?

DO THEY ALWAYS HAPPEN IN THREES?

HOW MUCH TIME DO YOU USUALLY LOSE WHEN ONE HAPPENS?

DO YOU WAKE UP IN THE SAME PLACE YOU BLACKED OUT IN?

WHAT DO YOU MEAN "NAKED AND COVERED IN MUD FROM HEAD TO TOE?"

ONLY MUD, OR ARE THERE LEAVES AND STICKS TOO?

He replied to her texts as he had replied to others' questions. There was nothing new in her inquiry. Everything had been asked and answered, rephrased and answered again exactly the same way as before. He had to keep telling himself that *she* hadn't asked those questions before, but it didn't make the process any less annoying for him. *What was the use really? She would just come to the same dead ends he and four other people had, and then where would he be?* He was getting sick of rehashing the one thing that he couldn't make any sense of. All thinking about it did was drive him crazy.

Logan escaped into the world of *COD* with Andrew and Mark. Rob was gone, and they were too glad about it to question where. Thus, in celebration, they'd invited Batu up to join them. They'd actually coaxed a controller into Batu's hand, and Andrew was patiently attempting to explain the concept of a first-person-shooter video game to a person whose entire gaming experience reached its pinnacle with the Atari version of *Space Invaders*. While that was going on, Mark and Logan started a game from scratch so that Batu could have some visuals to go along with Andrew's explanations. Logan had just demonstrated how to switch cameras (that you could change the perspective at all was a wonder to Batu), when his cell phone beeped, and the distinct sound told him it was a text.

Since his phone was on the coffee table and his hands were occupied with the controller at the moment, he opted to let it be. *Whoever it is can wait until the end of the round.* Mark, however, was not as patient, snatching the RAZR off the table and flipping it open. "It's a text from a girl named Lillie," he informed everyone. "It says, 'Do you sleep naked?'" he snickered after opening the message. "Sounds like Mr. Michaels has himself some plans for tonight," Mark continued to giggle as he pressed buttons.

"What are you doing, man?" Logan dodged an enemy soldier.

"Typing a reply," he grinned.

"Give me my phone, buttwipe, before I tea-bag your man!" Logan growled as he pressed pause and grabbed the phone just before Mark could press send on the message: YOU COULD ALWAYS COME OVER TONIGHT AND FIND OUT. *She'd be **real** receptive to that!*

"What does he mean 'tea-bag?'" Batu asked just as Logan deleted the message. Since Andrew was already playing commentator, he'd let *him* answer that one. He had sent Lillie the response NO. when Batu said, "Oh. I thought it was used to make tea."

They were having coffee after class on Tuesday, since Logan hadn't woken at an early enough hour for them to meet before. He had to admit that it was pretty nice having a kind of routine with her. It didn't make him feel trapped as he had thought it might. He looked forward to it. He wasn't sure how he felt about it when he had that self-revelation, but it was true. That didn't mean he was becoming monogamous either. Like she'd said, they weren't dating. Their relationship was just the way he liked them to be—no strings. It just happened to last a lot longer than what he was used to. Things weren't perfect for him, since they weren't sleeping together, but Logan decided he would take what he could get.

Like always, she was sitting at a table, waiting when he got there. Even though they weren't together, he bought the coffee. She habitually offered to pay, and he continued politely refusing to let her. He knew it was archaic and chauvinistic and whatever else people wanted to call it nowadays, but he still felt it was his place, and if he couldn't afford to buy her coffee, then it was time to get a job.

When he returned from the counter with her Frappuccino and his own cup of coffee, she was intent on some handwritten notes in front of her. "Whatcha readin'?"

161

She looked up at his question and smiled her friendly smile at him, the one that was his favorite. "Just some things I found interesting. Thanks for the coffee."

"No problem," he passed hers to her and sat across the tiny table. "What makes that so interesting? Is it for a class?" Lillie was an archeology major, and she was always reading and researching ancient societies and people. She'd told him archeology was like watching a story come together, climbing in an author's mind and watching the whole scenario come to life piece by piece.

Her laughter trickled over him, and he wondered if it was possible to drown in that sound. "You think all I do is study, Mr. Party-Now-Class-Later?"

"I'm guessing the correct answer would be 'no,'" he sipped his coffee.

"That's right," she told him in the tone a trainer might use with an obedient dog. "How in the world can you drink that stuff?"

"What? My coffee? Easy. I just tip the cup and drink . . . *very* carefully," he grinned.

"No. Really. I don't see how you can drink it black, for one thing, and hot in the afternoon for another." She treated him to another dribble of giggles.

"I drink it black because, unlike most people, I actually like the taste of coffee. And since when does the time of day dictate the temperature of my coffee?"

"I like the taste of coffee too, as long as it's got sugar and cream and whatever else they add in to make it sweet and delicious. And the time of day *always* dictates the temperature of my coffee! Why else do you think I get lattes in the morning and Frappuccinos in the afternoon?"

"If you drink lattes in the morning and Frappuccinos in the afternoon, what do you drink at night?" His curiosity was piqued.

"Espresso, of course!" Her smile called him a simpleton.

"Oh, of course," he tapped his forehead lightly with his palm. "You know, if I didn't know any better, I'd think you were a hippie coffee snob!"

"You take that back, Logan Michaels, or I'll go back to being the Ice Queen," her eyes of beryl were sharp enough to slice, ". . . and you *know* I will!"

"I didn't say you *are* hippie coffee snob," he clarified hastily, knowing she'd make good on her threat.

"It isn't like I refuse to drink anything that isn't Starbucks. I just have my preferences; that's all," she spoke primly. "I'll bet you do too when it comes to alcohol and women. And you don't get called a snob!"

"What can I say? It's a man's world, and you're just living in it." He was smart enough to duck so that her fist missed his face.

There was a brief silence during which he supposed she was giving him the silent treatment, but he didn't plan on letting her build up any momentum. She returned to staring at her notes, or at least pretending to, so he swiped a page from her stack.

"Hey! I was reading that!" She glared right through him.

"And we were having a conversation here," Logan reminded her as he scanned the words she'd written in bright blue ink. It seemed that these notes concerned the symptoms he'd been researching himself, though he only read through a few lines before she grabbed the paper from him and put it back on top of the others. "Is all this stuff about me?"

"I'm not done yet, but it's what I've managed to find so far." She sent him another smile, but this time it was full of embarrassment.

"Any theories?" He was impressed at the amount of material she'd come up with in just a few days' time. There had to be four or five sheets of legal paper covered in notes on both sides.

"One or two . . ." she began, but shook her finger when he opened his mouth. "Don't. I don't have enough info to share them with you yet. You'll hear them soon enough," she laughed as he attempted a pout of disappointment.

Chapter 11

Logan debated all morning during classes about going to his appointment with Dr. Miller. He had used up his freebies with the three sessions he'd gone to previously, and if he kept this up, he was either going to have to make adjustments to his budget or attract the attention of his father, who monitored the depletion of Logan's college fund as if it was the last money in the world. When given the choice of spending the money on alcohol and/or treating a chick to a meal as a prelude or postlude, or seeing Dr. Miller, the decision was clear cut. The only part that bothered him was wondering if she was actually on to something with the whole PTSD thing, and he was giving up too soon. Then again, he'd seen her three times, and she still wasn't able to make a definite diagnosis, and they couldn't start treatment for lack of that. *But what if I really do have PTSD and those pills or the hypnosis or whatever actually can get rid of the blackouts? And what about the pills? How the crap am I supposed to explain the monthly bill for Paxil on Dad's credit card? Walk up to him and be like, "Surprise, Dad. Your oldest son is not only a disappointment, but I'm mentally unstable to boot?" Philip would definitely be less than thrilled. But wouldn't it be worth hacking off the old man if it got rid of the blackouts in the long run? Just how long a long run are we talking about, though? Face it, Logan, if you jump into this with both feet, you're probably going to wind up with a standing appointment at a shrink's office for the rest of your life. Wouldn't that be better than losing 18 hours, doing Lord-knows-what, every month for the rest of your life?*

The internal argument raged in the same cyclical pattern well into lunch. He was finished with class and had made himself a sandwich while he continued to cogitate. He was half done with it before he realized that he hadn't even tasted the first bite. "Dang! Maybe I am crazy." He took a swig of Gatorade and decided, *To hell with it! If Miller can't find the answer, maybe she knows someone else who can. Dad can go screw himself; he's done it to everyone else anyway.*

He started the Camaro, ready to hand the Counseling Center $40, when his cell buzzed. "Crap! Lillie." He'd completely forgotten to meet her at Hill of Beans, which had somehow become an everyday thing. "Hey," he picked up and wondered if she was sitting there, sipping a Frappuccino from a blue straw.

"Where are you? If I didn't know any better, I'd think you were in bed with some chick. Wait. . . I don't." The ice she spoke with chilled him even through the phone.

"If I was, I wouldn't have answered," he tried to joke. The silence on her end had his explanation rushing out. "Really. I'm on my way to the shrink right now. Sorry I forgot. Can we do something in about an hour and a half?"

"Why are you still seeing that psychiatrist? I thought you said she told you that you weren't crazy." The ice had been replaced with confusion.

"She did. But she thinks I have PTSD and that it's somehow causing the blackouts. She says if I keep coming, eventually we'll figure out what the trigger is, and then we can somehow get rid of them." *I hope.*

"And how much are all these sessions costing you?" Now she was skeptical.

"The first few were free, but it's forty a pop from now on." He didn't blame her. He didn't even want to think about how much he'd wind up spending.

"That's ridiculous! Logan, you don't have PTSD. To have PTSD, you'd actually have to have had some sort of terribly traumatic experience that would scar you for life and make you stress out. Have you ever seen anybody die or be killed?" She was obviously trying to poke holes in Miller's logic.

"No." He wasn't going to let her.

"Have you ever been in a major accident and seen any graphic wounds or whatever?" She sounded like she was sneering.

"No." He wasn't about to cop to something like that and then have to invent details. That kinda crap would only come back to bite him.

"Then what could you have possibly experienced that would make you have PTSD?" She had a point there, not that he was telling her about it.

"Dr. Miller says she thinks I got lost in the woods as a child and that the blackouts are being caused by some sort of external trigger that goes back to that experience." There, he was sure she couldn't refute that . . . could she?

"And how in the crap did she come to that conclusion?" *Apparently she can.*

"She hypnotized me, and while I was under, I remembered being in the woods, walking around, searching for something and being really, really hungry.

She thinks it was a repressed memory." He doubted she could come up with a better explanation.

"Logan, promise me you won't go to see Dr. Miller today." She couldn't, so it seemed her next plan of action was to change the subject.

"Why? I think she could be on to something." He had the urge to defend the shrink, though he wasn't sure why.

"She's not. Just trust me on this. Don't go. I think I've figured it out. Meet me at the library in fifteen." Since when did she get to tell him what to do?

"I can't." *That'll show her.*

"What have you got to lose? If I'm right, you save way more than $40. If I'm wrong, you can call the Counseling Center tomorrow, tell them you were sick, and reschedule. No harm; no foul." *Why in the crap does she have to make such a logical argument?*

"Well . . ." He was at a loss.

"Come on, Logan. Man up. You know I'm making more sense right now than Miller ever has." *How does it feel, Michaels? How does it feel to be outwitted by a girl?*

"Fine. Make it twenty. I gotta re-park my car." *Don't feel too bad, she is a smart chick after all.*

"Good," and she was gone.

Logan walked into the library wondering what was wrong. It felt a bit surreal, skipping out on his appointment. Not that he hadn't cut class a few times when he found a more educational opportunity elsewhere. Still, he wasn't one to shirk responsibilities. His father had made sure of that. And going to his appointment with the shrink felt like one. *Get a hold of yourself! You act like you're ten years old and about to get grounded for doing something bad. You made a decision; now*

168

you're stuck with the consequences. He shook the guilt to the back of his mind when he found Lillie at one of the tables near the entrance. She was in her element, surrounded by reference books, yellowing journals and what looked like more than twenty smaller nonfiction books that he bet were drier than his high school English teacher's classes. Given ten minutes, he was positive he would fall asleep. He got closer and recognized her ever-present stack of notes. It seemed to have grown since he saw it last at Hill of Beans. He wasn't sure if that was a good sign or a bad one.

Lillie didn't see him until he sat down in the chair directly across her. "Hey you."

"Hey," she smiled briefly, and then her attention went back to the book she was reading. He noticed the pen and ink sketch printed on the opposite page. It seemed like a sinister picture, but he couldn't quite make out what the subject was, since it was flipped from his point of view.

"Looks like you've done a little more than just look into my situation." He eyed the mountain of work she'd done.

"Yeah. Once I got going, things sort of snowballed, and it was hard to stop. But I tend to go a little overboard when I'm researching something I'm interested in." It looked like her snowball had started an avalanche.

"You're interested in me?" He felt the cocky grin curling his lips.

"Not you, so much as your problem, but yeah." She seemed to take delight in deflating that grin.

"And what makes my 'problem' so interesting to you?" His rapid recovery time came in handy. His

169

question was quick and meant to measure her reaction time as well.

"Logan, have you ever had the feeling that you were on to something? Maybe you couldn't explain it to anybody, but you knew, just *knew* that you were right?" She was fast; he had to admit it. The girl was fast.

"You mean like intuition? Or a hunch?" Again he found his eyes on the shadowy illustration, which his own gut said wasn't a good sign.

"Exactly," she nodded and began to sort through the loose leafs she'd collected. Most were notebook paper filled with her neat script. Others, he thought, were Xeroxed articles taken from newspapers. Still more were pages printed from the Internet. Everything he saw had been annotated. There were copious notes squeezed into margins, whole sections of text blocked out in blinding yellow and pink, and word after word underlined in red, as if tiny claws had scraped away the words' surface to expose the meat beneath. "I've got a hunch about what's happening to you . . . but I'm not sure you're gonna like it."

"I wasn't too fond of what the shrink said either," he turned his palms up, waiting.

She blew a bit of breath up from the side of her mouth. "I agree that there's something going on with you, but the changes that you're experiencing aren't some sort of mental malfunction. I think they're purely physical."

"But the doc said—"

"The doctor you saw wasn't looking for anything outside the realm of medicine." She hesitated again when the surprise surfaced on his face. "That's why he didn't find anything wrong. The psychiatrist won't find anything either, though it seems she's doing a more thorough search. Neither of them will find anything because what I think we're dealing with isn't something that can be explained by science."

"What do you mean, 'it can't be explained by science?' If it can't be explained by science, then it can't be explained at all." He couldn't figure out where she was going.

"What about miracles?" She stared at him as if that might somehow change his answer.

"I don't believe in them." They were like luck. He knew that if a man was smart enough, he could make his own luck, and if that was the case, how could miracles exist?

"Or faith?" Nerves definitely weren't her dominant emotion now. He could almost see the heat simmering through her skin.

"I don't have faith in anybody but me." He told the truth, but as soon as he said it, he saw a shift in her and regretted it. He wasn't sure if she wanted to crumple to the floor or crouch for an attack. He wasn't fond of either option, so he didn't give her the chance to choose. "Just what do you think we're dealing with here?" Now he was the one with the fire in his veins.

"The stuff of legends. The supernatural. Shape shifters." She had to be kidding.

"Shape shifters?" He almost laughed.

"Can't you see, Logan?" *How can* **she** *stand there and look at* **me** *like* **I'm** *crazy?*

"How could you possibly know what was happening to me? You've been gone all summer." He made what he thought was an excellent point.

"That doesn't mean I can't see what's right in front of me. I'm surprised you can't." She was smirking now.

"What are you even talking about?" *She can't have any idea.*

"The weird stuff that's been happening to you. You've been trying to figure it out for months. You wrote the dates down right here." She picked up his notebook pointed at the neat columns he'd entered on the inside cover. "Do you know what they mean yet?"

"Very observant." He tried to look as nonchalant as she did. He'd only brought the stupid thing out of habit, and now she was using it against him like evidence in court. He wouldn't intimidate that easily.

"Three nights in a row, happening once a month. You're researching hormones and body changes. You have blackouts and headaches. Probably aggression too. Am I right?" Her hand was on her hip and her eyebrow arched. She had him.

"So?" What else was there for him to say. Denying was useless. "The doc swears I'm not dying, and the shrink says I'm not nuts."

"Of course you're not nuts!" She threw up her hands.

"What's that supposed to mean? You think it's normal to wake up butt naked and covered in mud on your bedroom floor with a headache fit for an elephant and no idea what the crap you did during the past six hours?" He was losing the hushed whisper that they'd been using in deference to others in the room, but he didn't care if he was talking too loudly.

"No. Not normal exactly, but I think I can explain it." She put a finger to her lips.

"How much you wanna bet?" He obliged, but only slightly.

"I don't. But I do think I can help you." She paused to gauge his reaction.

"No you can't. No one can. Not until I figure out what it is I'm missing. There's got to be an answer somewhere, and I'm going to find it." He shook his head. There was no way she knew something that two doctors didn't.

"I've already found the answer. Logan, you're a werewolf."

Chapter 12

The girl is freaking insane; it was all he could think. What else was he supposed to think when someone stood there and told him something so ridiculous? *No rational person would come up with an explanation like that. Maybe she's been studying and staring at books too long. That's it. Has to be. We've been spending time together for about a month now, and in all that time, I've never heard or seen her do anything that might make me think she was crazy. She just needs a break, that's all. She's spread herself too thin studying for classes and doing all this outside research for you too.* Logan felt guilty. What did he expect her to do? What made him think that she could help him? She was an undergrad just like he was. And science wasn't even her field. He could tell that she was the type of girl who wanted to help everyone she could, and what did he do but go and take advantage of that fact. Well, this was the consequence for being so self-centered. She'd begun to slip, and it was all his fault. He didn't plan on sitting around, doing nothing either. He would fix it.

"Logan?" Her voice reminded him that he hadn't said a word, and she was waiting for some sort of response to her announcement, though he wasn't sure what the appropriate one might be.

"Lillie, I really appreciate all the research you've done. Why don't you let me take you out for more

174

than just coffee tomorrow night, as a way of returning the favor? I mean, I know it won't be equivalent time wise, but it's something." He hoped he sounded sincere. He really was grateful for her help, even if it didn't solve the problem.

"I can't *believe* you're still trying to hit on me! We've been through this. You're not worth it to me." Her reaction was not what he was expecting.

"If I was trying to hit on you, you'd rip me to shreds. Plus, you're not my type, remember?" He could fire low blows too.

"It doesn't matter! I tell you the answer you've been searching for, and all you can say is thanks?" She sounded more angry than hurt.

"What do you want me to say? That I think you're crazy? That this whole conversation is ridiculous?" But then so was he.

"If that's what you think," she nodded.

"Well it is! They aren't even real, and you're telling me that I'm one of them? I hate to tell you this, but you aren't dreaming me up. *I'm* real." He wished his eyes could be as sharp as hers.

"I never said otherwise. You're real. I'm real. And so are some things we don't want to believe in. There's more to life than just what we can see." Unfortunately, her eyes were the ones doing the pinning at the moment.

"So now you're gonna go all mystic on me? Talk about magic or monsters or whatever?" He ignored them.

"No. I've got proof, Logan. That is, if you're willing to hear it." The ring of her challenge met his ears.

"Fine. Try me." But he already knew she would fail.

175

"Look at these." She put a stack of *The Technician*'s back issues in front of him. "In every one of them there's evidence." She picked up one of them, flipped to the news briefs and pointed to an entry:

THE CHANCELLOR'S CAT, MR. FUZZWHISKERS, DISAPPEARED LAST NIGHT. A CAMPUS FRATERNITY PRANK OR HAZING RITUAL IS THE SUSPECTED CAUSE.

"And then a month later. . ." She showed him another issue:

CATNAPPING CRAZE. WHAT BEGAN WITH THE UNEXPLAINED DISAPPEARANCE OF THE CHANCELLOR'S CAT HAS NOW BECOME A WIDESPREAD EVENT. CATS AND OTHER SMALL HOUSE PETS ARE GOING MISSING FROM ALL PARTS OF THE NCSU CAMPUS. IN THE PAST THREE DAYS ALONE, 20 ANIMALS HAVE BEEN REPORTED LOST OR STOLEN.

"And the month after that:"

A WOLF WAS SPOTTED IN A WOODED AREA ON CAMPUS LAST NIGHT, ACCORDING TO A POLICE REPORT FILED ANONYMOUSLY. THOUGH THE SIGHTING CANNOT BE CONFIRMED, AND THERE IS NO EVIDENCE THAT SUCH AN ANIMAL WAS ACTUALLY ON THE NCSU GROUNDS, MANY ARE ATTRIBUTING THE RECENT STRING OF PET DISAPPEARANCES TO THIS PREDATOR. THE PRESENCE OF A WOLF ON CAMPUS IS UNLIKELY BUT NOT IMPOSSIBLE. . .

"And most recently." She handed him an issue dated only a week ago:

176

TWO PIGS, THREE GOATS AND SIX SHEEP WERE
STOLEN FROM THE AGRICULTURAL DEPARTMENT OVER
THE PAST THREE NIGHTS.

"What do any of these articles have to do with me?
They're all about animals disappearing." Logan asked.

"The animals are disappearing because you're eating
them." Her answer would have been funny if she
hadn't been so serious.

"You think *I'm* the wolf somebody reported to
UPD? That sounds more like some drunk dude making
a prank call or doing a dare to me than hard evidence
that I'm some sort of wolf." He hoped to bring her
back to Earth from wherever she'd gone.

"But look at the dates, Logan. All the incidents
coincide with the dates of your blackouts, and all the
blackouts coincide with the nights of and surrounding a
full moon. You said yourself that you have absolutely
no idea what happens for six hours. Think about it.
You wake up naked and dirty on your bedroom floor.
Under hypnosis, you remember wandering in the
woods somewhere, starving. What if you're filthy when
you wake up because you've spent the night romping all
over the woods on campus as a wolf, and while you're
doing that, you work up an appetite. Thus, the shortage
of small pets on campus." *She actually sounds logical in her
own head!*

"You're saying I ate these animals as a midnight
snack?" This time he couldn't help laughing.

"That's precisely what I'm saying." She stayed
serious.

"That's impossible because even if I was turning into
a wolf somehow, I'm allergic to cats!" *There! Refute that!*

177

"The man in you is allergic to them, but is the wolf?" *How is it that the illogical person is actually winning the argument?*

"This is crazy. You know that, right?" He reminded her.

"Why? There are lots of shape shifting myths in Europe, South America and all sorts of cultures. And there are some historians who think that there's a little grain of truth in every myth or legend that just gets more and more distorted over time. What if there really are people who transform into animals? Is it really so hard to believe?" *What kind of question is that?*

"Yes." It was the most polite response he could think of.

"Instead, you'd rather believe that you suffer from all these symptoms because you got lost in the woods as a child and repressed the memory? How does that make any more sense than my theory?" Her anger was not assuaged.

"Maybe because Dr. Miller's theory is actually plausible, and yours isn't." *Screw politeness.*

"If that's the case, then why haven't you had these episodes all your life?" She was like a machine. She just kept pushing.

"I could ask the same question about your theory." *Finally, Logan scores a point.*

"I have two ideas about that. The first is that you've carried the genetic mutation responsible for the transformation all your life, and it lay dormant inside you until you were exposed to some sort of trigger." *How could she be proud of herself for coming to that conclusion?*

"And we're back to the trigger thing again. That's all I'm looking for. A trigger. And you give me all this

178

crap about being a werewolf? It sounds to me like you weren't able to find an answer to that question either, and to keep from coming back empty handed, you came up with this ludicrous theory, but when we get right down to it, you have no more clue what caused all this than me or Miller or anyone else." *Chalk up another one!*

"Would you be kind enough to let me finish please?" she raised a brow. "Thank you," she told him when he was quiet. "Now, I admit that I'm not sure of the trigger, but I think it may have happened just before the symptoms began to manifest themselves. But I'll come back to that. My other idea is that maybe there was no trigger because you somehow contracted the ability to transform like most people contract a disease. It might even be easier for you to look at it that way, like this is some disease with unpleasant symptoms, and we're searching for a way to cure it."

"That's the way I *was* looking at it, when I thought I had an actual physical disease. But wait . . . oh yeah . . . the doctor ruled all that out, didn't he? So then I started looking at it like it might be a mental disease and started seeing a psychiatrist. But wait . . . oh yeah . . . *you* said that my shrink was wrong. You said I couldn't have PTSD because there was nothing traumatic in my past. Yet both you *and* Dr. Miller are looking for a trigger *in my past*. You gotta make up your mind. Do you agree or disagree with her because you seem a little confused." He had never been so frustrated.

"I'm not confused. I just need a little more time and data before I can find the trigger." *Can she actually **hear** herself?*

"That's what Dr. Miller said too," he grinned, catching a whiff of victory.

179

"Fine. If you're so set on her being right and me being wrong, then keep going to her and spending your daddy's money. But don't come back asking for help when her food journals and therapeutic hypnosis and prescription drugs don't work."

"Lillie. Don't take this personally. It's not that I don't like hanging with you. It's just that I don't like for things to be illogical. Why don't we go grab some coffee or an early supper and forget about this whole thing, okay?" He put a hand on her shoulder in what he hoped was a companionable gesture.

"I'm busy," she shrugged it away and began to put away the things she'd brought with her.

"Well, call me when you get over being busy. We'll have that dinner then," Logan told the top of her head as that was the closest thing to her face he could see. Then he grabbed his notebook and walked away feeling like he had just kicked a puppy.

Logan tried to put the whole episode behind him. If Lillie was going to ignore him, then that was just something he would have to put up with until she got over her mad. Until then, he'd give her some space, but that didn't mean he had to agree with her preposterous theory. He called the Counseling Center and made another appointment, the only problem was, Dr. Miller couldn't work him in until October, which wasn't too bad because it gave him almost a month to sneak $40 from under his father's nose. He just hoped that Miller found the trigger quick, before he couldn't hide the expenditure anymore.

Between classes and avoiding Rob like the rank scumbag he was, Logan played the occasional game of *Halo* or *COD* with Mark, Andrew and Batu, who had become the newest convert to the all-consuming realm of video games. Watching Batu watch other people play was almost as good as playing himself, though it lacked the thrill of the competition. Logan knew that the games depended on timing and strategy, and he practiced his moves just like everyone else, but Batu was different. He seemed to be a prodigy. Like the *Rain Man*-idiot savant of the gaming world, without the idiot part. He was still a bit socially awkward, but Logan attributed that to the poor dude's extreme case of culture shock, since it was gradually getting better. Once he got a feel for the controller and the basic concept of video game play, Batu could watch Mark or Andrew or Logan execute a difficult move only one or two times, and then execute the same move perfectly on the first try. It was maddening to someone who had to practice to get those moves right. If he hadn't already been one of them, the boys might have banned Batu from the Xbox like Rob had been, but Batu was practically their little brother, and nothing he could do, no matter how annoying, would get him kicked out of the group.

And when he wasn't playing the Xbox, Logan had his share of company, though not as much as Andrew. There was no one else Logan knew of who was quite as successful as Andrew Stevenson was with the women, and there was absolutely no way of competing with him, which caused Logan to wonder why he should bother. He would only look pathetic for trying, and who was there to impress anyway? Mark was impressed by anything Logan did, since Logan frequently took pity on his pathetic lack of skills and tossed a few chicks his way. Rob's opinion was moot, no matter what it was. And Andrew? He could never be as impressed by anyone else's rate of conquests as he was of his own. So, Logan called a girl when he felt like it, slept alone when he didn't, and did a little drinking either way.

He spent one of those nights with a redhead named Kristy as payback for a favor for Mark. She had bronze skin, the kind so golden Logan wondered if she'd asked George Hamilton for tanning tips, and bright blue eyes. Her hair was straight and long, coming to the middle of her back. He generally preferred shorter hair, but the miles of copper looked good on her. But the arresting thing about her was her smile. It was quick and bright and flashed at him like the bulb in a camera. She was a girl who knew how to laugh, and often. There was nothing Kristy wouldn't joke about and no time too serious for her to make one. *Now **this** is more like it!* he sighed as they both caught their breath. There were no confusing new rules he had to discover or a delicate balance he had to maintain. All he had to do was what he had always done, and both of them would be happy with the result. There was flirtation but no banter or argument. No pain or anger or rejection or loss. Only pleasure. Hollow and fragile, but pleasure nonetheless. When she left 317 the next morning, they both had smiles on their faces.

It was several more days before Logan found himself amidst a serious conversation with Andrew, which as almost as rare for him as a vacant Friday night. "Dude. What's wrong with you? If I didn't know any better or wanted to get slugged, I'd tell you you were acting a heck of a lot like Rob," he dodged Logan's fist. "But I don't want that happening, so I'm not gonna say that. I *am* gonna tell you that you've been a real pain for the past three weeks, and that isn't like you. I know it works for Christian Bale in *Batman Begins*, but seriously, Logan, you're not that hot."

"Thanks, man," Logan answered morosely.

"It's a tough job," Andrew admitted.

"How do you even have time to notice what I'm doing? You're never here, and if you are, your door's shut. Most of the time, you're in class or with a girl, or in the same class with a girl." And Logan figured he was too distracted during those periods to notice much more than the chick in front of him.

"I'm just good like that," he grinned, but it didn't work as well on Logan as it did on the girls he was trying to seduce. There was a limit to his power, after all.

"It's not really a big thing. I'm just in a pissy mood. Rob's in a pissy mood twenty-four, seven. Can't I be in a pissy mood, even for a little while, without you getting all over me about it?" *At least I don't walk around with those aviators glued to my head and a glass of scotch permanently attached to my hand.*

"Not if that 'little while' has gone on for weeks. Why not just get laid?" That's what the whole world boiled down to for Andrew.

"I have! Remember the redhead, Kristy?" *It's not like I'm a monk!*

"That was like a week ago. The post-sex high's long gone by now. Get another girl. I'm sure you have no shortage of them in your phone book, but if you do, you're welcome to copy a few outta mine," Andrew sent Logan a benevolent smile, as if he'd just donated a thousand dollars to Logan's cause.

"Chill. I'm not Mark. I can get my own girl, if I want one. But that's not it. I guess I'm just disappointed that Miller hasn't come up with anything yet, and the end of the month is coming, which means sooner or later, so are three more nights of blackouts." He dreaded them like he'd dreaded visits to the dentist as a kid.

"I know what you mean, man. It does suck that you can't find the trigger." Andrew grabbed two beers and offered one to Logan.

"It really does. And I don't even know when to expect it again. Sometimes it happens once a month, and other times I find it happening twice a month. All I know is, it happens, and it's as annoying as crap when it does." Logan popped the top and took a sip before all the foam evaporated.

"Maybe Mark was right about the moon being the trigger. Have you checked into that?" Andrew sat in the chair across from Logan and propped his feet up on the coffee table, since his mother wasn't there to object.

"What's with you and Mark?" *And Lillie*, he added mentally. "It's got nothing to do with the moon. If it did, then how could it happen twice a month?"

"Have you never heard of a blue moon? It's a month when there are two full moons." Andrew looked at Logan like he'd called *Fight Club* a stupid movie.

"Well, what about the fact that this hasn't happened all my life? The moon's been changing all month, every month of my life, and nothing like this ever happened to me before April Fools' Day." Logan reminded him and regained a bit of dignity.

"Maybe it's kismet or karma or whatever. Maybe the universe is punishing you for some sort of outrageous evil you've committed," Andrew laughed.

"Sure it is, and that's why Batu is stuck downstairs, and we're stuck up here with Rob," Logan agreed.

"Hey! You mean *you're* the reason Batu got kicked out and Rob got put back in? The more I think about it, the more this cosmic punishment thing makes sense." Andrew totally missed his sarcasm.

"Dude! There is no cosmic balance or sense of right and wrong. Life's just a collection of events, and the way people react to those events determines the course of their lives. It's nothing more complex than that. There is no fate, or if there is, fate is just what you make for yourself. You're a man of science, or you're on your way to being one. Don't tell me you come down on the side of intelligent design or creationism or whatever!" *Why did all the educated people in his life suddenly have to become totally irrational at the same time?*

"I'm not exactly sure what I believe about that sort of thing. I've never been a very religious person, but the deeper I get into molecular biology and stuff, the more I see that life and life cycles aren't as random as we like to think they are. I'm not sure I'd swear that something as complex as human life forms is the result of a random fluke of nature or natural selection," he crawfished.

"Well, when you can tell me how to stop blacking out and doing whatever I do during that time, I'll quit being so pissy. Until then, you and Mark are just going to have to deal with it," Logan returned to the previous line of conversation.

"Here's hoping the shrink finds a solution to your problem quick, then," he toasted Logan and took another drink.

Logan and Mark went to Wal-Mart to buy groceries, and Batu tagged along because, since his magical initial experience with the store, he had never turned down an opportunity to return. It was Logan's custom to make a list of necessities before he went shopping, and then once he got to the store, he began at the back on the side that wasn't food, gradually working his way toward the front and then across to the food section, which he also tackled back to front. That way they wound up conveniently close to the front of the store when they were finished.

They were in the cleaning aisle, getting detergent and Pledge and toilet bowl cleaner, most of which Laurie informed Logan they were almost out of when she'd cleaned the place a few days earlier. Batu was still amazed at the sheer variety of scents that fabric softener (both liquid and sheet form) was available in. Personally, Logan didn't give a crap what his sheets and towels smelled like, as long as they were clean, but Mark and Batu were not so easily satisfied. Each of them was busily opening and smelling all the bottles of liquid softener the store had to offer. Logan was getting incredibly bored of this endless compare and contrast and was about to just pick one for the two idiots, so they could move on to another aisle, when he caught a movement behind him and to the left from the corner of his eye. He turned, and there was Lillie, on her toes, grabbing a bright green container of Gain. It was the first time he'd seen her since leaving the library the day she went loopy on him. He wasn't sure if that was because she was bent on giving him the cold shoulder or because he was determined to ignore her. *It is what it is*, he thought and debated on breaking his silence. What could he lose? If she snubbed him, it wasn't likely that either one of his friends would notice, since they still had their noses stuck in different jugs.

"Hey," he said, facing her fully.

"Hello," she responded with the clinical smile she'd used the first time he ever saw her.

"How are classes?" He wasn't about to let the conversation end there.

"They're good. Nothing like actually digging in the field, but then nothing is really," she confessed.

"Is that what you were doing this summer while you were off-campus?" He asked the question out of genuine interest.

"Yeah. I grew up in Manteo, not far from Roanoke. I've always wanted to dig there, and I finally did." The wistful look on her face told him it was true.

"I'm glad you accomplished what you wanted," he smiled at her authentic expression.

"Well, I didn't totally accomplish my goal, since we still have no idea what happened to Virginia Dare and the rest of the colony, but I haven't given up hope. One of these days, I'm going to make a significant discovery at the site, which will be the key to unraveling the mystery, and I'll be the next Howard Carter, the biggest name in the field of archeology." She was joking, he knew, but she was passionate about it. *She really is interested in uncovering the stories of the people of the past and what happened to them. She seems . . . fulfilled.* It made Logan wonder if he'd ever cared about anything as much as Lillie cared about anthropology.

"Are you into ancient Egypt?" He could tell she hadn't expected the question any more than she'd expected him to understand her reference. She was quick to mask it, but not quick enough.

"Not really. I prefer Eurasia. The Anglos, the Normans, the Gauls. And their lore. It's actually my favorite part of studying their cultures. How the assorted conquests spread certain stories from culture

187

to culture, distorted others. How the heart of most stories is common from people group to people group. Only the surface details change. It's a pretty cool illustration of the way mankind essentially remains the same from generation to generation, though we like to think we're very far removed from the more savage way of life." When she spoke, it was as if she was relating the most exciting story she'd ever heard to her closest friend.

"Logan's a savage all right," Mark teased, having overheard the end of Lillie's sentence. "If I were you, I'd be careful with my heart around him. He has a rep for ripping them to shreds."

"Thanks for the advice," she sent Mark that smile she saved for strangers, then turned to Logan. "See you around," Her words were crisp and cool, having lost the heat of the moment before. He nodded politely and watched her slip away.

"Why'd you have to do that, man? After all the chicks I get for you?" Logan demanded. "*I* don't ruin *your* game like that."

"How could you? You've never had the chance," Mark replied flatly.

Logan groaned. By now he knew before he even opened his eyes that his bare back was laying against the industrial carpet. He could feel the dried dirt caked over his skin and knew. *Two seconds earlier I was blissfully unaware of my condition, and now I can't even remember what came just before those two seconds.* It was sick, really. Sick that he could only recall annoyance and discomfort. But the more he tried to remember, the more nauseous he actually became, so he gave up thinking about how cruel irony was and went to shower.

188

He was used to the headache. He was used to the cleaning and the laundry. The only thing that bothered him about the blackouts was the unanswered question of why and how. There was also the question of when, but it wasn't as far up on the scale of annoying as the other. Every time it happened, he rehashed the same cyclical process of questioning and logic, and every time it happened, he came up with nothing. It defied logic that this could have been the seventh time he was experiencing these blackouts, and he had no more information, even after analyzing them, than he did after the second one.

Since it was just half-past six, he took pity on Andrew and Mark. If he couldn't find an answer, and two doctors couldn't find an answer, and finding the answer made a smart chick like Lillie go crazy, then there was no way his two roommates could find it. He tried to reconcile himself to having three sequential nights of blackouts once a month for the rest of his life. But that thought was so freaking depressing that he couldn't come to terms with it without buying a couple more bottles of Jäger and getting it with a few more girls. It was even more depressing when he had to write last night's date beneath the others: 09/25/07. So far he'd lost approximately 114 hours of his life to this thing, and he didn't even know what it was. To say that things "sucked" didn't even come close.

Chapter 13

Lillie smiled as Logan entered her area of the library after his classes that afternoon. *I was expecting something more like a smirk. Then again, she never does what I expect her to do.* He knew he was taking a risk, coming to her section again, but every time the blackouts happened, he felt driven to search the same sources over again. It was as if he was a detective, combing his case files, hunting for the one clue that he'd somehow managed to miss. The one that was standing between him and the answers he needed.

He gathered the same texts he had before and sat at a table to begin scouring their pages. Logan got through several paragraphs before she set a Post-It on the table beside his notebook. It listed additional Internet sources on medicine that he hadn't tried, since WebMD had steered him wrong in the first place, baffling him again. *If she's so convinced that science won't provide the answer, why is she helping me keep investigating that angle?*

He moved to a computer and began systematically searching all the sites she had listed for any relevant information. Despite the new sources, he was unable to find anything more than what he already knew and had read three or four times before. He tried not to be disappointed. *It's not like the info was going to magically appear in print where it hadn't been before. I didn't think it would. I just wanted to look again so I could feel productive.* There was nothing that could be done to halt this cycle anyway. *No matter what, I'm not going to remember tonight or tomorrow night either.*

The more Logan thought about it, the more furious he became. It was Lillie's fault that he missed his last appointment with Dr. Miller, and if he hadn't, maybe they could have found the crapping trigger by now. He was losing eighteen more hours, all because she thought he was some sort of mythological creature. It was ridiculous! *No wonder she's been nice to me today. She knows this is her fault, and she feels guilty!* He wanted to smack himself in the forehead at his stupidity, but didn't. She'd see that he finally made the same connection that she'd made hours, even days before, and he wasn't about to let her in on that. *I'm glad she feels guilty. She **should**.* He wasn't going to take pity on her and say anything to assuage her feelings. He *knew* how awful self-imposed guilt could feel. Hadn't his dad let him suffer that way countless times? Yet the comparison had him starting.

Since he had been old enough to make his own choices, Logan had tried with his entirety to do and be anything but what his father was and would do. It was knee-jerk now, the rebellion that he'd begun when he answered the office door to find that first brunette with too much make-up on to be a lady and not enough clothes on to cover her chest. Just as the repulsion was that came every time he thought of his father and what he did, what his mother let him do. The one thing that had never made any sense to him was her silence through the whole thing.

He had to be careful not to become what he had sworn against. Ignoring Lillie did nothing but bring

191

him closer to that end; thus, he had to thank her for her attempt at help and hear any apology she was ready to give. *She will not suffer at my hand.* As soon as he thought it, he knew the vow was sacred. As sacred as the one before it. The one it tied right into.

"Lillie." She looked up from the computer when she heard her name. He was standing on the other side of the counter. "Thanks."

"You're welcome, Logan," she smiled, but it only spread halfway across her face before dipping into a frown. "You look tired. Are you–Did it happen last night?"

"Yeah." He was suddenly uncomfortable looking her in the eye. There was more concern there than he had ever seen, and it was unnerving.

"Give me a sec," she began to type something on the keyboard. "Are you all right?" she looked at him again, and he had to force himself to meet her eyes.

"Tired, but otherwise okay," he kept his voice even, but that was a challenge.

"I'm sorry it's happening again. I was hoping it wouldn't . . . that I was wrong." She sounded like she really meant what she said. *Have I ever met a girl who meant a word she said before?* That was probably why he couldn't look her in the eye. *She breaks every rule I've ever played by.* Her version of the game confused him. It annoyed him. And yet he kept taking every turn he could get.

"Not your fault . . . exactly," he grinned, knowing she couldn't help herself.

"What is that supposed to mean?" Her change of tone had his grin getting wider.

"Just that if you'd left me alone, I'd have been to see the shrink by now, and I might know what the trigger is." He held up his hands as he didn't feel like losing any limbs.

"I *told* you what the trigger is, Logan. It's a full moon!" Her hands were also up in the air, but not in surrender.

Here we go! "Right."

"No. Seriously. You can check the lunar calendar. If I was a betting woman, I'd bet you $1,000 that tonight is a full moon." If she was angered by his sarcasm, she didn't show it. "Go check," she pointed to a vacant computer in a bank of others against the wall. "I dare you."

Those three words alone would have been enough to have him doing it, but they were accompanied by a smirk and even a raised brow. The combination was just too much. Though he imagined she was laughing her guts out at his retreating back, he headed in the direction she had indicated. He couldn't hold back the curse that slid between his teeth along with his breath when he Googled "2007 lunar calendar." The full moon was tonight. Acting on impulse alone, he checked the calendar for August's blackout dates and found that they corresponded to the full moon and the two days surrounding it. He got the same result when he checked July and June.

Logan couldn't breathe. He felt the second that his throat closed up. It was the same second that he realized with frightening certainty that Lillie wasn't crazy. She was right.

~

Lillie had been keeping an eye on him from her station behind the counter since he sat down at the computer. She wasn't sure how Logan would react to what she was sure he would find when he took her advice. She knew him to be a guy who operated on logic alone, and though she thought of his as a hollow existence, she was empathetic to the confusion he must be feeling. *Maybe now he'll understand that there are bigger things. More than logic and reasoning. Maybe now he can find meaning.* She hoped it was true. Otherwise, it was such a waste.

He pushed up suddenly from his chair, shoving himself back from the desk and onto his feet in one flash of motion. He was leaning over and had his hands braced on his thighs. It looked like he was trying to catch his breath after a long run. *He's having a panic attack!*

She was standing next to him as quickly as she could manage without attracting the attention of every person in the vicinity. "It's okay, Logan," she draped a hand over his shoulders. "Just take deep breaths, all right?" He was still gasping. "Focus on breathing in through your nose and out through your mouth, Logan. Nice and slow. In through your nose and out through your mouth."

Lillie exaggerated her own breathing so he could see and imitate. After a few reps, he had caught the rhythm, and his breathing pattern mirrored her own. "Good," she told him when he finally straightened. "That's good. You all right now?"

"I think so," he nodded. "If anybody can be all right after finding out that they're a living piece of mythology. And I suppose you want to rub it in my face. Go ahead."

"Logan. I don't want to gloat. It isn't about me being right and you being wrong. It's about you finding

194

the answer. It may not have come in the form you were looking for, but the important thing is that you've found it now," she patted him with the hand she'd had wrapped around his shoulders. It had slid off when he straitened, but he didn't shrug it off now. She took that as a good sign.

"But now that I have it, I have no clue what the freak to do with it. I mean, *how*? How? *How* does a normal guy wake up one day as a wolf?" He had a wild look in his eyes and, if it had been any other situation, Lillie would have made an awesome crack about the irony of his statement and his ability to have that particular look. But that look told her he was scarily close to losing his tenuous grip on reality, and that was not something to joke about.

"We'll figure something out," she made sure to look him in the eye as she assured him.

"How? There's no research about this kind of situation!"

"That's where you're wrong. Why don't we go to Hill of Beans? You look like you could use some espresso or something . . . strong. You look really pale."

"I think it's gonna take something a little stronger than coffee to make me feel any better about the situation."

"Give me just a minute to get somebody to cover the last few minutes of my shift. Stay right here, okay? I'll be right back." She squeezed his hand, hoping that the physical contact would help her words feel more real. *Maybe he'll be more likely to listen.*

~

Logan watched her walk back to the counter and wondered that he was still conscious. Wondered that the floor was stable beneath his feet. Wondered that anything he'd ever believed was true. Wondered that she was so calm. *But why wouldn't she be?* **Her** *whole life wasn't insane.* He kept wanting to pinch himself so that he could wake up from this terrible dream, but he was pretty sure that people who were dreaming didn't have panic attacks when they found out they were wolves and then keep right on sleeping. He debated walking away. He could just walk back to 317 and never set foot in the library again. There were other ways to find information. *If I go now, I can pretend that I was never here. It never happened.* But she had already planted the seed, and the freaking weed would keep growing and growing, no matter how much he denied it. *Still. It was stupid to stand here and have a breakdown right in the middle of the library.* He needed air. It wasn't running away from the problem if he was only going out for air, was it? *No. It isn't.* He was sure it wasn't. He left his stuff where it was. *Who would want that crap anyhow?* And headed for the glass doors. It was only a little way to get outside. Things would be clearer. It would all make more sense. Be more reasonable if he could just get outside.

~

He was nearly running by the time she'd found a sub and turned in his direction again. *Shoot!* was all she had time to think before she dashed after him. The only reason she caught up to him so quickly was that he stopped just outside the door and seemed to be staring into space. "Logan," she called softly, since she was behind him and had no desire to spook him into taking off again. He turned at the sound, and he looked lost. Profoundly so.

She wanted to cry at his expression, but knew he wouldn't appreciate that. But he really wasn't that cold, bad boy, man-whore he wanted everybody to think he was. He was scared and human, and he needed help. She knew, without a doubt, that she would be there if he would have her. "I want some coffee." She tucked her hand between his side and his elbow and tugged him in the direction of Hill of Beans.

~

The woman picked the craziest time in the world to want coffee, but she was pulling him along, and it didn't seem he had much choice in the matter. He had to concentrate to keep up with her. Those slim legs of hers could go faster than he'd suspected. "What's your hurry?"

"Didn't want you panicking again. I figured if I move fast enough, you won't have time to analyze all the reasons why you can't be—"

"Don't say it," he broke in before she finished.

"—what we both know you are," she completed the thought without using the word just for spite. "The sooner you come to terms with it, the better."

"What's that supposed to mean?" He held the door for her.

"Exactly what I said," she whispered as they approached the counter. Their conversation stopped until she'd ordered her Frappuccino and a black coffee for him, paid for both before he could stop her, and they'd both taken a seat at a table.

"Tell me what you meant," he reminded her while she sipped placidly, like this was a habit of theirs.

"Being okay with your . . . condition isn't the end of things, Logan. It's just the beginning. Now that we know what's causing your 'blackouts,'" her use of air

197

quotations annoyed him. "We can begin searching for a way to cure it," she smiled her conversational smile, which annoyed him further.

"Don't talk to me like I'm your customer, Lillie," he heard the flatness of his tone and was glad she hadn't encountered the unvarnished edge.

"Try to think of it more in terms of a doctor-patient relationship. If you look at it from that angle, accepting that you're anthropomorphous, lycanthropic even, is really no different from accepting that you have PTSD." She moved her hand from the Frappuccino to lay it sympathetically atop his.

"It's all about perspective," Logan nodded and felt a sense of déjà vu when he recalled telling Mark the same thing. *It's just not so easy when you're on the receiving end, is it?* Hadn't he always believed that you got out of life what you made of it? Well, he'd just have to find a way to make the best of this too. Everybody, every*thing* had a tell, and once he could identify his opponent, finding the tell was just a matter of time. "You're right," he acknowledged, looking her in the eye, and was proud the words hadn't hung in his throat. "I won't deny it anymore. So, what's the next step?"

"Research," she grinned, probably at the groan he couldn't keep in. "Don't worry. Haven't I already proven I'm *much* better at it than you?" *Speaking of opponents . . .*

"You have the unfair advantage of working in a library," he pointed out.

"Don't forget my imagination. If it hadn't been for your lack of one, you might have made this discovery on your own. You did all the hard work for me: compiling data, eliminating mental and physical ailments, tracking symptoms. Yet you still couldn't put two and two together and get four." Here was the smirk he'd been expecting earlier.

"Hey! I *have* an imagination. How do you know I haven't imagined all sorts of things about you already?" He wagged his eyebrows and braced himself for her punch.

"I'm sure you have. You're a guy. The only way you wouldn't have is if you lacked equipment, and judging by your reputation, I'd say that isn't likely." It never came because she was as cool as any river he'd ever swum in and just as much of a shock upon impact. "Just because you had some absurd fantasy about me, doesn't mean you're creative, especially when it comes to using your bigger brain." She grinned wider than the Cheshire Cat.

He knew he was pouting, but he couldn't help it.

Chapter 14

Logan woke up on the floor again. It was the morning of September 27th, and he was in the middle of what Lillie called his Seventh Phase. In many ways, the situation sucked just as much now as it had the six times before. Though this time there was no uncertainty. He knew the answers he'd been bothered by for the past six months, and that made a difference. He was nauseated but didn't have to try to remember what he'd done. Didn't have to think back and make things worse in the process. He already knew he'd spent the night in the woods.

He was stepping into the shower when he heard Metallica thudding from his cell and cringed. He strained to reach it before his head burst into—he could actually picture it happening, his brains seeping out like juice from a freshly split watermelon. Talking wouldn't be fun, but that ring was even worse. "Hello?" He hadn't even checked the screen to see who was calling. He didn't want to risk taking the seconds to do it.

"Are you okay?" Lillie's concerned voice poked the bear that was shoving and clawing around in his head, and he almost lost consciousness. "Logan?"

"Ungh. I'm here. That's about all I can say," he whispered.

"Do you want me to come over?" her voice was coated in concern. Smooth. But it still stung.

"Can you whisper? Dang but my head aches," he mumbled.

"Do you need me?" she asked as quietly as she could.

"I'm good, thanks. I just need an aspirin big enough for a mammoth," he put a hand to his head and regretted the motion.

"If I didn't know any better, I'd think you had a massive hangover," she teased.

"I wish," he said without laughter. "I'm gonna crawl to the shower so I can look and feel a little less like a jungle savage, and then I'm gonna try to crash on the couch for a while before I go to my class. Sleep this monster off."

"Meet me at Hill of Beans after," she whispered.

"Cool," he told her as he hung up.

If only I could twitch my nose like the chicks on Bewitched *or* Sabrina, the Teenage Witch *or whatever. I'd be rid of this whole mess: headache, phasing, and all. But then I'd just be another mythical being, so what's the difference?* He laughed at himself and got to his feet.

Logan survived the next night and was glad to know that he didn't have to wonder when it would happen next. He'd found that lunar calendar on-line again and printed a copy, then posted it on the wall beside his desk. According to the pattern Lillie had finally found with the dates, he didn't have to worry about phasing again for twenty-six days. That gave them nearly a month to research thousands of years of legends and myths from cultures scattered across the planet. *It's times like these when I hate being so logical.*

School had never been the primary focus of Logan's life. He was generally good at it, hence the full ride, but

201

there were times when he had to work for the B or C.
His father had lofty hopes for Logan, but the 4.0 was
gone the minute he stepped into World Lit. Preston
had the brains. *He* was the one who would have the
perfect GPA and the shot at an Ivy League. Logan did
all right for himself, escaping the shadow of the great
Philip Michaels and his demands, but if Logan was
silver, Preston was gold. Thus, when October faced
Logan across the table and dealt him nothing but midterm exams and projects with a sadistic smile, he took
stock like any good player and hoped for some decent
hole cards.

He was thigh-deep in books and study guides one
afternoon when Andrew and Mark barged into his
room. "Holy crap, bro! How many days you been
holed up in this cave?" Mark stepped over one of
Logan's piles of data. "It's starting to look as bad as
our side!"

"Hey! I can't help it that Financial Management of
Corporations is about to be the death of me!" Logan
said to cover his embarrassment. *The place really **is** a sty.
How the crap did it get this bad?*

"I guess so. I'd swear it's been more than two weeks
since you've had a woman in your bed, and I thought
that'd never happen!" It was Andrew's smart mouth
this time, which was good for Mark, since he might not
have survived, had he said it.

"Sometimes a guy's gotta take a little time for
himself," Logan muttered, knowing he should be glad
that the guys hadn't noticed before now. *Has it really
been a little more than six weeks? What the freak is wrong with
me? Shouldn't being a wolf mean that I want it **more** often
rather than less?*

"Well, that time's up, pal. Get this mess shoved somewhere, and call a girl before your *buddy* starts thinking you're a monk. You're starting to rival Mark in the longest dry-spell contest," Andrew grinned. "You can't leave me out here to face myriad single chicks on campus all on my own. I know I'm good, but even legends like me have their limits."

"Besides, you'll probably be more productive and crap if you find a way to relieve some of your stress," Mark nudged him companionably. "Plus, Fall Break starts tomorrow. You can't spend the whole four-day weekend studying."

"Y'all are hard to contradict," he sighed. "I'll give Joan a call as soon as I finish what I'm doing and save this. It'd suck a mother if I did all this work and lost it now."

"If you're not on the phone with her in ten minutes, I'll call her myself," Andrew threatened. "Better yet, I'll give her number to Rob," he amended when Logan rolled his eyes. Mark gaped at the idea, and Logan's death glare made it clear that there would be no need in taking such strong action, so Andrew chuckled and dragged Mark out before he recovered the power of speech.

Logan did call Joan, and it conveniently turned out that she was free for the night. Time was, he would have been a bit more stoked at the thought of a girl spending the night, especially since it hadn't happened in a while and he didn't have to be up early for class the next day, but he was distracted. He couldn't get too psyched about getting some when the thought of being . . . what he was skulked in the back of his mind. *Does being—what did Lillie call it?—lycanthopic mean that even when I'm human, I retain certain characteristics? What if I'm more*

203

aggressive? What if I accidentally get violent or lose control? He hadn't been nervous about performance in what felt like decades. But that was before he had to worry about more than satisfying his partner. That was before he had to worry about endangering her life.

The more Logan thought about it, the more he didn't feel comfortable taking that sort of risk with a girl who had no idea what she was walking into. It wouldn't be right if she wasn't aware of the situation, but it wasn't like he could walk around with his condition common knowledge. He'd get locked in a padded cell somewhere, which wouldn't be good when it came time to phase again. He still wasn't sure what he did during the nights of the phase, but he knew that whatever it was couldn't happen if he was locked in a mental hospital. *Someone was liable to get hurt.*

He couldn't be responsible for that. He was okay with being irresponsible in his own life as far as pickling his liver and "endangering his eyesight," but seriously hurting anyone else in the midst of the debauchery was never part of the equation. He always gave up his keys. He always suited up. He always satisfied her first. If anybody was at risk in the situation, it was him. The addition of this new variable totally threw him off. He was good at math ergo, business major, but that didn't mean he could always solve for x.

There was no way he could plan for and take precautions against killing her. *If I lose control of myself for 18 hours every month, who's to say I can control myself all the rest of the time? Sex is a primal act. What if, when I'm in that primal mind set I can't control myself?* It wasn't that much of a leap, considering how animalistic his body became during the phases—enough to destroy his sheets and have him waking up a mud-man.

But what about the six other phases? Haven't I slept with plenty of girls in between them? And those girls weren't hurt. They had just as much fun as I did. What made this last phase any different than the others? He realized that it wasn't the phase that was different at all. The difference was simply that he had knowledge of the phases now, when it happened that he hadn't had before. The question then became, *Does my knowledge of what's causing me to phase make me any different, any more dangerous than I was when I was phasing and didn't know why?*

He was calmer once he found his answer. There were plenty of girls who'd shared his bed since April Fools'. None of them came close to dying, so he didn't need to worry about Joan or any future partners either. They were safe as any woman could be in a frat boy's bed. *On second thought, they're probably lots safer with me than they would be with somebody like Rob!*

Being with Joan drove Logan loco. Totally loco. He had always thought of himself as the king of the one-night-stand. Unlike a large portion of his sex, he was the master of ending the night (or day, depending) amicably. To his knowledge, there weren't any bitter chicks who lit bonfires on Valentine's Day and watched his picture go up in flames as they sucked down entire bottles of wine with a side of chocolates. He enjoyed being able to say that since neither Andrew nor Rob could share that boast. They didn't really give a crap if the girl went to bed liking one guy and woke up hating his evil twin, but Logan wasn't that blasé. He liked girls, legitimately liked them for more than just being sex pots. He liked having a few female friends he could hang out with. Granted, that hanging out usually ended with both him and the girl naked, but he was capable of

appreciating her body and personality equally. He cared
whether they left his bed happy and always tried to
ensure that happened. Too many times he'd heard how
women felt like objects, used and discarded. Too many
times he'd seen his father do just that.

It irked him that, with Joan against him, he couldn't
concentrate on her. He looked at her but didn't see
Joan, or maybe it was that he *did* see Joan. He was
finding faults he never noticed when he was with a
woman. Why look for them when there was so much
good at first glance? There was really no need.
Granted, he had his types. The ones he liked more
than others. But he was able to find something pretty,
if not downright beautiful about almost all of his
partners. So why were Joan's eyes too far apart and her
nose too narrow? Why was her hair too short and her
grin too quick? Why did the jut of her chin seem too
strong? Though there wasn't really anything wrong
with the overall package, he couldn't seem to help
himself. He was cutting her into pieces and didn't like
what he saw.

Joan didn't like what she got. She didn't stay for
breakfast. She didn't kiss him goodbye. Logan was
certain. It wasn't the first time he'd failed to please a
girl, but it was the first time he could recall it happening
since early in his teens. He was angry at himself for
Joan as much as he was for his pride. He never should
have done this. He knew he wasn't in the right frame
of mind to enjoy it, and why do it if he wasn't getting
any enjoyment? It wasn't fair to the girl, and that
angered him more than the blow to his ego. *Didn't I
swear I'd never leave a girl empty-handed?* But that was what
he had done. He'd used Joan just as his father used all

those bimbos, but he was worse. *At least Dad enjoyed himself. I can't even pretend to claim that I did. And at least those girls got something out of the deal—money, clothes, jewelry, anything as long as it hushed them, kept them discreet.* Joan had gotten nothing. Not even pleasure. When she left, pulling the door to as she went, Logan felt like *he* was left holding the losing hand.

He didn't bother calling any other girls that weekend. *What was the point?* But Mark was right. There was only so much schoolwork a man could do before all the letters crushed together into a thick black blur. He had a tension headache, or maybe it was from his laptop's backlit screen. Either way he couldn't look at words and numbers anymore. The characters were too jumbled up to have any meaning for him at all. He shut down the computer and looked at the clock. It was 5:30 on Sunday afternoon. He hadn't seen anything but the interior of his room, the hallway, or his bathroom since right after Joan left Thursday morning. He was studying, but he was also avoiding Mark and Andrew with a new determination that was eclipsed only by the familiar determination to avoid Rob through any means necessary.

Holing up meant no TV on the couch in the living room, but it didn't mean he couldn't sneak out and see if Batu was downstairs. *He has no idea that I'm in the midst of a dry-spell, so he can't rag me about it!* The sheer genius had Logan pressing his ear to his closed bedroom door and wishing he had a water glass and the skills to use it. He didn't hear anything on the other side, but he waited a good fifteen minutes before he turned out the light and eased the door open. Andrew's was shut, and Mark was nowhere in his line of sight. *This is as safe as it's gonna get*, he reasoned and slunk down the short corridor into the living area, hardly daring to breathe.

When he reached the open area, he saw that there was no need for his deliberate quietude. Mark was passed out on the couch with his mouth open wide enough that Logan bet he could fit his entire fist into it. There was no way his footsteps would bring Mark out of that coma. He wasn't even sure a freight train right next to the boy's head would do the trick. Still, he was careful to keep all his keys closed in his fingers. He didn't want to chance bringing Rob out of his den, if he happened to be back there somewhere. He shut and locked the door as softly as was humanly possible and dashed down the single flight to 217 before anyone knew any different.

Batu came to the door after only a couple knocks. "Logan. Please come in. How are you?" he smiled warmly enough despite retaining some of the stiff formality that comes from only having textbook knowledge of a language.

"Doin' good, Batu. How're you?" he returned as he followed Batu inside. The apartment was an exact replica of 317 save the furniture arrangements and personal effects. The color scheme had even been duplicated. It was a bit surreal. Almost like walking through a mirror to the other side, if such a Carrollinian concept were possible. The scary part about being on "the other side" was, once a person was there, it was hard to tell the difference between that place and the place from which he'd come. It was a little like being in a dream and beginning to suspect that it was a dream. *What's real? What's imagined?*

"I'm good. Please sit down," Batu gestured, refusing to sit before Logan did. "How are Mark and Andrew?" he inquired when they were both in chairs.

"They're good too," Logan told him and wondered what he was doing here. "Well, it's been three months now. What do you think of your new digs?"

"Digs?"

"Yeah. 'New digs' means the new place you're living," he explained.

"Ah. I see. I like the apartment here because it is just the same as the one upstairs, but I do not like my roommates so much as I like you and Andrew and Mark. The other fellows are not quite so nice as you. But you are likely glad to have your other friend back in 317," Batu tried to look contented, but failed.

"Actually, the three of us'd rather have you in there with us than Rob any day!" Logan grinned when Batu did.

"Then perhaps we can make arrangements to be roommates once again in the new semester."

"No can do, pal. The contracts we signed are for the entire school year, and by the time we have to sign another one, I'll be graduating," Logan hated the way Batu's excitement was extinguished, so he tried to soften the blow. "But you might talk to Mark and Andrew. I'm pretty sure they'll still be around."

"I will see," he shrugged. "How are your classes?"

"They're about to kill me. We've got midterms coming up next week, and I lost three nights in a row to those freaking blackouts week before last, so I'm running pretty far behind right now." Logan was honest. There was no reason not to be.

"Can none of the doctors diagnose you?" Batu seemed surprised.

"Nope. The MD couldn't find a thing, and the shrink thinks I have PTSD, but that in itself is crazy, so I've pretty much given up on science." *But there was no need in being **too** honest with him, either.*

"You do not trust his opinion?"

"It's a her actually, and no, I don't trust her opinion because in order to have post traumatic stress disorder, I'd have to had experienced something really scary as a kid. I didn't, so she has to be wrong. Plus, I don't feel like paying her forty dollars per visit when all she does is ask questions without bothering to answer any of mine." Logan shook his head.

"I do not blame you for being concerned, but it is sometimes possible to find answers in areas other than science," Batu's face was serious when Logan glanced up to check.

"What d'you mean?" *Oh, Lord, not you too!*

"Perhaps you should look inside yourself for the answers you seek." Batu sounded like some sort of spiritual guru.

"I *have* been looking inside myself. I've been looking inside myself and wherever-the-crap else I could to find them, and in case you haven't noticed, I'm kinda at a loss." Logan tried not to let the caustic edge in his voice become too sharp.

"No. You have been looking to science for answers. You have been looking to others for answers. Now you should look to yourself." *More mystic mumbo-jumbo.*

"And how in the crap should I do that?" Logan demanded.

"To become enlightened, you should meditate and study." *I wonder what he would think if I told him what really happens.*

"I'm not into religious stuff, Batu." Logan hoped that would put an end to it.

"Why?" Batu seemed taken aback. *No such luck.*

"I just don't think there's anything out there that's mysterious and can't be explained. And ever since humans became intelligent enough to prove or disprove anything, people have been trying to find out if God's really out there. In all that time, we've been able to prove that the world was round and that it's made of atoms and part of a vast, ever-expanding universe, but we can't find any evidence to show that some sort of higher being created it or humankind. We can't find it because it isn't there." He hoped Batu understood enough to leave it alone.

"Do you not have faith?" Batu seemed saddened and confused, and he still hadn't clued in to Logan's aversion to the subject.

"The only thing I have faith in, the only thing I can trust is myself. It's the only thing I have control over." Logan didn't want to upset Batu, but that was the way he felt. Batu would just have to deal.

"I think you have not been able to find the answers to your questions because you have not been willing to let go of all your concerns. You must find peace within yourself to learn about your existence." *Who are you, Gandhi?*

"I'm not questioning life or existence, Batu. I'm questioning why these things are happening to me." Logan tried logic again, although he wasn't sure why. He was beginning to wonder if logic still worked in this wacked out reality.

"But in questioning why things are taking place in your life, are you not, essentially, questioning your existence? It is only natural. All people have questions

211

about life. It is why so many people groups have the same stories to explain mysteries: the creation of the world, the stars in the sky, the seasons, the history of the nations." *Obviously it doesn't if Batu can use it against me!*

"You mean myths? Legends? Made up stories of giants and monsters?" Logan raised a skeptical brow.

"Yes. They may not be correct, but they can contain some bit of truth," Batu nodded. *You can say that again.*

"You're a smart guy. Are there any Mongolian legends you know that contain little bits of truth?" The startled look Logan was met with showed him that he'd been a bit harsher than he'd intended.

"There is a legend in my culture that I believe is appropriate. It is the Legend of the Grey Wolf, which tells where our nation's greatest warriors come from." Batu smiled. "It is said that there was once a great battle, and the only person who lived was a young boy who was badly injured. He was found and tended to by a she-wolf, Asena. When the boy became well, Asena bore his children—ten male creatures who were half-wolf and half-human. One of these is the first of the Khans, an ancestor of Genghis himself." *You've got to be freaking kidding me!* Logan hoped he hadn't paled when he felt his stomach plummet the first time Batu mentioned "wolf." *What are the odds? . . .*

"Do you really think Genghis Khan was part wolf? That somewhere in his family line was the spawn of some bestial union?" This time Logan did laugh. There was no other logical reaction.

"Of course not. But I do believe that within every great warrior, there is a part quite similar to a wolf. A warrior must be cunning and ruthless, shrewd and strong, even wild and aggressive. Those are similarities, yes?" *Maybe the dude's got the right idea about this enlightenment crap after all.* "Do not worry, Logan. If you want, you can find your answers. You know where to look."

Chapter 15

Lillie didn't see Logan again until three days before the night they predicted he would begin his Eighth Phase. Midterms had kept both of them too busy to do more than send a few texts back and forth. It had been just under a month, not an unreasonable amount of time when he thought about how long it had been since he'd seen some of his frat brothers, or his parents and brother for that matter, but in the case of the latter, there could never be an unreasonable amount of time and space between them.

He wasn't sure how he felt about the pressure that gathered in his chest at the thought that he was walking in the direction of Hill of Beans and Lillie. He told himself it was nerves; after all, she'd called him the day before and said she finally had time to do some research if he was in. How could he not be? It was his life, wasn't it? He was losing 18 hours every month they didn't figure out some sort of cure for his condition. They had something like 78 hours to research before he phased again, and considering how much material they had to sift through, it was no wonder he was feeling anxious. The odds of preventing the next phase were not in his favor, and he just wasn't looking forward to prowling the woods for three nights straight and three mornings of waking up with Krakatoa exploding in his head.

A month's space had Logan feeling that she had done something different with herself, but he couldn't be sure. Maybe it was just the light, or the residual stress of midterms, or the effect of the color she was wearing now–green–as opposed to the one she'd been wearing the last time he'd seen her, not that he could recall it.

"Hey," she gave him a half-smile as he sat across from her and slid a latte to her.

"Hey." He wondered if it was her hair. Maybe it had grown a quarter inch. Or maybe she'd had it trimmed when she went back to Manteo for the long weekend. His first instinct when he'd left Batu's that afternoon was to tell Lillie about his freaky little psychic ex-roomie. Then he talked himself down because he was sure he'd look like an idiot telling her how this nerdy Mongolian had scared him crapless. But he had sent a text, just to be friendly, and that's when he found out she couldn't have met him anyway. She was at home with her parents, and he was on campus, hiding from his roommates. *It was a dang good thing she was out of town*, he decided.

"Do I have foam on my nose?" she demanded. Her question seemed pretty random until it hit him that he'd been inspecting her like she was a contestant in a wet t-shirt, and he was the judge.

"No. It's just . . . something different about you. That's all," he shook his head and tried to do the same with the notion, but wasn't successful.

"Is that your version of an attempt at being charming?" she didn't hide the smirk in her cup the way she tried to.

"No. If I wanted to charm you, you wouldn't have to wonder. You'd know you'd been charmed the second you walked out of my arms and realized you couldn't really live until you were wrapped in them again," he winked and was ridiculously pleased that there was fire in her eyes that were locked on him.

"I can't speak for myself, but you're just as obnoxious as you were when I saw you last." She smiled like she'd just told him the sweetest thing she could possibly say.

"As long as I'm no less handsome," he grinned and sipped his coffee. He took the bitter flavor with relish. Its sharpness told him this was real; if nothing else had been since the last time he'd sat across from Lillie at this table, he knew this was real. *Finally.* "So what's the plan, Indiana Jane?"

"There's absolutely no way we can go through all the popular legends and their variants in three days, so we need to narrow them by relevancy." She said as she reached into her bag and pulled out her notes. *I swear they multiply faster than rabbits*, he eyed the stack.

"How do we do know which legends are relevant?" He had a feeling he wasn't going to be getting any sleep for a while.

"You're gonna hate me for saying this, but we need to find out the trigger." She was looking at her handwriting and shuffling the papers, but he wasn't stupid. She was smiling bigger than Dallas.

"Who are you, Dr. Miller? I thought we'd already done that. Lycanthropy trigger equals moon." Was he never going to escape that freaking question?

"No. I mean, you're 21 years old. If you'd been born a—" she was startled when Logan strangled on a sip of coffee, "if you'd been born with the condition, you would have always been affected by the cycles of the moon." She had sobered enough to make eye-contact again.

"You're saying something happened to me that made me susceptible to it?" he cleared his throat. *Great. What else am I susceptible to? Am I gonna wake up one morning and be a zombie too?*

"Yeah. And that something had to happen between the full moon in March and your First Phase in April. The date would be somewhere between March 5th and March 31st."

"I was here on campus the whole month except for the trip to Breckinridge we took during Spring Break," he shrugged.

"You didn't leave Raleigh anytime other than that? Are you sure you didn't go home for a weekend or something?" She was incredulous. *She doesn't know me at all.*

"I'm positive," his mouth and stare were firm; she had no more room for questions.

"I'd venture to guess that since this is your seventh full semester on campus, the trigger isn't here. If it was, you'd have been phasing way before last March. That means you must have come into contact with it when you went to Colorado," she deduced.

"That means we're screwed," he corrected. "Who knows what I touched when we stopped for food or gas, or *where* we stopped, for that matter."

"I don't think the trigger would be something so mundane that you didn't notice it. Lycanthropy isn't some extreme form of the common cold. If you encountered the trigger, you'd be aware of it. Did anything weird happen?" she waited for his response.

"It was a college dude's dream," he smiled as he thought back to that idyllic week. "We drank. We

217

gambled. We skied. We had girls. We drank some more . . . Hey! D'ya think Jen could've given it to me?" *How do you even protect yourself from something like that?*

"Jen? Logan, it's not some STD," she shook her head and laughed at his audible sigh of relief.

"Well if it isn't catching, then how did I get it?" They both heard the raw frustration in his voice.

"I didn't say it wasn't catching. It just isn't catching in the ways you're thinking. You can't get it from someone breathing on you, and you can't get it from having normal sex," she cut her eyes at him at the word "normal."

"Are you suggesting that I did a freaking wolf?" *What kinda wack-job does she think I am?* He'd spoken louder than he meant to, and several people at the nearest tables looked over at him.

"No. I just meant that you'd have to be exposed to blood to contract it, I think," she answered him as calmly as if she was explaining how to use the Dewey Decimal System.

"Exposed to blood? This is sounding more and more like AIDS all the time . . ." he muttered. "Maybe I should get tested."

"It might be a good idea, considering the obscene amount of partners you've had, probably in this school year alone," she spoke plainly, but held up a hand when he looked affronted. "I'm just saying. Anyway, didn't you say you just had a full batch of medical tests done, and everything came back clean?"

"Oh yeah," he could breathe a bit easier when he remembered that.

"But I don't think this genetic mutation or chemical reaction or whatever can be detected on any of the tests we have right now anyway. If it could, the general population wouldn't think of what you are as a myth."

"You actually think there's science behind this crap? That's the big difference between you and me. I *know* there's no science behind it. I know that because two different doctors, people who deal with science on a daily basis, couldn't find anything that pointed them to lycanthropy."

"Of course there's science behind it. Just not modern science. There are things modern science can't explain, and those phenomena, in turn, spawn legends and myths that fill in the gaps science leaves. How do you think I was able to figure out what the blackouts were a symptom of? I used the scientific method to weed through and find the valuable information, form a hypothesis, test that hypothesis, and prove it to be true. I assure you, Logan, the whole process is very scientific." She had her arms crossed and seemed quite professional. *Maybe she could be the new Buffy.*

"And you intend on using that same scientific process to locate the trigger and find a cure?" he almost covered the doubtful timbre.

"Do you see any other way of approaching this thing?" her hand was on her hip, and her eyes had gone a hard, sharp green that he knew he'd do well to watch out for.

"I guess not. It just sounds like this cure is going to take a while to find, if we ever do." *So much for this ever being over. . .*

"We will. How do you think the actual existence of your kind has been kept secret for so long?" The spark inside her that seemed so dangerous when burning against him now seemed almost determined enough to glow well into eternity if that's what it took.

"So I have a 'kind' now?" he pretended offense.

"Yes. Admitting it's the first step to recovery." She kept a straight face. *She'd be a beast at five-card.*

"What's the next one?" he couldn't help the grin.

"Nailing down a timeline for the week that you were in Colorado, as best we can." Her pen was spreading blue loops smoothly, evenly across the page. The curves undulated with her thoughts, and he wondered if she even tried, or if the ideas flowed from her mind to her hand pre-organized.

"And then?" Because he knew there would be.

"Then we do a little digging to find out what happened up there that did this to you. Once we find the initial cause, we can eliminate the legends that contradict or neglect to mention that cause and what we know to be the truth. It'll make the task of finding a cure much easier." Her eyes were sharp now too, but instead of heat, they were sharp with cunning–the pleasure of a puzzle. And one she could solve.

He had never thought before, how those in her field were continually faced with questions, questions whose answers they sometimes dug for their whole lives and never unearthed. The low margin of success would annoy him. He was a numbers guy. He liked a good puzzle too. But his always ended with a definitive answer. He always found what he was searching for. He suddenly wanted the same for her.

~

For all her newly acquired knowledge of the history and possible causes of his condition, Lillie could offer no suggestions on how to make surviving his eighth phase any less infuriatingly miserable. Logan had to deal with the filth and discomfort and lack of sleep just as he had before and power through them. He had no

220

choice. For that Lille was sick. Disgusted with herself. He was looking to her for answers, and she was failing him.

When Lillie looked at Logan, she saw a destructively handsome man. But one who was lost, just as the psychiatrist had surmised, only he didn't know it. Wouldn't admit it to himself, or perhaps he couldn't. He was a tough one, but he wasn't as strong and cold as he wanted the world to believe. She'd known that the day he'd come back to the library—come back when it would have been easier on his ego to stay away. The fear had drowned out the pride. He was human. He needed a lifeboat just as much as the next guy. It didn't matter if he'd been swimming on his own for years. The water he was treading now was chilly and deep. She only hoped she could reach him in time.

She called him on the morning of October 25, after his first night of the phase. She pressed the numbers and watched them appear on the screen one at a time until all seven were there and let her finger hover over the "call" button until her screen light went out. It took her three tries. He picked up on the first ring, and she wasn't sure whether to be relieved or upset.

"Yes." In one word, she heard everything. The nausea. The ache. The anger.

"What are you agreeing to?" she pitched her voice as low as she could.

"You called to make sure I was still alive, right? I was answering your question." His voice sounded rough enough to scrape into her ear. She winced.

"Did I wake you?" Hers came out soft in comparison.

"No. I guess the change does, though, I'm not sure if it happens when the moon sets or when the sun rises. Either way, I woke up around 5:30." At his mention of time, she checked her watch. It was just after six. She imagined he'd had his shower by now and decided that wasn't a safe thing to think about. Not when she had stopped worrying about how he was feeling and started picturing how he might look.

"Do you want to meet after class?" She said to keep herself from asking about his head.

"If it's all the same to you, I think I'd rather pass out for a few hours," his words hurt when they scratched through the phone.

"Of course," she nodded, though he couldn't see. She couldn't blame him after he'd roamed the woods all night, eating who-knew-what, since he'd scarfed all the house cats a few phases ago. *The Technician* told them he was going after farm animals, now that the smaller domestic animals were gone. She prayed he didn't get through all of those before they found a solution. If he did, he'd have no choice but to go after a human.

"I'll call you when I wake up." That was all he gave her for goodbye.

But he didn't. Nor did he call her the next morning after he phased or the next. Lillie wanted to call and check, to make sure some member of campus security hadn't seen him prowling in the darkness and shot. That he wasn't lying crumpled in the forest, a pale heap amongst green and brown. But she'd chew off her own fingers before she let them dial his number again. It didn't matter that he hadn't left her thoughts since she'd closed her phone on the end of their conversation. It didn't matter that she caught herself

222

praying for him to come striding to her section of the library, ready and willing to hit her with so many slights she could barely think to make a loaded reply. It didn't matter. *She* didn't matter.

~

When Logan woke in his bed Sunday morning, he rolled over on the mattress in sheer relief. He had several things to sigh about. The bed was soft. He and his sheets were just as clean now as they had been when he went to bed last night. His head wasn't pounding, and he wasn't sick to his stomach. It was way past five thirty. The phase was over now, and he wouldn't have to deal with it for another month. And maybe, just maybe, he and Lillie could pinpoint a cure for this thing before the moon was full again. In celebration of all these things, he closed his eyes and went back to sleep.

That afternoon Andrew decided to organize a little get together. He called dozens of girls, asked Logan to do the same, sent Batu an IM that said "get your butt up here," sent Mark to the store for "supplies," and hoped that Rob would stay wherever Rob was for the duration. Logan scrolled through his address book and sent messages to Alexa, Ashlee, Beth, Betsy, Buffy, Dana, Deena, and Dina, Elizabeth, Heather, Holly, Kat, Kate, and Kelly and stopped short when he got to Lillie. *Crap!*

He had broken his own rule, the one about not stringing a girl along. It was a strange rule for a guy to have, but he usually kept it with no problems. He'd spent years learning what not to do from his old man, and those years told him that his father was a master stringer, with his business partners, with his wife, with his whores.

223

How can I fix it? If it had been any other girl, he'd just call her up and invite her to the party tonight and make sure she knew she was expected to stay over, but Lillie wouldn't be mollified by those kinds of things. He'd be lucky if she didn't use that sharp tongue and wit of hers to cut off his manhood and send it back to him in gift-wrapping. *No. This is going to have to be done face-to-face.* And a personal encounter might be even more dangerous than a phone conversation. Sure she could eviscerate with words, but that would hurt a lot less than a swift kick below the belt. He would be a fool if he thought she didn't have some muscle hidden in the legs of her slacks. She was an archeologist, and she'd just spent the better part of the summer at a dig. But he didn't see any way around it. With Lillie, it was all about saving face, and emailing, messaging, or calling would not help him do that. *I wonder if I still have that cup left over from intramurals sophomore year.*

On Monday, Logan looked up the library's number on NCSU's website and called to see when Lillie would be in. He knew she had most of her classes in the morning so that she could work in the afternoons and early night shifts, but he wanted to be precise. He wanted the espresso to be steaming when she found it on the circulation counter. Then when she picked it up and saw the note on the coffee sleeve, she might be more receptive to coming to the table he liked in her section so that he could apologize. She also might bring the coffee and scald him with it, but that was a chance he was going to have to take, though he was banking heavily on her desire to avoid scenes at work rather than being the cause of one.

He was in line at Hill of Beans by 5:40 and had the cup on the counter at three minutes till. Logan made sure the dude who was waiting on Lillie so he could end his shift knew that his ability to use his right hand for more than waving at people depended on his guarding that coffee like it was gold until Lille got there and making sure she knew it was hers. Then Logan sprinted to the table to wait.

It was seven after six when he looked up and saw her coming in his direction, the espresso in her hand. She stopped just short of the table and leveled a look that threatened to impale him and pin him to the shelf behind him. "Have a nice nap?" Her voice was even sharper than her eyes.

"It was decent," he tried to smile instead of flinching. She continued to stare. "I'm sorry about that, Lillie. I really am—"

"I'm not one of your one-night-women, Logan." The slant of her eyes sliced him again.

"I know that. I wasn't trying to blow you off." He put up a hand for protection.

"I think I liked you better when you had the guts to be honest," she slashed again.

He could feel himself bleeding out right there in front of her. All the words he'd thought could explain and appease ran too quickly through his mind and mouth for him to catch. His chance at salvaging the situation slipped away, drip by bright drip. "I'm sorry."

"You said that before," her lips twisted with the shaft of her eyes, and he found that he couldn't breathe.

"It's the truth," he whispered.

"No. The truth is you aren't sorry, at least about me. You're sorry that you've screwed up and lost your little automatic research assistant, but you couldn't care less about me." She twisted again.

"I swear, it isn't like that, Lillie. I just needed some time alone." he shook his head. It sounded empty, even to him.

"Is that what you tell your bimbos when they wonder why you haven't called? Face it, Logan. I was right. You're vapid and shallow. You use women to get what you want, and then discard them when you've played out your hand. Well, you don't get to burn my card, mister. This time, *I'm* the one who's getting a new hand, and all you're gonna be left with is a pile of ash." That the description fit his father to a T made Logan as sick as one of those headaches he kept during the phases. He couldn't help himself. He blanched. Joan's face turned up in his mind. It was all he could see.

He couldn't let Lillie see him the way Joan did, look at him like he was a disappointment. The way his father did, like he was trash. He blinked until the faces were gone, and the only one before him was Lillie. "I'm sorry. I never meant to hurt you. But I have to do this on my own."

Chapter 16

For a brief second or so, Lille contemplated throwing the espresso in his face and then seeing how he fared on his own. But there was something in his face that made her think he might be sincere. He had paled at some point during the exchange and looked almost sick. "Are you okay?" She hadn't forgiven him yet, but her anger and hurt had softened.

"No." He told the truth, and she knew it.

"What makes you think you have to do this alone?" She sat down across from him and deliberately took a sip of espresso.

"I just do. You sympathize. I get that, but there's no way you know what I'm going through, and any help you offer me is nothing more than an educated guess." Bleakness echoed in his voice.

"So you're an island. You happy with that, or do you wanna become a peninsula?" She was having none of his pity-me party.

"It doesn't matter whether I'm happy with the situation or not. I can't do anything about it. I just have to make the best of it." His whining grated. She couldn't take much more, or she would have to slap him.

"That's crap, Logan. So what if I don't change with the freaking moon? I can still help you. If we work together, we can figure something out. If you work

227

alone, you might come to the same solution, but that would take at least twice as long. Do you really want that?" She tried logic.

"Do you really wanna be friends with a myth?" he raised a brow.

"Jesus ate with the sinners and tax collectors. I figure I can drink coffee with a myth," she smiled as she took a dramatic swig.

"I am sorry about last week, Lillie," he held her gaze.

She had never met anyone who was able to make such powerful connections with eye-contact alone. When he leveled his eyes with hers, there was no way to look anywhere else. No way to blink. No way to break that link. It was a tool, she knew, to seduce mostly-willing women into his bed, not that he needed much coercing to get those girls to do his bidding. She'd always despised them, the ones who thought with their passions rather than their heads. They were just as bad as the frat boys they slept with who thought with their lower heads. Now she pitied them. When he turned those steel gray eyes on them, they were as good as done.

~

The month of November passed quickly for Logan. It always did. If he could make it to Thanksgiving Break, then he knew he could survive the semester, since there were only two weeks of classes after that before finals. He and Lillie communicated somehow every day via text or phone call or having coffee. He wasn't a fool. He knew how close he had come to losing her. The thought of having her everlasting derision had kept him up a couple nights after he brought her the apologetic coffee in the library. *Why?* he asked himself as he laid in the dark. *Why does this one*

228

matter? The one who shows absolutely no interest in me whatsoever? Sure she cared about him, but he could tell that it was in a totally platonic way. *Out of all the girls in the world, what makes this one different?* The answers evaded him in those moments of wakeful unrest, and his final conscious thought was of a waterfall of ink black hair and forest green eyes.

He was pleased at the rate that he and Lillie could eliminate extraneous lore. The sheer volume of legends and myths concerning any sort of shape shifting creature was enough to make him want to settle for losing 18 hours a month for the rest of his life and be done with it. There was no way. He was like a high school freshman who'd somehow wound up in a class full of graduate students, swimming in books and names he couldn't read, sinking in words he didn't understand, reaching for purchase but finding only page after page pouring past him, pushing him farther down into confusion. But Lillie was a natural. She dove into the texts and had no trouble bobbing back to the surface any time she pleased. She could sift through the muck that sucked at his toes and swallowed him bit by bit—feet, ankles, calves—without the slightest fear of sliding any deeper than she wanted to go. Lillie could tell with only a surface reading if a version could possibly be applicable to his situation. Logan had to read them carefully to discern their merit. If she was a fish, he was a bird, wary of wading any more than he had to into the unknown.

Some of the first stories to land in what Logan thought of as the Load of Crap pile were the ones that Hollywood had popularized: super-strength and speed, increased aggression, and retaining a human intellect.

Though they couldn't be positive about the first three, he and Lillie reasoned that if he possessed those powers, there was no way he could have gone undetected by UPD or the forestry service for so long. And they were sure that he carried no trace of humanity with him when he shifted into the lupine form. If he had, surely he would remember the experiences in more than his subconscious. Unlike pop culture's depictions, it seemed that when Logan was a wolf, he was just that–a wolf; and when Logan was a man, he was only a man. There was no in between. No shared consciousness. He was no Jacob Black.

The more they read and eliminated, the more impatient he became. He wanted something to show for the work they'd done. The pile of questionable material was still much bigger than the Potentially True pile and the Load of Crap. They'd been at it three-and-a-half weeks, and still they had isolated neither an initial trigger nor a cure.

He had been hoping that they'd solve this thing before his ninth phase. According to the calendar, he was set to shift in the middle of Thanksgiving Break, and he was worried about how the wolf was going to find its way back to his bedroom at his parents' house, a place it had never been. Lillie was more worried about what he was going to hunt in Asheville.

"Are you sure you can't just tell them you have to study?" she asked.

"Am I hearing things, or did the good little Catholic girl just encourage me to lie to my parents?" Logan smirked.

"I did not just encourage you to lie to them. I encouraged you to come up with an excuse to stay on campus so that we wouldn't have to worry about you waking up in a strange place totally nude. If you told them you had to study, it would be the truth. You just wouldn't be doing the kind of studying they'd think you were." She tried to hide her instantaneous aggravation, but he caught a hint of it before she covered it with her prim explanation.

"Much as I'd like to, I can't avoid going home this time. I haven't been there since Christmas Break," he sighed.

"That's nearly a year!" Lillie looked astonished.

"So? When was the last time you were home?" He cocked a brow and aimed his question.

"I was home for Father's Day in June. We usually all get together for the Fourth, but I was doing the dig at Roanoke, so I missed that this year." Her face told him more than her words did just how sorry she was that she hadn't made that family gathering.

"Do you spend every holiday together?" he heard the tone of his voice and knew that detached was better than envious.

"We do Easter, Mother's Day, Father's Day, Fourth of July, Thanksgiving, and Christmas," she shrugged. "And I try to make it home for my parents' birthdays too, but that doesn't always happen." It was no wonder she didn't understand him. They didn't live in the same world. "Does your family never get together?"

"They do, but I only go back when I have to, which means that if I've called on Mother's and Father's Day, I can put it off until Thanksgiving." His words seemed to appall her, but she changed the subject without saying anything.

"Since there's no getting out of it, we need to figure out what to do about you waking up naked who-knows-where." She picked up a book.

231

"That may not be such a bad thing, depending on the where," Logan grinned and wished she was like his usual girls who would get distracted by that small movement.

Lillie didn't bother to glare but kept her eyes on the page she had begun to reread.

It took everything Logan had to steer the Camaro in the direction of his parents' house after class on the 20th. He could have waited until the next morning, but why postpone it? He was going, and whether he left sooner or later wouldn't improve anything. His car was built for sport, but he didn't enjoy the curves of the highway or push the speed limit as he might have on another day. The best part about the break would be starting the return trip to Raleigh.

He pulled onto the winding half-mile private drive that led to his parents' house and slowed his car. Philip hated loud engines that intruded on the seclusion he'd created for himself, no matter that his own car was quite capable of snarling like the cat it was named for.

Before he left campus, Logan had decided that he'd make as few waves with his old man as he possibly could this time. Surviving home for five days while phasing three times would be hard enough. Once the trees opened up to reveal the house, he turned off his Alpine and AC/DC. Another concession. Then he parked around back so that his parents' cars weren't blocked in. He wiped his shoes on the mat at the back door and knocked.

His mother's distorted face appeared on the other side of the beveled glass, and she opened the door with a smile, as he'd known she would. "Logan!" she cried, as if she hadn't spoken with him the night before.

"Hi, Mom," he stepped into her open arms and gave her a squeeze because he was supposed to. She held on long after he'd loosened his grip, and he thought he felt a sob on his shoulder.

"How was your trip?" She stepped back before he could be sure. Ginnie Michaels looked the same as she had for as long as Logan could remember. She was a petite woman with the creamy skin and auburn hair that her Celtic ancestors were known for. She wore her hair chin-length like Jackie O and never left the house without pearls in her ears, powder on her face, and diamonds on her fingers. Today she had on gray slacks that told Logan she wasn't expecting any company. His mother never wore casual pants in front of anyone but family. He had never seen her in shorts.

"Fine," he answered and wondered how long she was going to keep stretching that smile across her face.

"Did you leave your things in the car?" she looked at the floor near his feet.

"I've got everything," he shifted the duffel to his left hand so that it was no longer partially hidden behind his back. Her smile slipped a bit, but she caught it before it left altogether.

"Your room's ready," she spread it back in place and moved aside. He went several steps toward the stairs before he took a hit to his knees and almost face-planted.

"Logan!" He looked down to find Preston wrapped around his legs.

"Hey, Pres." It had been nearly a year, and Logan could have sworn, in that length of time, his little brother had grown at least six inches. He stood awkwardly for a few seconds more before the little boy released him and looked up.

233

Preston had their mother's complexion, but he'd gotten their father's hair and eyes, so he was a freckled, seven-year-old version of Logan. That was why Logan hated to look directly at the kid; it was like looking at his own younger self. He fought the urge to shudder and tried to remind himself that the boy couldn't help what genetics did to him.

"Are you gonna be here *all* week?" Preston was eager to know as Logan, whose legs were finally free, started towards the stairs again.

"Yep. All week," Logan answered flatly while he went and knew without looking that Preston was following right behind.

Logan managed to avoid any contact with his father until Wednesday night, and may have been able to do so a little longer had it not been Preston's birthday. But that meant Philip had to have dinner with the rest of the family and couldn't get by with having it sent to his home-office. When his father sat down at the end of the table, Logan coolly returned the look he got, though he knew that he should have deferred. *I'm not a child that you can intimidate with a stare anymore.* And he was not the first to break eye-contact. Philip did that when he bowed to pray, causing Logan to bite the inside of his cheek to keep from laughing at the hypocrisy of his father feigning devoutness. *He has to be one of the most dishonest people I know, and here he is praying for blessings in return for service. He'd take the blessings all right, if there was anyone up there to hear his request, but he won't serve anyone other than himself,* Logan scoffed into his napkin after passing his plate.

When everyone's plate was full, Preston could keep quiet no longer. "Dad, did you know that Logan's gonna stay 'til Sunday?"

"That's nice, son." Philip momentarily stopped cutting the roast beef on his plate. "But I think you've got more exciting news than even that. Isn't someone at this table turning seven today?"

"Yes, sir," Preston grinned. "Can we have cake and presents soon?"

"After dinner," his father nodded.

Ginnie tried to engage her men in conversation throughout the meal, but Logan was pensive, and Philip made no more concessions to Logan's presence than his initial acknowledgment, so the dialogue involved only Preston and his mother, with his father and Logan nodding occasionally and making one-word responses when necessary.

Logan speared a piece of potato and thought of Lillie. She would be eating dinner with her big, noisy Catholic family. He could see them clustered around a table that was too small for the group, but no one would notice because they were too busy enjoying themselves to complain about the closeness. They probably weren't the type to complain about that sort of thing anyway. He imagined they wanted the closeness while his own family sat poles apart at a table large enough for twelve. Holidays were made for that kind of people, the kind who were sincere when they slapped you on the back as they welcomed you home. The kind who were family in more than name only.

Preston was ecstatic when he opened Logan's gift, an "Ultimate Bumblebee" Transformers action figure that not only transformed from robot to Camaro, but also came with sounds and was able to respond to the noises around it. Though it had been Ginnie's idea, Logan had to admit that it was a pretty cool gift for a little boy, or at least he would have thought so at Preston's age. But then came the gifts from their parents: a Nintendo Wii and several games and accessories, some pretty extensive Lego sets that could make the Death Star and the Millennium Falcon and ships from *Pirates of the Caribbean*, Transformers and Spider-Man action figures, and an Xbox 360 (which Logan coveted because it was newer than his and less likely to get the Red Ring of Death), and he promptly forgot all about Bumblebee. The second Preston ripped the last of the paper off his presents, Philip headed for his office, his exit unnoticed only by his youngest son. That Ginnie covered her husband's absence didn't surprise Logan, but it did infuriate him.

She dashed to the kitchen and returned with the cake. It was baked in the shape of Preston's favorite Transformer, Optimus Prime. It had arms and legs, and the icing on its head was stiff enough that it had been shaped into the many contours needed to create the Autobot's distinctive face, and it had been dyed the appropriate colors. The thing was so realistic that it seemed to be only an enlargement of the plastic toy Preston had just unwrapped, and if Logan wasn't sure that it was edible, he might have questioned whether it was actually a cake. *Even for Pres, that's a little extreme.* He glanced at his mother, who was beaming as she cut a piece for the birthday boy and added a scoop of ice cream to his plate before passing it over. Preston took it with a gigantic grin and plunged in. Ginnie looked at Logan, perhaps to ensure that he wanted a plate of his own, but he turned away and went to his room.

It all made him sick. The falseness. It pressed in on him every time he came back to Asheville. The house, the grounds, the whole freaking town was nothing but an empty façade. And when he was there, he felt empty too. He was Neo, and there was no way out of The Matrix. Morpheus had given him the red pill, and there was no spitting it back out, but instead of being free, he was back in the grid, and all the horrible knowledge he'd gotten from his trip "down the rabbit hole" remained. He pitied those who were naïve and thought that being rich or successful was everything, and then again he didn't. They were content, just as Preston was, to be at the mercy of people like his father, and *he* was the one who couldn't find contentedness—not in things, not in people, not in God. It was all hollow. Stupid to believe or trust in any of that. It would all disappoint, without fail. He liked to think he was better off knowing. That way he wouldn't get hurt. Lillie, as grounded and sincere as she was, would eventually get crushed, either when her religion failed her, or when the ones she loved most betrayed her. He hated it, but there was nothing he could do except hope that it wouldn't happen or that he wouldn't be the one to do it.

Chapter 17

He opened his eyes and hoped that he was in the woods that surrounded his parents' place, but he wasn't sure. He did know that he was damp and cold. He stood up and walked a few paces in the direction he was facing. He had taken the precautions that Lillie had suggested–leaving his window open and making sure there were recently-worn clothes with his scent on them nearby. They were hoping that even though the room wasn't permeated with Logan's scent like 317 was, the wolf's nose would be able to find it on the clothes and follow it back to the house when he looked for a place to curl up for the day.

He went a few steps farther and could tell by the light that there was a break in the trees, so he was at least heading toward some form of civilization. *If it isn't my parents', I'm screwed*, he thought, but walked a bit nearer to the edge of the trees. He poked his head around one of the grayed trunks and didn't recognize the house he was looking at. *Screwed sideways*, he corrected. *How the crap can I explain to some strangers why I'm a mud-covered streaker and not get arrested?*

But it was either crouch in the woods all day, cold, filthy, and starving or grow a pair and see what happened. So Logan looked for a sizable leaf–recognizing that he had real pity for Adam and Eve–

found one large enough to do the trick, covered himself, and made a dash for the garage.

He hugged the exterior wall of the garage and made his way behind it. *There has to be a back door around here somewhere.* He kept moving as quickly as he could with bare feet and tried to use the landscaping for cover. When he had almost reached the back door, he saw to his right what looked to be a wire fence, dividing this property from a neighboring one. On it, there was a sign declaring that THE LAND BEYOND THIS POINT IS THE PRIVATE PROPERTY OF PHILIP MICHAELS. NO TRESPASSING.

By the time Logan made it back to the house, he had missed three calls from Lillie. He tried not to sigh when she picked up with panic in her voice. "Are you okay?"

"No worse for wear." He didn't know what he thought about her tone. It was nice that she wanted to know what he was going through, but with girls like her, a little attachment was often too much attachment for his tastes. It was natural, he guessed, for him to be important to her—she was to him, though he wasn't sure why. Still.

~

Lillie was livid. Worse than, except that she couldn't think of a better adjective. *How could he be so blasé about waking up in strange woods totally vulnerable? It was dangerous, that's what it was. He could get arrested, or worse, shot,* she fumed as she listened to the arrogance on the other end of the line.

"You shouldn't take chances, Logan. This is the second night it's happened in a row, and you barely got back into your window yesterday morning. For

239

goodness' sakes, just come back to Raleigh before something bad happens. It's Saturday. You've done Thanksgiving with your family. What's one day? It isn't like twenty-four more hours will make up for the year following that they'll have to wait to see you again." It was low, she knew, but she didn't care if he was aggravated, just as long as he was safe and alive.

"I can't stay in 317 forever, Lillie. What am I supposed to do when I graduate? What about the poor SOB who inherits my bedroom? It's gonna be hard to explain when he wakes up one morning to find the place trashed and a naked dude on his floor!" His chuckle had her wishing she could reach through the receiver and throttle him. *We'd see just who was the poor SOB then, wouldn't we?*

There was no reasoning with him. The guy drove her mad. *Mad's just about right. I've gotta be mad to get so emotional over a hedonistic frat boy*, she rolled her eyes at her own weakness and wondered when it had come to this? When had she come to be more interested in a guy than school? More interested in a present mystery than the marvel of uncovering the past? Or the lure of a future dig in the Amazon, or Papua New Guinea yielding the secrets of time?

The thought that had tears gathering so fast that she almost didn't have time to wipe them out of her voice before he heard them, that he might not come back from Asheville, had her hands trembling, and she used that. Used the fear and other emotions that sprang up inside her and poured out in drips and waves. Turned them into anger and unleashed it all on him.

"If you want to get killed by some redneck with a twelve-gauge and a thirst for blood, go right ahead. You can call me *if*, by some miracle, you make it back to NCSU. Otherwise, I'll just assume that I can go back to doing something in my free time other than scouring ancient texts about overgrown, idiotic, undomesticated canines."

~

"I didn't ask for your help, remember? You offered. You don't have to do anything you don't want to. No one's making you except maybe your overactive sense of social responsibility. Or is it guilt?" The thought struck him just as hard as he hoped it did her. In the second he said it, he knew that it wasn't true, but he used it anyway, slashing like claws. "That's it, isn't it? You're doing this in an attempt to work your way into heaven. How many Hail Marys does this cancel out? Just tell me they made you a decent offer, at least made it worth your while to put up with the abomination."

~

That he could suggest it ripped at her, even as she could see the situation from his side. She ached, but not for the hole he'd just torn out. She ached for the one she couldn't feel, but knew was there, swollen and festering, an infection spreading unchecked over time. "Please, Logan. . ." Lillie whispered, her hand pressed against her chest, and in the silence she added, "Come home."

~

Logan parked in the closest vacant space, the one Rob liked to put his H2 in because it was on the end, and the vehicle parked there was less likely to get smashed by a drunk driver a la Stella. He had a little laugh to himself as he dialed Lillie and swung the duffel from the back seat over his shoulder. *He'll be so pleased!*

241

"We've got a problem," Logan told her the second she picked up.

"What?" her voice cracked in his ear.

"It's a Sunday. During Thanksgiving Break. Hill of Beans is closed and so is the library."

~

The thought bloomed in her mind and was beautiful to her before she found the sticking point beneath. *My apartment.* She could see him there, *wanted* him there but knew what he would want when he got there, even if he knew better than to expect it. That was most of the reason that they always met and researched at a public place. She wasn't willing to take any risks, not with a man like Logan. Still, her place was better than his. She wouldn't be at a disadvantage. "How about my place?"

~

Lillie's living room was as he'd expected, clean, organized and neatly crowded. She had a nice couch and coffee table, a couple of chairs, bar stools for the counter, a tiny TV, black and white film posters on the walls, and a few prints of ancient landmarks. On every flat surface there was at least one picture frame, and most of those frames held the same faces captured at different ages and places. The rest of the space was filled with books, hardback and paper, fiction and non; issues of *National Geographic* and other anthropological magazines, and DVDs. Hundreds of them. Mostly black and whites, but a few of the films were in color. He noticed her apartment smelled lightly of powder or soap and clean laundry.

She sat him on the couch, pressed a chilled can of Coke into his hand and rushed down the hall only to return with a familiar notebook and an expandable file

242

folder which seemed to be barely large enough to hold the stack he swore had tripled in thickness since he'd seen it only just before going to Asheville. She curled into the chair across from him with the table between them and began to flip through her pages. Logan cracked open his Coke and took a sip.

"I think I've got some Ritz crackers and cubed cheese if you're hungry." He shook his head at her offer, then realized that she hadn't looked up.

"Mom wouldn't let me leave without breakfast," he voiced the answer so she'd know. She nodded, but that was all the answer he got. "Is anything in those pages important enough to share?"

Lillie's viridian eyes shifted from the papers to his face, and she tucked the edge of her lip between her teeth. "It's the trigger. I think I've found a possible cause . . . but I can't prove it yet."

"That it's only a hypothesis hasn't stopped you before," he quipped, looking for a laugh, but she sent him the smallest smile instead.

"That night in Breckenridge? When you got hurt in the woods? I don't think you fell and cut yourself on a rock, Logan. I think you were attacked."

Chapter 18

Even when Lillie showed him the news clippings detailing the carnage from the cabin at their resort she'd copied from the digitized files in the library, Logan had a hard time accepting that some other lycanthrope had murdered those children and their sponsors that Jen had told him about. *But it would make sense.*

"Say it was a lycanthrope. Okay. That explains why it looks like a wolf attack. What about the door? Even lycanthropic wolves don't have opposable thumbs, and apparently we don't have any supernatural powers. That theory also doesn't account for the missing girl. And why that particular cabin?" He wanted them to be on to something just as much as Lillie did. He just knew better than to get excited before all the details were smoothed out.

"Slow down, Logan. I think I've got all the answers you want. That the killer is a lycanthrope explains everything. Just let me print a few copies of something," she put a hand on his arm, and it seemed she was willing him her patience.

"The lycanthrope theory washes, Logan. It washes, and here's why: Sarah Abbot, the missing girl. *She's* the killer." Lillie had to hold up a hand to keep him from yelling at her outrageous claim. "Just listen. Sarah Abbot's body was never found because she didn't die. She didn't die because *she* is a lycanthrope. Think about it, Logan. When you wake up the morning after, where are you?"

"My apartment." He sat next to her on the couch and shoved his hand through his hair.

"That's right. Do you know why? Because even if you don't share a consciousness with the wolf, he subconsciously remembers your scent. In the same way, you subconsciously remember his treks through the woods, as evidenced by that quack's hypnoses. And how does the wolf get back into 317 without opposable thumbs?" She waited for his answer.

"The window?"

"Exactly. That's how Sarah Abbot got into the cabin, and she chose that particular one, and *only* that one, because it smelled familiar to her. She returned home, or the closest thing to it she could manage."

"I haven't killed anyone, Lillie."

"No, but you've annihilated the entire feline populace and moved on to the Ag department's livestock. Breckenridge is a tourist trap. There probably isn't an animal bigger than a squirrel for miles. You're just lucky the campus is so big."

"So if Sarah is a lycanthrope, where is she now, and how did she become one? Don't we still have to figure that out before we can stop this thing?"

"I don't know yet, Logan. But I will."

"I hope you know soon. I'd rather not spend the next forty years in jail for a murder I didn't consciously commit," he sighed.

"At least you wouldn't have to worry about going home," she shot him a sideways look.

"There is that."

He didn't leave her apartment right away like he'd planned. He figured that he'd excuse himself the second they were done discussing the research and deciding the next step to take. And there was a moment, a second's slight hesitation, when he could have risen and made some sort of stupid excuse to get himself out the door. But the silence came, and he let it pass without moving. This was new territory, Logan realized. He had gotten pretty good at keeping the innuendos to a minimum with Lillie, but he was aided in that they always met in a public place. This was the first time they'd ever spent any time together in private. Without the barrier of social expectation, he wondered how long he would be able to pretend he didn't want her.

"Got any plans tonight?" She spoke, and he realized that things had been quiet for a while.

"Seeing as I was still supposed to be in Asheville right now, I'd say not," he grinned.

"Well, I have a plan."

"Is that supposed to surprise me?" he raised a brow.

"No. But I do have one. We can just hang out for a while, until it gets dark, and when the moon comes out, I can watch the magic happen," Her voice sounded rational. He knew it did, but then why was what she said with it so ludicrous?

"Magic? Did you just say *magic*? Lillie, this isn't some slight of hand, Siegfried and Roy crap. In a few hours I'm going to turn into a freaking wolf!"

"I know that, Logan. As I recall, *I* was the one who informed *you* of the situation," she rebutted.

"Hooray for you. Here's a cookie," he told her dryly.

"I don't want your imaginary reward," she shoved away the empty hand he offered her. "I just think it would be a good idea for me to observe you—" He glared at her. "—I mean the wolf in action."

"And where in the world did you read that the definition of a 'good idea' is 'one that can get you ripped to pieces?'" Logan shook his head. "You *are not* going to observe what the wolf does, do you hear me, Lillie? You aren't going to do it because I don't want to be rinsing off what's left of you in the shower tomorrow morning."

"You aren't my boyfriend, Logan. You can't tell me what to do," she reminded him with arms crossed and eyes narrowed, sharp as shattered glass.

"Just because I don't have a title doesn't mean I can't stop you from getting yourself killed. I may do a lot of things you don't approve of, but that doesn't mean I'm a monster or that I was born without a conscience. You are not going to follow that wolf tonight. You're going to stay in this apartment all night long. You're not going to open the door for anyone or anything until the sun comes up. *That's* what you're going to do." He wasn't backing down.

"What makes you so sure? The last time I checked, you lose consciousness when you phase. Therefore, I can do whatever I want to tonight, and there's no way you can stop me!" The smile on her face was torturous.

"Lillie, you're staying put, even if I have to tie you up to get you to do it. I will not have you out there where it is. I won't have it!" He relaxed the fist he hadn't felt form.

"Logan, you've phased on twenty-four nights, and nothing's happened to me. What makes tonight any different?" The arrogance on her face didn't prove she'd won. It only proved that she was irrational.

247

"You weren't out looking for me those other times. Purposefully trying to find me. It isn't too hard to avoid a wolf if you don't go walking in the woods," he admitted. "But this isn't just walking in the woods, Lillie. This is putting on a red cape and carrying a basket of goodies to Grandma."

"If I recall, Red was the one that survived the story, not the wolf," she was smirking.

"That's not the point. It's too risky," he sighed and tried to decide how to make her see reason.

"Isn't it more risky to wait until you've blown through every woodland creature in the county to start trying to track your movements? Until you've got nothing left to feed on but human flesh? Isn't *that* too risky?" Her mouth was a thin line, and he could see the anger in her sea-green eyes, turbulent as a hurricane.

"I wouldn't let that happen." *Can't. If it comes to that I'll...*

"How would you stop yourself? You aren't even Logan when you're in that body. You're just a . . ." she broke off.

"A wild animal?" he supplied. "Wild animals can be caged, Lillie. Put down if need be."

"But that's different, Logan. Killing the wolf would mean killing you too," she looked at him, and those eyes were soft with rain.

"If it means keeping everyone else safe, then that's what I'll do," the note of finality he heard in his own voice was as surprising to him as it was to her. He hadn't known how he felt about it until just now, but in an instant he was certain. He knew how this was going to end.

~

"You can't just give up like that. There has to be another way. A cure," the desperation flooded into her face, and he turned away.

He cleared his throat, still facing the other direction. "I didn't say I was going off into the woods in a little while with a katana to commit hari-kari. We can keep looking. Keep trying. Surely you've come across some options we can try."

"Well, you aren't going to be too happy about the ones I've found so far," she sniffed, calmer now that they were talking business again, and she could pretend that she hadn't just had a flash of his body laying on the ground, lifeless and covered with red. "Most of 'em are pretty gruesome."

"I'm a guy. We live for gore," he faced her again, and she saw that he was grinning. "What do the myths say?"

"Some cures are the same no matter the trigger. Others are specific to the cause of the lycanthropy. The most common solution is killing and subsequently beheading the wolf, but I won't be a party to murder, so that's off the table. Another way is crucifying the wolf," Lillie shuddered at the thought. Crucifixes hadn't really bothered her because she'd grown up with them all of her life, but since she'd seen *The Passion of Christ*, she couldn't look at one without thinking of those scenes. She'd had nightmares for weeks afterwards. Movies didn't usually affect her like that, but knowing that the production crew had taken pains to create the most accurate depiction of a crucifixion as possible had somehow made watching it worse.

"If it's all the same to you, I'd rather we find another way," he put a hand on her shoulder. Lillie marveled at the way its warmth flowed into her. She wondered what it would be like to be wrapped in one of his hugs before she could distract herself.

"Well, I don't suppose you'd be willing to convert back to Christianity?" she tried to look hopeful.

"I don't think it counts as conversion if you aren't actually sincere," he smiled as he shook his head.

"Why are you so difficult?" she teased. "You don't like any of my suggestions!"

"Well, find me some better alternatives," he demanded with a wink.

The sigh she heaved was meant to portray exasperation as she shuffled through her research to find something less unpleasant. "We could always try wolfsbane . . ."

"Isn't that the lupine equivalent to rat poison?" he asked dubiously.

"The stories aren't too clear about whether the patients were actually able to survive this treatment. In most societies, death was considered a successful cure." It was getting hard for her to keep a serious expression.

"It sounds like an *un*successful cure to me," Logan frowned.

"Told you you wouldn't like what I'd uncovered so far. There's also removal of the wolf's skin. . ." Lillie looked up in time to see Logan's revulsion and smothered a snicker. "Or we can get a priest to perform an exorcism."

"No."

"Oh, come on! An exorcism wouldn't be as bad as getting skinned alive," she nudged his ribs.

"Maybe you haven't seen *The Exorcist* movies or *The Exorcism of Emily Rose*, but I have, and I do *not* want to be strapped down while all sorts of crazy crap's happening all around me."

"It's just a little Holy Water mixed with a few phrases of Latin," she shrugged. "The rest is only Hollywood."

"Yeah? Tell that to the chick with the green bile spewing out of her mouth and her head spinning around and around on her neck!" *Is he really serious about finding a cure, or not?*

"Would you let me smack you on the forehead three times with a knife or a stick from an ash tree?" she asked after flipping a few more pages.

"Now there's a remedy I can deal with, as long as I don't end up with a concussion or scalped." Logan actually looked a little relieved.

"I can also scold you three times using your Christian name," she returned to the page and read a bit further. "But you'd have to tell me your middle name."

"Logan," he spoke crisply.

"I thought that was your first name," Lillie asked in confusion.

"I'm named after my father, Philip, but I've always gone by my middle name to differentiate."

"So where does 'Logan' come from?" she couldn't help but ask.

"Mom read it somewhere," he shrugged.

"It suits you better than 'Philip,'" she smiled at him. "Less pretentious, but only slightly so." *Philip Logan Michaels.* Lillie tested the sound in her head and decided she liked it.

~

"What're you smiling about?" he wondered. A smile from most girls was a good sign, but he could never be too sure about one from Lillie.

"Even though you're very annoying, sometimes you can be entertaining too," she shrugged. "Besides, I think I just won the argument." *There it is, the **real** reason behind her happiness.*

"How's that?" Logan resisted the urge to cross his arms.

"You just okayed two options for attempting to cure your lycanthropy, and *both* of them entail me going out and following you tonight, especially if we want to get this over with before the next phase."

"You neglected to mention that I need to be the wolf for those remedies to work, and since I do, I revoke my previous approval of them." He was proud that he hadn't raised his voice. It had taken some doing, but he had not altered his tone. "Therefore you have no reason to go out and track it. Under no circumstances are you to leave this apartment."

"Again, how do you plan on stopping me?" she arched a brow in challenge. It was obvious that force wasn't going to work, since he couldn't make good on any threat. And he'd tried logic too, but it had failed him because women defied logic. Logan only had one mode of recourse.

"Lillie," he took her hand in his and peered into her golden-green depths. "I need you to promise me you won't go out of the house tonight. Please. I'm asking you to stay here tonight just like you asked me to come home today. I came home for you, Lillie. Now I need you to stay here for me." With any other girl, he could tell if she was receptive. Lillie wasn't as transparent. As he waited for her answer, he appreciated the way her hand fit in his. He had already known it would be slightly calloused from the digs she worked. He had held countless women's hands in his, and he wondered if it was her unattainable status that made it feel different, better than any other he could recall. *That's it. Just wanting what you can't have. Human nature, after all.*

Lillie peered back at him, but her face was empty of all emotion. Again he thought about how great she would be at cards. *She'd teach Rob a thing or two about ice, that's for sure.* For a moment, he thought she was going to pull away from him; instead, she squeezed his hand and drew a breath. "All right, Logan. I'll stay," she whispered. "I'll stay."

Chapter 19

Forget beheading or crucifixion; finals week was going to be the death of him. That's what Logan decided when he woke up that Monday. Whatever had possessed him to take classes at the precise times that meant he had tests three days in a row? After the third night, he and Lillie had put the lycanthrope issue aside and spent two weeks studying for exams. She was as serious about preparing for them as she was about finding a solution for his problem. She was carrying eighteen hours and should have been more frantic than he was. But Lillie was Lillie, and that meant that even under extreme pressure she was as organized and efficient as a machine. Notes and books were annotated and color-coded, and she had worked out mnemonic devices for all of the material she was a bit iffy on. It was almost sickening.

"Where are you, man? It feels like I haven't seen you in, like, a freaking month," Mark's call disturbed the silence of Lillie's living room with Lacuna Coil.

"Studying, which is probably where you should be too," Logan answered, though Lillie looked through him like his study hall teachers used to when they caught him shooting paper balls into a trash can.

"Aw, c'mon, dude. Lighten up. All you have to do is pass with a C. You don't think you've spent enough

254

hours in the study room during the semester to do that?"

"One of these days, my dad's gonna start wondering why it is that I haven't joined the company if I don't get outta school pretty soon. I don't want that to happen 'till I'm already done and long gone from Raleigh." Logan rolled his eyes.

"Who *are* you, and where the crap is my roommate? The only thing you've had time to hit lately is books, and that just ain't like you, man."

"Shuttup, Malone. The only reason you even give a crap about my social life or lack of one is that if I don't have a girl, then you don't either," Logan growled. There was silence from the woman beside him and the other end of the line. He slid a hand over his face. "Look, man. I didn't mean it the way it came out. I'm just running on nothing but Red Bull and about two hours' sleep. Can you cut me some slack? I'll be human again by Friday."

"Oh really?" Lillie smirked. "I'd like to know how you're gonna pull that one off with such short notice."

"Is that a *chick's* voice I hear? You're with a chick. I *knew* it. Logan Michaels studying for finals. Yeah, right! That'd be just as likely as Rob Norton developing a personality," Mark snickered. "No wonder you're so pissy that I interrupted."

"Well . . ." Logan had been careful not to talk about Lillie in front of the guys. He wasn't sure why he felt the need to keep her a secret, but he figured it had something to do with his having an actual friend who was a girl might make it seem like he was losing his touch, and he wasn't having the likes of Rob thinking something like that about him. There was no way.

"Well, I'll let you get back to your 'studying' now, bro. I just called to let you know that we're partying at the house tomorrow night. You can bring the book you're looking at with you if you want to. You never know when you might need something to read." Logan could hear Mark's grin even though he had hung up. When he looked at Lillie, she was laughing. "What?"

"Logan Michaels, I do believe you like to talk the talk more than you walk the walk." Lillie's face was a blank page when he looked at her to read her expression.

"Are you talking smack?" he raised a brow, not daring to be very hopeful.

"Absolutely. Logan Michaels, the infamous lady-killer. How true can it be if your own roommates are starting to question your seductive abilities?" The smile that settled on her lips was soft. *She's evil.* He worked to push back the thoughts that had just formed in his mind.

"In case you haven't noticed, I've been a little preoccupied lately. I mean, it's kinda hard to concentrate on seduction when you're trying to make sure your less-civilized side doesn't slaughter half the student body."

"Would your frat brothers buy that excuse? 'Cause if they would, I've a mind to sell them the Taj Mahal too," she crossed her arms and seemed unimpressed.

Logan was confused. It felt like she was encouraging him, and there wasn't anything wrong with that, but after months of being rebuffed, he wasn't sure what to make of this new attitude. He debated responses for a moment. "All right, Snow White. Care to put your money where your mouth is?"

"Last I checked, you didn't think I was your type," Her eyes were molten emeralds, and he couldn't think anymore.

"Last I checked, you didn't think I was yours either." He leaned in and waited. She didn't recoil. His kissed her, and though he expected ice, there was only warmth.

When he could form coherent thoughts again, Logan pulled back and dreaded the intensity of her anger. *I'm exactly what she accused me of being. Exactly what I swore to her I wasn't.* "I'm sorry."

"Why?" Lillie inquired, and for once, Logan didn't have to question the meaning of her smile.

Somehow he had almost made it through four finals in three days, and he felt confident that he wasn't going to be repeating any of those twelve hours in the last semester of his college career. He may not have made A's, but not everyone was as studious as Lillie Thackery. Logan hadn't seen her since that last study session at her place, but they'd texted in between cramming and taking tests, so he didn't feel bad. It wasn't as if he was avoiding her. He just needed some time with the guys to release the pressure that had been building since he saw his sadistic finals schedule. After all, that pent up stress was to blame for what had happened between them. Even though she didn't seem offended by his breach of trust, he wasn't going to let it happen again. Couldn't. *It wouldn't be worth the risk. If I lose her because of hormones, how will I ever get my life back?* There was no way he could find the answer by himself. He just wasn't good enough at research. And even if he did, how could he administer the cure alone when the vast majority of them seemed to require him to be in his lupine form?

Logan wasn't thrilled about how important Lillie had become. By necessity, he depended on her to keep his secret, to help solve the problem. He didn't like strings. They made things too tangled, especially when he wasn't as detached from her as before. He had wanted her from that first encounter in the library, but as long as they were both erecting walls, keeping distance was easy. Now all of a sudden, Lillie was tunneling beneath hers and his, like an underground spring trying to bubble up to the surface. He could build a dam, but it would only hold for so long. *And then what?* Logan shook his head to disperse those thoughts and wished he'd never kissed her.

~

Lillie was happy to be finished with exams. It wasn't the material, but the testing schedule that was grueling. Now she was looking at a month's break before beginning her last semester as an undergrad. She knew she was going to take an anthropology internship in the spring, which would count for six hours and Anthropology of Religion and Applied Anthropology to complete her twelve-hour scholarship requirements. It would be the lightest semester of her career, but she felt like she deserved it after taking no less than sixteen hours for seven regular semesters and working digs every summer in between. She would make it to May, and then she would start working towards Ann Arbor and the University of Michigan.

But for now, she would not think of the future. She put on her pajamas and slid beneath the covers with a cup of cocoa and her worn copy of Anya Seton's *Katherine*, and into the Middle Ages. Ever since she'd first heard the story of Katherine de Roet and John of Gaunt, Lillie had been captivated. So little was known about the couple–their homes and possessions were all lost to antiquity, but their offspring, the Lancasters, through their descendants, continued to influence the politics of the modern world. This was what had made her want to be an archaeologist, the idea that two people could love each other for their entire adult lives despite their society and culture deeming them unfit mates and that the reverberations of that love could still be felt six hundred years later. That such a passionate story had survived the centuries despite the loss of so many details inspired her to find and give voice to the hundreds of thousands of other stories that had been lost to time's destructiveness. She fell asleep later on, after reading of Blanche's death, and dreamt of a tall, dark man with a powerful kiss.

~

Logan woke the morning after his last final and found that he was not alone. Her long brunette hair spilled out around her face and from what he could tell, she had an athletic frame. The thought had him cursing beneath his breath as he nudged her awake. Sleepy blue eyes blinked back at him, and he was relieved enough for a quiet laugh. He traded places with a pillow and whispered, "Sorry. I'm gonna take a shower. Go back to sleep," but she had already snuggled into the downy form and didn't hear him.

"I see you finally let yourself have a little fun," Andrew grinned from his prop behind the bar. He had been sneaking one of Mark's Pop-Tarts.

"I don't remember letting myself, but I think I did have a pretty good time," Logan went to the cabinet to see what provisions they had.

"Large quantities of PGA punch and Jäger will do that to you, man. Besides, since when do you ask for permission?" Andrew wiped a crumb from the corner of his mouth at Logan's prompting.

"Good point. And since when do you get up alone on a Saturday morning?" Logan spotted a box of Bisquick and reached for it.

"Since I needed time to crash after finals and get rested up for a brunch date I have in a while with one of the Chi O's," Andrew finished the last of the Pop-Tart and went to see if there were any cartoons on.

He made pancakes for himself and Tayte and Andrew, and he figured that if either of the other guys were home, he'd be sharing with them before the morning was over, so his stack kept getting taller. While he was flipping yet another cake in the pan, Tayte poked her head out of the hallway with a grin, and he wondered why he'd been nervous. The facial structure was totally different. The mouth too pouty, the nostrils a bit too flared, the eyes just the slightest bit too wide-set. And none of those were bad things. Tayte was definitely the prettier of the two.

When she had gone, Logan went down to get Batu, who was now almost unbeatable at *Halo* and *COD*. He didn't want the poor little guy feeling like Logan was ignoring him, and to be honest, Logan couldn't remember the last time he'd hung out with him.

They came back upstairs to start the Xbox Live tournament and recruited Mark to play. Andrew was invited, but he only had about fifteen minutes before Stephie expected him, and she was not one to keep waiting. That meant they needed to include Rob if they wanted to use all four players. Mark lost the round of Rock, Paper, Scissors and had to invite his closest neighbor into the game.

Rob agreed with little coaxing and with their team complete, they began to attack the Covenant. Aside from the frequent scotch breaks, Rob was a decent teammate, but even if he hadn't been, 317's occupants would have been victorious because of Batu. It didn't seem to matter what world they were in. Batu could blend in with his surroundings and decimate the other teams before they even realized he was there. Eventually Mark and Rob tired of shooting grunts with Needlers and riding around on Warthogs while Batu singlehandedly massacred every soldier in sight, and then it was just Logan and Batu.

"Did you find the answers you were searching for?" Batu asked as they looked at the stats of the round they had just finished. Logan had been trying not to notice the discrepancy in the number of kills for his player and Batu's.

"Answers?" Logan turned to him.

"That explain why you are having blackouts," Batu elaborated.

"Not exactly," Logan fiddled with the camera joy stick on his controller. "Or at least now that I've found a few of the answers, I have more questions than I did."

"If you found the answer to your question, how can that create more questions?"

"I'm not sure how it happened, man, but it did," Logan shrugged.

"Still, you do not seem as lost as you once were. I believe you are on the right path," Batu nodded.

"I'm not so sure about that, Batu. Does your country have a saying like 'Hell hath no fury like a woman scorned?'"

"Not exactly, but I have heard that it is not wise to anger a woman, particularly one you care for."

"Well, that's where my current path seems to be heading, straight for hell," Logan could see disaster ahead and wasn't looking forward to it.

"I do not know much about women, Logan, but I do know my people say that it is easier to catch an escaped horse than to take back an escaped word," he suggested.

"Um, thanks, man. I'll keep that in mind," Logan pressed start on the next round.

Lillie's text woke Logan up from his cat nap late that afternoon:

CAN YOU COME OVER TONIGHT?

GUESS SO. HAVEN'T GOT ANY PLANS. He tried to sound neutral, though he hadn't been able to shake the thought of her since he imagined he had woken up beside her.

GOOD. WANT TO SEE YOU BEFORE I LEAVE FOR HOME.

WHAT TIME? He held his breath.

NOW?

SEE YOU IN 20. He closed his phone and rose to get dressed.

Lillie's living room was slightly less crowded with books than the last time he'd seen it, almost as if she couldn't stand to leave some of them behind in Raleigh for a month while she was in Manteo. She asked him in, and he went to the couch, expecting her to sit in the chair across the coffee table from him, like she had done the last time he was here. She sat on the other end of the couch. "How did finals go?" she started the small talk.

"I think they went all right, how about yours?" He was relieved he had something to say.

"I'm feeling pretty great now that they're over, and I get a month-long break," she sighed.

"That *is* awesome," he smiled. But the truth was he would almost rather keep taking finals than have to spend thirty days at his parents'. "When do you leave for home?"

"In the morning sometime," she waved a hand in the air. "Just as long as I'm there before dark. What about you?"

"I'll get there eventually," he turned his palms up and lifted his shoulders.

"Do you know when you'll be back on campus?" She seemed to be surrounding him with the depths of her eyes.

"Probably right after Christmas. I always try to make it to the New Year's party at the house," he swallowed to keep from gasping and had to remind himself there was plenty of air.

"Of course." They shone like jade when she nodded.

"When do you plan on coming back?" he forced his lips to ask.

263

"The Sunday before the spring semester starts. I like to stay as long as I can during Christmas Break since I won't be back home until March." She swept a few strands of her dark hair behind her ear, and he wondered how soft it would feel as it slid between his fingers.

"That'd be a good thing, in my book," he reminded her.

"Let's not talk about your parents, Logan," she bit her lip. "It makes you melancholy."

"Melancholy," he raised a brow as he tested the word. "That makes me sound distinguished."

"What?" Confusion was plain on her face.

"Only refined people like Cary Grant or Gregory Peck or whoever get melancholy. The rest of us ordinary people just get sad and depressed."

"Logan, I'd say you're anything but ordinary," she smiled, and as he watched the curve of her lips, he wanted to taste them again.

"Seeing as how I'm a lycanthrope, you have a point," he brushed the urge away and noticed how close she was sitting. There were barely six inches between them.

"That's not what I meant," she shook her head and laid a hand on his, then pulled it over to her other one.

He still wasn't sure what to do. With any other girl, this would be a cue to begin seduction, but it was Lillie, so he didn't move. "Maybe we could order pizza and watch one of the three billion movies you have here," he gestured toward a stack of them with his free hand.

"I'm not that hungry, but you can order something if you want." Somehow she had laced her fingers into his, and her palm was pressed tightly to his own. He could feel the calluses. *This isn't right. She's not one of your kind of girls. She doesn't know what she's doing.*

"Lillie," he breathed. "I thought you didn't want this, that you only wanted to be friends."

"That was before I knew you. When I only knew the person you pretend to be," her voice was soft, so different from her normal tone of scathing confidence. It couldn't have been a tremor he heard; Lillie was never unsure.

"That person *is* me. I *am* shallow and vapid. I have sex and get smashed and don't give a crap about the consequences."

"You don't care about the consequences for yourself, Logan, but you're anything but careless with other people. That's why you're hesitating now." She was right, but there was a part of him that wanted to take what she was offering, to drink until his thirst was slaked, but what would be left for her?

"I don't want the same things you want. I can't give them to you," he tried to take his hand from hers.

"I'll take whatever you can give me, Logan, because I know what I want, and right now that's you. Just you." The truth was crystal in the ocean of her eyes. He let it wash over him as he pressed his lips to hers and drowned in the taste.

Chapter 20

"Are you all right?" It was the third or fourth time he'd asked her, and each time she'd said she was fine, but he couldn't help himself. It was as if he'd just dropped one of his mother's Capodimonte flowers, and he had to keep looking to make sure it was still in one piece. There had been tears. Logan had seen them and had no idea what to make of them. They didn't always mean pain or regret, but Lillie's motivations were never as clear to him as other women's were.

She turned her face to his, and they were almost nose to nose. There was a curve to her lips. "I'm exquisite." The contrast of her eyes against the burgundy sheets and golden-edged comforter made them deeper somehow, though he had thought them fathomless before. "How are you?"

"I'm good," he smiled and wondered if his complete lack of guilt made him despicable. He lifted a strand of hair out of her face and tucked its darkness behind her ear. Logan couldn't explain it, but the action made him eager to kiss her again, though he should have had his fill by then. "You hungry now?"

"I could eat a little. You want still want pizza?" she teased.

"I wouldn't turn it down," he grinned. When she stirred beneath the covers, he laid a hand on the soft skin of her bare shoulder. "Stay here. I'll make the call," he said and then pressed his lips where his hand had been to please himself. She laughed and caught his chin, tipped it up for a taste of her own before snuggling back into the covers. "What? No argument?" he raised a brow.

"Absolutely none." She laughed again as he sat up, shook his head and reached to the floor for his jeans.

Logan left Lillie's a bit before midnight, since she had to finish packing and head home the next morning. He wasn't fond of her making the drive with only a few hours' sleep, and that was sure to happen if he stayed until daylight. He told himself that was why he had to leave, but even such a logical reason was almost weak enough for him to ignore. *Her roommate'll be back soon*, he tried again, but Lillie unintentionally negated that when she mentioned that Cayla was seldom there, since her parents lived in town, and she only had the apartment because it was covered by her scholarship. *Since when do I need an excuse to walk away?* He couldn't remember that ever happening before, and *that* was reason enough to go.

"I'll send you a text when I get back to Raleigh," she said as he watched her from the other side of the doorway after he'd talked himself out there. "Be careful when you phase. Call me if you need to."

"I will," he looked at his feet, the concrete beneath them, anything but her eyes.

"Merry Christmas," her voice came to him, clear and even.

"You too," he still hadn't looked up. He didn't want to see what was in her face, but curiosity had him peeking. It was as smooth as glass.

"And happy New Year." Her wish was genuine; he could see it, hear it too.

"Yeah. You too. Save that first kiss for me," he winked now that it was safe.

"Only if you will," she smirked and pulled the door to between them.

~

Lillie was spent. The breathless euphoria was past now, and she let herself sink slowly into the couch once Logan disappeared behind the door she had closed. She felt free; the dam had been broken, and she had poured out all of herself. Yet she was not empty–she had never felt so full, overflowing. But she was tired. She covered herself with the soft afghan she kept thrown over the back of the couch. As she snuggled into its warmth, Lillie closed her eyes and imagined that she was wrapped in Logan's arms instead and drifted to sleep with damp cheeks.

~

Logan awoke with a start, a sob echoing in the recesses of his consciousness. He stood and began the trudge back to Philip's property. He wished for his watch or that he could use his senses to tell the time of day in this body the way he was sure the other body could. As it was, he only knew that it was morning, and it was *cold*. Freaking frigid. He wondered if he was going to make it back to the house before losing an extremity or two. The stupid wind wasn't helping either. *If I ever get back, I'm gonna spend the next twelve hours in the Jacuzzi.* He concentrated on that thought as he hugged himself and walked, sucking the air in and out of his nose since his mouth was clamped shut so hard his jaw ached. *What I wouldn't give for a jacket right now.*

By now he knew which direction would take him to his parents'. This made his third time to have to streak from these woods back there. Logan could only guess that Raleigh was in the general direction he had been heading before phasing back. He tried not to think that he'd be doing the same thing tomorrow morning and Christmas Morning as well. It was just too depressing.

He went a little farther and stepped on something sharp. His toes were numb, but, unfortunately, his soles weren't. He lifted his foot and found a jagged rock. He stepped carefully over it and kept moving. The cut would clot eventually, that or freeze over. There was nothing he could do about it now anyway. And the longer he stayed out here, the colder he got.

When he finally climbed back into his window, he heaved a sigh at the simple delight of being warm, relatively speaking. He scooped up the clothes he'd left by the window, half-hoping that their scent would be strong enough to attract the wolf, though it hadn't worked any of the other nights he'd phased. Logan headed quietly to the bathroom he and Preston shared to get rid of half the forest's floor that was covering him. *It sucks that the Jacuzzi's in Mom and Dad's wing. Else I'd be about to slide in next to those amazing water jets instead of cleaning up first*, he thought as he turned the knob and stepped beneath the spray that wasn't warm enough. The air hissed between his teeth at the sharp change in temperature. After a second or so, the water was steaming, and he soaped himself up, watching the filth fall to the tile beneath him.

Logan had always been a clean guy, or at least he'd thought so until he'd become a lycanthrope. He hadn't *known* clean before. *But I do now.* He rinsed his hair again and felt to make sure there was no debris left.

269

When he was satisfied, he stepped back under the water and saw that the stream hitting the floor was clear. He shifted his foot to center himself and glimpsed a pink tint where he had been standing before it was washed down the drain. *Crap!*

He shut off the shower and stopped long enough to grab a towel before dashing into the hall. The cut on his right foot had made a plenty of prints leading from there to his bedroom door, and, he imagined, from there to his window. *Maybe Pres isn't up yet.* Logan grabbed several feet of toilet paper (since he didn't want to explain bloody towels later) and went to wipe up the evidence.

He was about three prints from his door when he heard Preston's voice behind him. "What're you doing, Logan?"

"Nothing. Go back to sleep. It's Christmas Break." Logan reminded him without turning.

"What are you doing with the tissue?" he seemed closer.

"Cleaning up the floor. Go on, before Dad finds out you're up. You want to sleep in, don't you?" That was his trump card. Logan had to hope it would work. Bluffing adults was one thing. Bluffing Mini-Me was another.

"Is that *blood*???" It was too late. That morbid curiosity Logan himself still felt was in Preston's voice. There would be no way of getting rid of him now.

Logan miraculously kept from sighing. "Yeah. I cut myself somehow, but it's no big deal." He turned and saw that Preston was completely engrossed in the remaining footprints.

"It looks like a lot. Can I see?" *Did his eyes actually just **sparkle**?*

"If I show you, will you leave me alone? Mom'll kill me if the maid finds dried blood on the hardwood."

When Preston nodded, Logan lifted his right foot and revealed the slash of red across his sole.

"It's still bleeding," Preston observed as a bright drop hit the puddle where Logan's foot had been.

"Yeah. Can you get me some Band-Aids?" Logan tore off some of the paper and pressed it to his foot. Like Logan knew he would, Preston went without another word. *He might be annoying, but the little guy does come in handy every once in a while.*

When Preston returned, he brought an entire box of Band-Aids, some Neosporin and a handful of paper towels. "It says on the commercial that you can clean up an entire mess with just one," he answered Logan's raised brow. "But I brought extras just in case."

"Thanks, Pres," Logan told him as he took the bandages and salve. When he was done with his foot, Logan saw that Preston was covering each print with a paper towel and then stepping on it with his own foot before moving on to the next one.

By Sunday morning, Logan had a new plan. He was sick of streaking from a random spot in the woods back to his parents', and, after the close call with his foot the day before, he wasn't sure he could risk it. That was why he'd gone out after lunch yesterday and left some sweat pants and tennis shoes in the fork of a tree trunk close to where he always awoke. *Why the crap didn't I think of this **before**?* The first time still would have been tricky, but the other four mornings would have been a lot less complicated and cold.

He was a great deal warmer as he ran back to the house, and the trip seemed to go faster, but that was probably because he didn't have to try to run and cover himself simultaneously. When he got back to his window, he was still a little chilled, but he was nothing like the popsicle of the day before. It wasn't until he walked out of the bathroom after his shower and nearly into Preston that Logan realized he had a problem.

"Whoa," was all he had time for before the questions started.

"Why are you up so early again today? And what were you doing yesterday when you cut your foot, anyhow?" Preston wondered.

"I'm up early because that's what I got used to during the semester," Logan shrugged.

"Liar. You've slept way later than this every day you've been home except yesterday and today." Preston's eyes narrowed, and Logan wondered if *he* made the same face when *he* knew he was being conned.

"I just didn't feel like spending the entire day in bed. It's kinda a waste of a break if you spend the majority of it asleep, don't you think?"

"I don't believe you," Preston announced, and Logan could see that it was true. The little boy before him was no longer curious about what his big brother had been doing. Now he knew Logan had a secret and was hurt and angry that he wasn't in on it.

"Too bad," Logan sidestepped Preston and headed for his bedroom door. "Because that's the only explanation you're going to get," he said and closed the door behind him. He set his alarm for a little after nine and fell back into bed, hoping that by the time he woke up, Preston would have given up standing outside the door and trying to stare a hole through it and gone off to annoy someone else.

Christmas morning was a tad tricky. Logan awoke near enough to the tree he'd stashed his clothes in that he wasn't very chilled, but if prior experience told him anything, it would be after seven by now, which meant that body temperature wasn't his main concern. He also knew by prior experience that Preston would have gotten up at least an hour before to see what Santa had brought. Thus, his absence might have already been noticed.

He was winded when he got back to the window and stepped through. *What if Pres told Mom about yesterday morning and the morning before?* There would be no way to pass it off . . . unless he claimed that he had been out all night with a chick or was nursing a hangover in his Camaro.

His friendship with Lillie had taught him how to cover the evening absences by checking the time for sunset/moonrise and making sure to be "out with friends," "in bed" or "studying" by then, but there was no way to cover for a morning absence, and especially not one on Christmas morning.

When Logan slid his window shut, he walked to the door and listened for any activity in the hallway. He didn't expect any since the festivities always happened downstairs in the den, next to the family tree, but he had to make sure. After creeping to the bathroom to wash all his skin left visible by the pajamas he'd grabbed, he headed down to face the questions, settling on the hangover excuse.

"Logan!" Preston yelled as soon as Logan had descended far enough to be seen. "I've been up for hours! It's *Christmas* morning! Where've you been?"

273

"That is an interesting question," Philip agreed, checking his watch. "You know we have a dinner commitment with your grandparents."

"I had a little too much party last night," Logan sighed. "Sorry . . . but it looks like you had a good time without me," he observed the pile of torn paper and toys that surrounded Preston and ignored Philip's scowl.

"I did! I got new games for the Wii and the Xbox, and new Transformers too! Plus I got a lot of candy and some DVDs, and best of all, a flat screen TV!" Preston was practically squealing by the time he got to the flat screen, and Logan winced, not only to make his cover story believable, but also because he was pretty sure the neighbors' dogs could hear the sound.

"That's great!" Logan really did have to work to sound enthused. *What the crap does a seven-year-old need with a 52 inch TV? Thank God I can leave on Thursday.* He bypassed the debris and sat on the opposite end of the couch from his mother who had yet to speak to him.

Ginnie seemed to become aware of his presence when she felt the couch move. She turned to him then, and he could see that the smile on her face was strained. "Merry Christmas, baby," she told him in a steady voice. She was nothing if not well-trained.

"Merry Christmas, Mom," he did his best not to sound angry. He wasn't supposed to see that she had been upset–probably over one of his father's girls, so he would try to pretend he was as oblivious as his brother. Being oblivious didn't mean he couldn't hug her, though, he decided, so he moved over and held her the way she had held him when he was little and was sad or scared or mad at the world. Her hugs were magic then, making everything okay as long as he was safe in her arms. It was Christmas after all, and it didn't matter that her stupid compliance had been as much the problem as Philip's indiscretion had. She deserved to be happy today just as much as Preston did, or more.

Logan couldn't figure out why she'd done what she had all these years, but part of him felt like she might have done it for him and Preston, and if she had, he didn't like to think about that. Logan told himself that she could have used Philip's infidelity as leverage, and even if she didn't want to end the marriage, she could at least get the upper hand and be paid well for her silence. But as far as he could see, all she got was anger and hurt. That was her own fault, not his. She should have had the brains to see that she could make a very profitable business deal, since those were terms Philip understood. Instead, she was stupid. She had been sitting pretty with a flush but had played like a fish and folded. For that, he could be angry, and he chose anger over sympathy more often than not. It was just easier. What difference did his reaction make for her anyway, when Philip held all the chips?

"Don't you wanna see what you got?" Preston interrupted Logan's ruminations.

"Of course," Logan smiled and knew his expression was just as strained as his mother's.

Chapter 21

His mother cried like she always did when he left, and Preston pouted, but Philip hadn't had any reaction other than reaming him for drinking too much and being hungover the morning before because he "knew better than to embarrass" his father in front of other people. Logan remembered his vow not to make waves, but it nearly took biting his tongue in two to keep from reminding Philip that *his own* behavior embarrassed Ginnie all the time, not to mention Logan.

Though Philip was unhappy about Logan's behavior, it seemed he was pleased when Logan handed over the mandatory printout of his grades for the fall semester. Philip had been irate when he learned that legally he could not have constant access to his son's grades the way he did to Logan's bank account, so as part of the conditions for providing Logan's living allowance and Kappa Sig dues, Logan had to inform him of all midterm and final grades every semester. This time Logan had stayed under budget and kept a 3.25, so after the lecture on propriety, Philip showed his approval the only way he knew how. He shoved a roll of Benjamins in Logan's hand, turned back to the work in front of him, and dismissed Logan from his office.

"It was great seeing you too, Dad," Logan muttered after he'd closed the door.

The three-and-a-half hour drive back to Raleigh was a welcome one for Logan. After spending all of Christmas day pretending that he enjoyed being with his family, he was craving extended solitude. He left as soon as lunch was over (since Ginnie wouldn't hear of him leaving before that) on the 26th.

When he got on campus, it was almost like Pompeii. Everything was there, just as it had been when he left, but there were no signs of life anywhere. *Is this the way Lillie feels when she walks onto a dig?* He wasn't sure where the thought came from, why an empty campus had made him think of her, but he shook it away. She wouldn't be back for nearly two weeks, and he'd gone longer than that without talking to her already. He hadn't heard from her since he left her apartment that night, and he was glad he hadn't. It meant that she'd been serious when she said she didn't need strings. Maybe their relationship didn't have to be as doomed as he thought . . . or at least maybe not as destructive.

There were only a few cars in his lot, but he took Rob's spot for the simple joy of it. Then he unlocked 317, and it was vacant too. The other guys would trickle in over the next few days, he was sure, since there was going to be a big party at the house on New Year's Eve, but that left him with a good chunk of time on his hands.

Logan considered calling someone from his address book that he hadn't seen recently, like Leesi, or Shari, or Marie, but it wasn't likely that they were in town yet either. He thought about playing a solo game of *COD* or *Halo* but considering the crap he went through with his last phase, he decided that he should order a pizza, pop open a can of Coke, and sift through some more of the questionable material waiting to be sorted into the

Potentially True pile or the Load of Crap pile. The going would be slow without Lillie's ability to finesse data, but at least they'd be a little closer to a cure by the time she returned than they were when she left.

It took him the rest of the year, all of five days, to hit upon something that looked promising. There was an obscure mention in a search engine's "Ask" section that he couldn't validate, but he liked the sound of nonetheless because it didn't involve torture or death for the man or the wolf. According to the entry, the condition of lycanthropy could be cured through "the highly dangerous trick of extracting three drops of blood while" the victim is "in the wolf state."

Though Logan wasn't sure how he could go about performing the aforementioned "dangerous trick," since it, like hearing his Christian name and being smacked on the forehead with a stick, required Lillie to be in danger, he wrote it down as a possibility and kept searching. There was no way he was going to let her get close enough to the wolf to draw its blood with a syringe. He had no control over the wolf, and judging by the disappearance of all those Ag department animals and pets, Lille wouldn't survive the attempt. *Small animals are one thing, but I am* **not** *having her death on my head.*

He kept picturing the carnage that the wolf had inflicted upon the unsuspecting sheep or house cat, knowing the same would happen to her, if he wasn't careful. That he had seen so many movies like *An American Werewolf in London* and *Silver Bullet* and cheap horror flicks when he was a teen didn't help the situation. In every scene he conjured, there was a bloody mess of bones and guts after the monster finished feeding. He wondered if the wolf was as messy as the fictional representations were. *There's only one way to find out.*

Logan's New Year's resolution for 2008 was to find a cure before he killed a human. He knew that the wolf hadn't killed anyone on campus because there were no missing students, but there were six days during November and December when he phased in Asheville, and there was no way for him to know what it had hunted in those woods. Asheville might have been ritzy and exclusive, prime real estate for humans, but he imagined that a wolf might find its selection of wildlife less than desirable, and he shuddered to think how close he was to houses when he awoke on the chilly forest floor. The walk back to his parents' took him fifteen or twenty minutes as a man, but he knew a wolf could cover the same distance much faster, especially if it was ravenous.

That was why, despite the fact that he normally disregarded any sort of tradition or notion, Logan set out towards the wooded area closest to Wolf Village with a topographical map and a compass on New Year's Day in 40° weather. He wished his phone had GPS, but he had a RAZR, and though it was cool and compact, it didn't boast that particular feature. Not that he had needed it at the time he bought the thing.

Taking a cue from Lillie, Logan had plotted out possible places that would make a good den for a wolf, circled them and identified their coordinates. All the information he found indicated that wolves sought shelter from the damp and cold under some sort of natural covering if possible, so that was where he looked first. Ditches, valleys, and gullies were the most likely places, and as he walked, he kept an eye out for carcasses that could have been left from October. It wasn't likely that scavengers had left him many clues after two months, but he would play what he was dealt and see if he couldn't parlay a win out of the hand.

Logan spent the rest of the daylight hours that week trekking through the wooded areas on campus, trying to look as inconspicuous as he possibly could. The closer it got to the 9th, the first day of class, the more students there were milling around who might see him and think he was insane. He figured the wolf would head for the nearest source of water, and Lake Raleigh just happened to be in the center of the Centennial Campus precinct and not too far from Wolf Village. The lake was also surrounded by plenty of tree growth on its west side. Those woods would be the perfect place, providing cover and water and probably a nice food source in the early phases.

On foot, there was no way Logan could cover that distance twice in the span of twelve hours in the daytime, much less in the dark, but a wolf could with little trouble, he suspected. As he walked, he considered how much easier it would be to find the wolf's den if he shared consciousness with it like so many of the lycanthropes in the myths and legends did. *Of course, if that was the case, I would've known why I was blacking out all along and might have been able to find a cure by now, and that would've just been way too easy.*

He kept moving and used his compass to make sure he was heading southeast, towards the center of the copse and eventually the shore, though he doubted he would get that far. Everything he read told him that wolves didn't actively seek out people but preferred to avoid them unless forced into civilization through loss of habitat, or if humans unwittingly stumbled upon their territory and the wolves felt threatened. Wolves, it seemed, were also more comfortable living in packs, which led him to think that this lone wolf would feel even more uncomfortable in close proximity to humans than if it had companions, which would drive it deeper into the trees. *Or it could be more desperate than other wolves and more prone to attack any humans it comes into contact with. Great! Now I feel much better.* The thought had him picking up his pace. *If this wolf's getting edgy from being alone, there's no telling what it might do . . . what* **I** *might do*, he corrected and trudged on.

Logan was searching yet another section of the trees near Lake Raleigh when his cell vibrated in his pocket. The guys had gotten used to him leaving out "at an ungodly hour" in the morning and not returning to 317 until well after noon, as well as his refusal to answer their queries, by the time Tuesday came around, so he wasn't sure who would be sending him a message. Instinctually, he meant to ignore it as he had been doing since New Year, but curiosity had him stopping to pull out his phone and check.

JUST GOT BACK ON CAMPUS. ARE YOU BUSY? Lillie wondered.

SORT OF. @ LAKE RALEIGH LOOKING FOR ITS DEN. he answered.

WANT HELP? she offered.

NO. WE CAN JUST MEET UP WHEN I'M DONE.

281

He figured his reply would tick her off, but by the time she found him, he would have wasted too much time standing still, waiting for her, that he could have used looking for the den. *Besides, this is the last day I can search, seeing as class starts tomorrow. After that, I'll only be able to look on the weekends and occasionally after class. It's a pity she'll be in a bad mood, though*, he shook his head. He doubted he would be getting that kiss she promised him now.

~

NO. WE CAN JUST MEET UP WHEN I'M DONE. *Of all the chauvinistic things to say!* Lillie was tempted to hurl her phone across the apartment. Instead, she opened a reply and typed "K." She wasn't one for using much text speak, so she hoped that he could translate her one-letter answer into the fury she felt, and if he couldn't, she'd make sure he knew it when they were face to face. To kill time, she began to methodically unpack her bags and sort her dirty clothes.

~

Logan wasn't sure what to expect when he knocked on Lillie's door that evening. But he wasn't an idiot. He came bearing pizza–the stuffed crust kind–and an espresso because it was getting dark, and to his way of thinking, that made it night no matter what time the clock read, which would rule out lattes and Frappuccinos.

She opened the door and was as much the Ice Queen as she ever had been. Her eyes alone burned like liquid nitrogen. He pulled a breath of air in through his teeth and smiled. Not the smile he used to get results, because that would certainly spark an explosion, but the one he used out of politeness, since

282

he hoped that would diffuse some of her anger. "Hey, Lillie. Can I come in?"

"Yes." The word cut him the way the wind could on a ski slope, if he wasn't wearing enough layers, though he was wearing his coat at the moment. She stepped aside and he came in, wishing for warmth but finding none.

"You hungry?" He set the box on the coffee table with her espresso and his coffee.

She shut the door, and by the time he had his coat off and was starting to sit, she was across from him. "What do you want, Logan?"

"I figured we could catch up while we ate, and then get back to the research." He made sure his voice was calm and evenly pitched.

"You want to pick up right where we left off?" Her mouth was straight, her eyes were narrowed sharply, and her brow was arched.

"Somewhere thereabouts," he nodded.

"*Now* you want help?" Her hand was gripping the espresso, and he could only hope that she didn't throw it at him. He didn't want to deal with severe facial burns on top of lycanthropy.

"Yes. I'm sorry about earlier, Lillie, but I figured it would take a while for you to find me, and it would just be easier if I finished up alone, and we went out together next time." *That's reasonable*, he assured himself.

"I'm sure you did." Even her expression was frozen. He watched as she took a sip, hoping the heat and flavor would help her thaw.

"I was thinking. Maybe we can find the den, and then set some sort of trap for the wolf. If we can catch it, maybe it would be safe for you to get close enough

283

to say my name or hit it in the head with a stick." He stared at the pizza box while he was talking and opened it to grab a slice when he was done. "I found another possibility too," he said, and when she didn't respond, he told her about the three drops of blood.

"What are we supposed to do with the blood after it's been drawn?" *Am I going crazy, or does she sound intrigued?*

"It didn't say in the answer, and I couldn't find the source that person used," he shrugged.

"I think we're better off using a silver dagger or something," she scoffed.

"You know where anything like that's laying around?" He couldn't hide the relief that she was getting to be in a better humor.

"Not offhand, but I'm sure I can find something," she showed him her smile for the first time that night, and he couldn't decide what was more painful, the ache it caused in his chest or the fire of her anger that had threatened to consume him.

Holy crap! he thought when he registered what had happened.

"What's wrong, Logan?" Lillie looked alarmed, and it wasn't just the level of concern in her eyes that he didn't care for. It was the strange new ache inside him that wasn't going away.

Chapter 22

For the second time in his life, Logan contemplated turning down a willing woman he was interested in, and for the second time, it was Lillie Thackery. The plain truth was she scared him. Always had. With her cool countenance, tremendous intelligence and simple beauty. With her innocence and her curiosity, her passion. She was a continual contradiction, and she confused the hell out of him.

Lillie had sat next to him on the couch and peered at him like she thought he might pass out, and he wasn't so sure he wouldn't himself. "Logan? You okay?"

"Yeah," he let out a breath. "I think so." He sat up and put his head between his knees because he remembered reading somewhere that it helped get rid of dizziness. By the time she brought him a glass of water, he had gotten a hold of himself. His hand was steady when he took the cool glass from her, but then his fingers grazed hers, and she smiled at him. His insides were quaking again. He took a sip of water as she watched, and then carefully set down the glass before he drenched them both. She was still smiling.

It was when she leaned in to kiss him that he came to himself enough to protest. *Once was one thing, but twice is too risky.* "Lillie . . ." but she cut off whatever he would have said. "Wait," he tried again when his

285

mouth was free. "Lillie, nothing's changed. You know that, right?"

"Yes. . ." she said into his ear.

"Are you sure . . . ?" he struggled to remember why he was arguing.

"Aren't you?"

~

Lillie sat up after her stomach rumbled the second time in the past few minutes. "Logan. . ."

"Hmm?" he opened his eyes.

"I'm gonna reheat a slice of pizza. You want some?"

He stretched before reaching for her. "I'll get it. How many slices d'you want?"

"Two," she decided, since she'd probably just burned enough calories to cover one of them. "And *I'll* get it, since I'm already partially up," she smiled down at him before squeezing his hand and heading for the microwave.

~

He heard the beep as she set the cook time for their pizza and rolled over. It affected him much the way an alarm clock did, driving away the last moments of comfortable bliss with the harsh reality of daylight.

Aren't you? Her question had been playful, and it was the last thing he heard before he let himself sink into her, but the tone of the question echoing in his head was totally serious. She was smoother than anything he'd ever tasted and three times as intoxicating. Which made the hand he was playing that much more dangerous. It was like she said before, he didn't give a crap about what happened to him, but he was getting more and more concerned about what would happen to her. So maybe he wasn't. Maybe he wasn't sure at all.

By the time Logan's eleventh phase started on the MLK holiday, they had found what they thought must be the wolf's den. It was in a small thicket made of some plants and bushes that grew beside the overhang of a rock. It made a cozy cave for one, as long as the tenant didn't mind the stench of urine and what was left of several unidentifiable carcasses.

It appeared to Logan that the bodies kept getting larger, which made him more anxious to end it all. If he hadn't killed anyone yet, it was just a matter of time before he would. And the notion that Lillie might be the next biggest body hadn't left his thoughts since it cropped up a few weeks earlier.

If he believed in that sort of thing, Logan could have said that he had a premonition back before finals, when it became apparent that there was no easy cure for his condition. He had known then that if it came down to committing murder or self-sacrifice, there would be no real choice. Logan found himself taking the same stance now, if not with even more certainty, due to the ever-increasing possibility of Lillie being the victim of that murder.

"Now that we've found the den, how do you plan on trapping yourself?" Lillie interrupted his thoughts. They were standing far enough away from the area that they hoped their scent wouldn't contaminate it.

"I was thinking maybe a steel trap," he answered, trying not to picture what the jagged teeth would do to his limb, should he be lucky enough to survive.

"And what do we use for bait?" Her elementary question surprised him.

"What do you think about a rabbit? We could get one from a pet shop." Again, he didn't like to think of what would happen to the rabbit, but sometimes pawns just had to be sacrificed, and cards just had to be burned. *In the end, the pot'll be worth it.*

"You mean one that would smell like humans?" she raised a brow.

Okay. So this won't be as easy as I thought it would be.

"Can you think of a better option?" he sighed. "We could always use scent block."

"Don't you think old deer pee would tip it off just as much as human scent would?" She was laughing outright now.

"Actually, it doesn't seem to mind my scent. In fact, it's attracted to it, according to you. So maybe I can just put some hamburger meat out here and—" He tried again, but she disrupted his suggestion.

"Okay. Let's say the ground beef actually works, and the wolf steps into the trap. *Then* what? That still leaves you in the wolf's form, albeit no longer as threatening. How is keeping you in one place for the rest of the night going to change anything? All that would happen is the wolf would struggle to get free until the sun came up, and then you'd wake up as yourself again except possibly with a chewed off hand or foot, or at least a very sore wrist or ankle."

How can I even call myself logical after that?

"So you think we should do nothing?" he couldn't hide his frustration.

"No. I think you should be okay with me waiting here for the wolf. Then, if-slash-when it does get caught in the trap, I could try as many of the 'credible' cures as possible. It's the only way for us to rule out any of the Potentially True ones and get any closer to ending this."

Though he wasn't "okay" with her being anywhere near the wolf, there was no recourse. Since there was no class on MLK day, it was easy to get the ground beef at Wal-Mart. The complicated part was trying to find a coil spring trap. Luckily, Lillie was a Jedi Master at research, whether it was academic or practical. With the help of the Internet, she located two stores likely to carry traps, and only one was open. She also pulled up driving directions, and it took them all of thirty minutes to get from her apartment to the store on Jamison Drive.

After talking to the salesman, it seemed they needed a coil spring trap that was at least 7.5 inches; otherwise the wolf might be able to work itself free. And even with a trap that large, the guy couldn't guarantee Logan that the wolf wouldn't chew free or even escape, if its foot was severed when it triggered the trap. Apparently things like that "just happen on occasion." In the end, it cost Logan about $30, but that seemed reasonable when compared with the cost of taking someone's life.

When he had read the instructions a third time, Logan carefully set the trap a couple yards from the wolf's den but near enough that he could still smell its scent. He made sure to camouflage the metal completely with leaves, dirt, and whatever else he could find before placing the raw meat in the center and hoping that something else didn't come along and try to get a snack before the wolf did. Lillie had postulated that as long as the trap was clearly in the wolf's territory, other animals would more than likely elect to avoid danger over grabbing a bite. He checked his watch and noted that if the predictions were correct, the sun would set around 5:30, and since the moon would have already been visible for an hour at that time, he had little more than an hour before he phased.

"Promise you won't get too close," he told Lillie a little later as he got out of the Camaro, which was parked along Trailwood Drive.

"I'll do my best not to get hurt, Logan, but if these ideas don't work, I'll have to set it free somehow," she reminded him. "We don't know what'll happen if it's still caught when you phase."

"It doesn't matter if it's still caught. You wait until I'm me again," he shook his head. "I *will not* have you mauled just so I don't have a broken wrist. If the injury carries over, I'll deal."

"You worry too much," Lillie smiled and pecked his cheek.

~

Lillie crouched behind some branches and waited, wishing they'd figured this out last fall, when it was still warm outside. She was far enough from the trap and the den that she figured the wolf wouldn't care even if he did pick up her smell, which she had attempted to mask with the scent block Logan insisted she wear. She had leather gloves on her hands, a latex camouflage face mask, and a small knife, a vial of Holy Water, and an iron magnet in her pockets. She'd wanted to bring a syringe, but there was no legal way of getting one quickly enough. *There's always tomorrow night.*

She checked her watch and saw that Logan should have phased by then, and the wolf was probably tracking its supper. Rationally, she knew that currently Logan *was* the wolf, or the wolf was Logan, but she couldn't reconcile the fact in her mind. There was Logan, and there was the wolf, no in between. Logan's body might be the same as the wolf's body, but the wolf didn't think with Logan's thoughts, didn't share Logan's memories. The wolf didn't hold her when he thought she was sleeping; Logan did. But Logan was right in that she had to be careful.

She whispered a prayer and momentarily wished for her rosary, but the beads might have made a sound. Not for the first time since meeting Logan Michaels did Lille wonder how a good Catholic girl had come to have a lycanthropic lover and be sitting in the woods after dark, waiting to catch a wolf. *Katherine de Roet probably felt the same way when she woke up one morning and was John of Gaunt's paramour . . . not that sleeping with a married man is in any way as physically dangerous as trapping a wolf, but it's an entirely different matter spiritually.* It was too late for guilt. She'd thrown her lot in with Logan's, and now she'd face the consequences. *Besides, maybe there's hope for him yet . . .*

Lillie lost track of how long she had been in her hiding place. It was too dark to see her watch, and she was afraid to press the glow-in-the-dark button even for a moment, but from the looks of the sky, there was still plenty of darkness left in the night. She occupied herself by trying to locate constellations, but sixth grade science and those brief dreams of being an astronaut were too far away for her to do more than guess at what she was seeing, though she had found Orion's belt. Looking at the stars made her think about what it would have been like here in the place she was crouching before the Europeans came to North America. *What would it have been like for those Catawba and Siouan tribes? Maybe the stars are the only thing that hasn't changed.*

291

When she thought of anthropology, she most often thought of the ancient cultures in foreign lands, swept away by time. Even when she thought of the colony at Roanoke, the people weren't indigenous. What had happened to them was a mystery, but the fate of North Carolina's original population was not. They might have had a vastly different culture from the Puritans who settled here, but they were not the mindless savages the English painted them to be. They were closer, more connected to the earth than the "civilized" destroyers who invaded their land. They had legends of a trickster wolf, a creature that shifted from man to beast and back again on a whim or because of a curse. *Perhaps they were much wiser than they've ever been given credit for.*

The snap of a twig startled Lillie, and she focused on where she hoped the sound had come. In the distance, it seemed that a figure was moving towards the trap, and she prayed that it was the wolf. That it would take the bait. That one of the remedies would work, and that Logan would be all right. It was all she could ask.

Silence. There was nothing else. She waited and barely dared to breathe. There were insects in the background that might cover the sound, but she wasn't taking the risk. She had almost decided that it was her imagination, and there was nothing interested in the bait, when she heard the sharp pop of the coiled spring shutting steel jaws.

Lillie didn't hesitate. She sprinted towards the trap, hoping it would all be over soon. She was almost there when she noticed that there was still silence. No snarling or gnashing of teeth. No howl of pain. Not even a whimper.

She froze, understanding that the wolf had not been fooled and was still free to defend its territory against any intruder.

Chapter 23

Logan awoke on his bedroom floor. *At least I'm in 317 and not having to run nude through the woods.* He laughed despite the throb of his head, but his next thought had his smile fading and his eyes flying open. *Lillie!*

He pulled himself off the floor and over to his nightstand, grabbed his phone, jerked it open, and pressed her number on speed dial. One ring, two . . . *Pick up, Lillie. Pick up the phone.*

"Hello." She answered on the fourth ring, just as he was about to curse out her voice mail.

"Are. You. All. Right?" he spoke each word separately so that he wasn't screaming as had been his initial inclination.

"I'm okay. Are you?" *What does that have to do with anything?*

"I'm aces," he dead panned. "Are you really? What happened out there last night?"

"Nothing happened. It triggered the trap but was smart enough to keep from getting caught." It appeared that she wanted to forget his first question.

"So you sat there until it took the bait and then went home?" He knew her better than that.

"Not exactly. I heard the trap engage, and then I went to see if it was there. By the time I figured out what happened, I was already too close—"

"Are you in your apartment?" he demanded while she was mid-sentence.

"Yes, but—"

"Don't move. I'm on my way." Logan shut his phone without waiting for her answer.

He could finally breathe again when Lille opened her door. He stepped calmly inside and shut the door behind him. Then he looked, really looked at her. She was wearing pajamas. Her hair was pulled back into a ponytail, and her face was bare, save a discoloration that shadowed her right cheekbone. Her hands seemed fine, as did her feet, but he couldn't tell about the rest of her, since it was covered in cotton clothing. "Lillie."

Logan wasn't sure if he had gone to her or she had come to him. All he knew was that he was holding on, and she was holding on, and neither one was letting go. After a moment, he pulled back and brushed his thumb over the bruise on her face. "Where else?"

"My left side and hip, where I fell. I blocked with my right. The gloves and mask took the worst of it," but she kept her eyes down.

"Show me," he didn't bother to check the coolness in his tone.

When she lifted her shirt, he could see the empurpled outline of each rib, and farther down there was an angry cloud of mottled mauve and gray brewing on her hip.

"Anywhere else?" He kept his expression still and his jaw tight.

She turned her back to him and took her top off, showing him several long scrapes that stretched across her spine but were thankfully only superficial.

295

"Is that it?" He waited for her nod, then took her hand. "I'm sorry. Lillie, I'm so terribly sorry," and then it was he who couldn't make eye contact.

"It's not your fault, Logan," she whispered as she put her head on his chest.

Logan had begun to fight an internal war. He knew that he should stay as far from Lillie as he could, no matter what form he was taking at the moment. He knew too that he had caused enough damage in her life, and leaving her to clean up the mess alone would only make it worse. Part of him wanted her help and support, part of him just plain wanted her, and part of him knew the others were selfish, a quality he despised. He got little sleep, almost nothing out of his classes, and blew off Andrew and Mark more times than he could count. He was beginning to feel like his father.

After that first morning of the phase, they didn't speak of the attack. Not even when the phase was over. When Logan slid into bed with Lillie each night, he pretended not to see the scrapes and bruises. When he woke up to leave before class, he tried not to compare their colors to those of the day before.

As soon as the danger was gone, at least until February, Logan retrieved the trap and sold it for cash at a sleazy pawn shop that had no cameras and asked no questions. They went straight back to searching for a cure, though Logan only did it for Lillie's sake. He knew death was the only option. He just wasn't sure how to get Lillie to agree with him.

Logan walked into his apartment a few mornings later, and the feeling struck him that he hadn't been there in a while. He wanted to dismiss it as untrue, but it wasn't. Lately, if he wasn't in class or serving his study hours in the library, he was either with Lillie in the library doing research and sorting info or with Lillie at her own place. He never brought her here and doubted she even knew which apartment he lived in. They met at the library or Hill of Beans or her apartment. He never suggested his, and she never asked. And it wasn't that he was ashamed that he had somehow become monogamous (at least for now); it was out of respect for Lillie. That she was willing to give herself to him was none of their business. He may not have been the most chivalrous of men, but he wasn't going to be responsible for ruining her reputation, not after everything else he'd ruined for her. She deserved better.

He stepped into his bedroom and peeled off the shirt he'd worn the day before. He was digging around in the closet for another when he heard a voice he assumed was Mark's.

"Logan? Is that you? I was beginning to think you'd moved to the library, as much 'studying' as you've been doing lately. That or you'd gone over to the dark side and become an antisocial scotch drinker like Rob."

"Since when are you keeping tabs on me, man?" Logan pulled his head out after finding something to wear and saw that he was right.

"Since when do you play things so close to the vest, bro?" Mark countered with a note of surprise.

"Since you started noticing my tells," Logan grinned.

~

Lillie was determined that she was not going to let finding a cure affect her grades. She was determined too that she would find the cure quickly. She had to.

297

She could feel Logan pulling away, letting go of
everything around him. He was preparing for the end.
If I don't find something soon, he's going to ask me to help him.
And though she might not be as sinless as she once
was, that didn't mean she was willing to commit a
mortal sin like murder. There were things even the
Pope couldn't absolve, and killing Logan would be one
of them. *How could anyone be absolved of sinning against her
own heart?*

~

Logan started keeping his study hours so that once
they ended, Lillie's time to monitor her section of the
library began. It maximized their research time.
Though she was shelving and helping customers, she
was close enough to help if he needed it. It was nearing
February and his twelfth phase, but after what
happened during the last phase especially, he wasn't
comfortable with the thought of her out there alone in
the woods with an animal that would as soon rip her to
pieces as look at her. Without the help of another
person, there was no way a cure, if they happened to
find one, could even be attempted. The one thing the
last phase had taught him was that he was playing with
fire as long as he allowed himself to keep phasing.
Sooner or later the wolf would deplete the wildlife in
the woods near the lake, and some human was going to
pay for it. If he believed in that sort of thing, Logan
might have prayed for success or luck as he turned page
after page in front of him. It all felt so futile.

He was sitting at his table in the library, staring into
the stacks to keep from having to focus on the lines
printed before him. His black coffee had long since
gotten cold. He was about to go down and get a fresh
cup for himself and a mocha Frappuccino for Lillie,

when he felt the presence of someone beside him and almost jumped out of his chair, knocking the chilled coffee over.

Batu's hand was quicker than Logan's and had the cup upright before more than a few drops could dribble from the hole in the lid. "Sorry, Logan. I did not mean to scare you."

"No big deal, man. How are you?" Logan shrugged and wiped the moisture with a crumpled napkin. *Lillie would be majorly P.O.ed if I got these books wet.*

"I am doing well, thanks. But I do not think you can say the same," Batu's look of concern appeared genuine.

"I've been better," he agreed.

"Is the answer to your question still bothering you?"

"You could say that," Logan nodded. "The solution to my problem is looking pretty dangerous. I'm not very happy about that."

"Life is dangerous, but we live it. Love is dangerous, but we fight for it. You have not been living or fighting recently, my friend." Batu's expression was sad, disappointed. Even harder to face than Philip's disappointment, but Logan wasn't sure why.

"It's not that simple," Logan shook his head.

"Oh, but it is. All you have to do is decide if you love her enough," Batu paused.

"But I don't—" Logan tried to stop him. *It hasn't gone that far. Couldn't.*

"*Do* you love her enough?" he repeated.

"Enough to what?" Logan sighed. It seemed ridiculous now that Batu had said it out loud. If Batu knew it, then Logan was only lying to himself.

"Enough to let her go."

Batu had no idea what he was asking. Breaking off contact with Lillie would be easy enough, but it wouldn't really keep her out of danger. *And it would only hurt her.* At least this way he wasn't facing his phases alone. *And who knows, if we keep searching, maybe we can find a way for me to take control of the wolf, and then I can drown him in Lake Raleigh.* But he knew that was too easy. He knew he should just go buy a gun and be done with it. *But what if that only kills me and not the wolf? Or what if it doesn't kill me at all, only makes me paralyzed or something. That would leave Lillie to deal with this alone.* It was just too risky. *What does Batu know anyway?*

Chapter 24

Logan awoke the night before his twelfth phase and reached for her. She was there, just as he knew she would be, a few inches away, sleeping on her left side. She had been worried about something for several days, but she wouldn't tell him what, and he knew better than to think it was the midterms that were coming next week. Lately, when she slept, she mumbled things he couldn't make out and clung tightly to him. They were nightmares, he was sure, but he could only guess at what was scaring her.

He figured she was reliving the attack in her dreams, and since he was about to phase again, he could see why she would be distressed. But he was going to take precautions this time. He had a plan—one that didn't involve her going up against a wild wolf with nothing more than a knife and a magnet.

~

Lillie awoke on the morning of Logan's twelfth phase and tried to snuggle into him. He wasn't there. She couldn't keep the coldness out of her. She had known that whatever was going on between the two of them was temporary, and she had told herself to be okay with that. Logan didn't pull any punches with her. He'd said from the beginning that he couldn't give her anything permanent, any sort of commitment. *That*

301

doesn't stop me from making a commitment to him. And that commitment would have to be enough.

Since she was too cold to sleep, she slipped into some pj's and headed to the kitchen. She made a cup of coffee and wished she didn't have to drink it alone. It was nice to come back to the world at the same rate as Logan did. *He always seems more vulnerable when he's just woken up. When his eyes are still warm gray and not cool steel.*

She was up two hours before she normally rose to shower and dress before her morning class. The thought of returning to bed crossed her mind, but she knew the combination of the coffee she was sipping and the vacant other side would keep her awake. *At least I can spend the time researching,* she smiled, humming a few notes from Thin Lizzy's cover of "Whiskey in the Jar."

~

Logan checked his watch again. He'd driven an hour out of Raleigh to Raven Rock State Park. He had about thirty minutes before he phased, and he wanted to make sure he had enough of his cologne to mark the path he was taking from where he parked the Camaro to the wooded area he was heading for now. By the time he was himself again, he would have little time to wander around and find the car if he wanted to make it back to campus before missing class. *If only there was some way I could keep covered until I get to the car . . .* but he couldn't come up with anything other than stripping down to his boxers and leaving the clothes he was already wearing in a pile not too far from where he sat and waited for the change. There was no guarantee that he would even be close to this place when he woke, but he figured it was better than not trying at all.

He awoke with a mouth full of leaves and a head that hurt like he'd downed a gallon of Jäger. Still, it wasn't the worst place he'd ever woken up in after a phase. At least he knew where to go to find his clothes and car. His step was much more energetic than it ever had been trudging back to his parents'. When he reached the Camaro, he checked his phone and saw that it was a few minutes after seven. *Awesome! I can just make it back to 317 and clean up before my 9:00!*

There were two missed calls from Lillie. He wasn't sure what to make of his inability to wait until he got back to Raleigh before he returned her call, but he pressed her speed dial anyway.

"Where are you?" There was no preamble, just the question.

"On my way back to campus."

"Did it run *that* far last night?" He picked up a note of hysteria in her voice.

"No. I drove out of town before I phased. Now I'm driving back."

"Want to eat lunch after class?" she seemed a bit calmer after his explanation.

"I'm not sure if I'll have time," he tried to soften the blow.

"I missed you last night. I couldn't sleep." Because it was Lillie, he knew that wasn't a ploy.

"I know," he kept his response short and toneless. That was best. "I'll see you after my study hours."

"All right, Logan . . . Bye." *Apparently she thought short and toneless was best too. I'll have to come bearing more than coffee if I want to sleep over Friday night.*

~

Lillie hadn't seen Logan since they'd gone to sleep Monday night. It was Friday afternoon, and the

303

distance was killing her. Sure he'd returned her calls every morning to confirm that he was okay and sat at his table and read through documents while she worked, but that didn't count as far as spending time with him. *It's okay though, because last night was his third night of the phase. It's safe for him to come back to me now.* It was the hope that she clung to so that her anger didn't get the best of her. She repeated it over and over to herself. *He **will** come back to me . . . He **will** come back to me . . . He **will** come back to me . . .*

And she channeled all her frustration into research.

~

It was another two days before he worked up the courage. He went with a latte and a new biography called *Royalty For Commoners: The Complete Known Lineage Of John Of Gaunt, Son Of Edward III, King Of England, And Queen Philippa.* It sounded as dry as anything his textbooks had ever used to put him to sleep, but he hoped that she liked it, and since the title included the name of one of her Facebook-professed interests, he was fairly certain that she'd appreciate it.

When he knocked on her door, it took her more time than usual to answer. He was starting to wonder if she was even at home, when he heard the lock click, and Lillie opened the door. Instead of an icy stare, she gave him a grin that swallowed him whole. "Logan, you're just in time!"

"Um, yeah," he followed her inside and shut the door, since she didn't wait, but turned to head to her laptop. "I brought you a latte and . . . a surprise . . ." The apology he'd been mentally composing disappeared.

"Thanks," she smiled again as she took the latte. "I can't believe it, Logan! I just can't believe it, but I think I've actually found the cure!"

It wasn't until she'd let the exclamation burst from her that Logan noticed the flush on her cheeks and the way her hands were trembling. "Lillie, why don't we sit down, and then you can tell me," he put his arm around her and led her to the couch. She sat without prompting. After a moment, he sat next to her and nodded.

"I'm not crazy, Logan," she took another sip of the latte she'd yet to set down.

"I didn't say you were, did I?" he raised a brow. "I just think you've had a little too much caffeine," and when he reached for her cup, she gave it to him.

She took a second, perhaps to form a sentence, before turning to him in absolute seriousness. "The clue was there all along, Logan. I just couldn't see it . . . but now I know how we can determine which myths might work for you."

"How?" he pushed his previous behavior to the back of his mind, since she'd obviously forgotten it.

"We need to find Native American myths. Ones involving a 'trickster.' Those are the most likely to explain how you came to be a lycanthrope and how to cure the condition." She smiled again.

"What makes you think that?" *It would really help your argument if you weren't grinning like a fool.*

"It was the girl. Sarah Abbot. The one who attacked you. Her family can be traced back to the Colonies. And most of the English settlers had contact with the Native Americans who lived near the settlements. Almost all the legends have those who weren't lycanthropic by birth contracting the disease

305

either through a curse or some other form of black magic. And since I'm not inclined to believe that you're some sort of immortal witch who survives on the blood of animals, that only leaves a curse. If that's the case, then I *know* there's an antidote. There always are in legends like that." She eyed him like he was simple or something.

"But why would an Indian shaman curse anybody? And how could that curse keep affecting people hundreds of years after it was . . . cast, or whatever, on a person?" *That makes no sense!*

"Think about it, Logan. The settlers basically came and took everything the Native Americans had because they thought it was some sort of a 'divine right.' But they didn't have any rights to the land at all. Didn't you say you were mad when the University made Batu move out of 317, but you understood why they did, since Rob was there first?" It was as if she could hear his rebuttal before he voiced it.

"Yes," he answered begrudgingly.

"What Batu would have done to Rob by staying is like what the English did to the Native Americans, only the Native Americans got it worse. Don't forget Jackson and his reservations and The Trail of Tears," The meticulous part of her could not be contradicted, it seemed.

"Okay. So maybe I can see why some chief might have wanted revenge on the settlers, but what about the longevity of the curse?" he pointed out.

"There are lots of curses in the Bible that last years and years, some of them 'even to their tenth generation' according to Deuteronomy," she reminded him. "So it's not inconceivable that a shaman's curse could cover a few hundred years."

"Okay. Let's say I buy all that. What about the cure you said you thought you'd found?" *He* reminded *her* of her initial claim.

"Well, I'm just thinking this is a *potential* cure. . ." she clarified, "but there are so many Native American myths concerning a person's reflection revealing his true self, that I thought maybe, if we could get the wolf to see its reflection, it would see the humanity trapped inside, and the curse would be broken."

"Don't you think the wolf sees its reflection when it gets a drink of water out of Lake Raleigh?" Logan was tired of playing along.

"Not a clear one. There are lots of ripples on the surface of the lake. For it to work, the reflection would have to be undistorted, completely clear." Again, she looked at him like he was a stubborn pupil.

"You want to use a mirror?" *This is insane!*

"Not just any mirror, but one with a silver backing."

Chapter 25

Lillie was taking no chances. None. Not after nearly getting mauled when their plan failed last time. That was why she planned to use a silvered mirror; if the silver didn't work, perhaps the reflection would. She set about trying to locate an antique mirror that was old enough to be backed with silver and large enough that the wolf, when confronted with the obstacle, wouldn't merely be able to jump over it. She found that the average size of a wolf was between two and three feet tall, and it could leap about sixteen feet. She wanted the mirror to be at least 30"x42", but hopefully they could find one bigger. That way the wolf could get a good look, even if it did manage to jump over the reflection. *Once we find the mirror, all we'll need is a way to ensure that the wolf encounters it. I just hope Logan won't put up too much of a fight . . .*

~

Logan was grateful to have Lillie distracted from his disappearance by her discovery. He just wished it made more sense to him. The logical part of him that had fought so hard against even the possibility of lycanthropy was fighting equally as hard against her theory that it could be cured with something as easy as a mirror, even if that mirror was supposed to be backed with silver. It was the same logical part of himself that kept protesting when he went to bed with her.

308

After the first couple times they were together, he was able to let himself sink into her so that the logic was drowned out. Aside from the times he drove himself so that the wolf would be out of range, he had no qualms about being with her. She was soft and sweet, and quenched something in him that he didn't know was thirsting. Now that logic wasn't so quiet. Now it was loudly objecting to their entire relationship.

As Batu had pointed out, there was no sense in lying to himself anymore. *I care more about Lillie than I have about anyone in* . . . but he couldn't remember the last time he'd let himself get attached to someone else. *I've gone too far. I need space.* But to make that space would hurt her, and like he kept telling himself, he couldn't do that anymore. She'd given him more of herself than she had anyone else, and he didn't take that lightly. *This is why I don't care for strings.* But the thought came too late. He was pretty tangled up in her now. *Still, attachment doesn't mean I can't have a little time to myself.*

"Lillie?" he asked as she lay next to him, wrapped in his arms and darkness.

"Hmm?" contentedness seemed to wash over her.

"I've got plans with the guys tomorrow night," he ventured.

"Okay." Neither of those two syllables contained any contentedness whatsoever. He waited for a continuation, but nothing came. Somehow the silence was worse than her anger or pleading.

"I'll try to be back before too late, but if we decide to have a *Halo* tournament, I may just end up staying over there. . ." he added, remembering that she had trouble sleeping alone.

"That's fine," she said as she snuggled closer into him. *Maybe things aren't as tangled as I thought.*

"Look who finally decided to come back home," Rob exclaimed when Logan opened the door to his apartment. As expected, Rob was lounging on the couch, drinking scotch, and *SportsCenter* was playing on the TV.

"I almost answered, 'Look who finally got a life,' until I realized you didn't," Logan countered.

"Where've you been anyway, Michaels? You've been AWOL so long, I was thinking about subletting your room," Rob took another swallow.

"I've been on campus. I can't help it if there's more to my life than a sports recap show and scotch," Logan walked to the chair opposite the couch and sat down.

"Did I just hear who I think I heard?" Andrew poked his head into the living room and seemed to confirm that Logan was there. "Bro!" Andrew yelled. "Mark! Logan finally decided to come out of hiding!"

"Midterms are over, and Logan's finally had enough 'studying?!?' This calls for pizza and poker," Mark decreed, coming out of his room.

"First one to fold buys," Logan agreed and reached for the deck of cards.

Andrew was forking over the last of his cash to the pizza guy while Rob shuffled the deck. He grumbled as he did it, but only because it seemed the required reaction. The game was put on hold temporarily while they each ate their own medium one topping.

". . . I just think that since Andrew was paying, we should've been able to at least get Papa John's instead of this cheap Domino's crap." Rob picked up a slice. "I'm just sayin'," he added when no one agreed.

"Shuttup, Norton," Andrew said over a mouthful of pizza. "You're eating it, aren't you?"

The game became serious after they ate, and though Mark was getting better at his poker face and reading what cards his opponents held according to their eyes, he was the next one to drop, leaving Logan and Rob to play for $400. Rob was the toughest of Logan's opponents because he was able to shut off all his emotions and calculate. Logan was Rob's toughest opponent for the same reason. And Logan had the scotch on his side. Rob was still drinking it like water, even though the pizza was gone. Logan couldn't even recall the last time he'd even had two fingers of Jäger, much less several high balls of it. All he had to do was wait Rob out. He'd get just loose enough for Logan to find a tell, and it would be all over. Until then, Logan would play it tight. And playing it tight was his bag.

It was two weeks until Spring Break, and Spring Break meant Logan's 22nd birthday. It also meant that he'd been a lycanthrope for a full year. Despite the hundreds he had in his pocket, Logan wasn't nearly as pleased with the world as he had been with the boys now that he was lying in a cold, empty bed. There was nothing to distract him from the situation, *but it's better this way. Better that she gets used to the space.* He knew that he was playing on tilt, and that was no way to behave in life any more than it was in cards. It was the best way to make a losing hand, and he didn't want that for himself or Lillie.

~

311

Logan hadn't been back to her apartment since the night he told her he was going to hang out with his roommates. It had been almost a week. She had quit coffee cold turkey because if she consumed even a milligram of caffeine after seven p.m., there was no way she was getting any sleep until after two. She had always thrived on her ability to never totally shut her brain down. Even when she was drifting to sleep, she could be contemplating some plan she had for the next day and promptly remember it come morning. But since Logan, there was no drifting off with some thought in her mind. There was almost no drifting off at all. She knew he wasn't trying to hurt her. He called or texted her at least once a day, and that was when they both weren't in the library.

Lillie surfed the net for antique or silvered mirrors while Logan searched stubbornly for a different remedy. But finding a mirror wasn't her most daunting challenge. She had a little bit of cash saved for buying movies or books or both, and that would do nicely. Plus there were plenty of antiques shops around Raleigh that were sure to have what she was looking for. The part that concerned her was getting the mirror into the woods. If she managed to find one as big as she wanted, she'd need help transporting it, and it was a safe bet that Logan wouldn't be thrilled to lend his hands, much less his car.

~

Logan was looking at Lillie through the glass walls of the Kappa Sig study room. She was as dedicated to her job as he had ever seen her, though he could tell by the look of her eyes that she was tired. The sight of her brought a wave of guilt that almost pushed him out of the room and in her direction. Almost. *I've made my choice*, he reminded himself. He was determined to wean her off of him, no matter how much it hurt. He'd take the withdrawal if he had to, just to keep her from OD'ing. *I owe her that much.*

Andrew and Mark had been making plans for Spring Break 2008 since the moment they recovered from their trip to Colorado. This year they wanted sun instead of snow, so they were heading to Ft. Lauderdale. Logan didn't dare risk it. His thirteenth phase was set to fall just as the week was ending. *Who knows how many people would die?* He tried not to think of the bodies of the youth group the Abbot girl left in her path. His victims wouldn't be teens going to learn the slopes. They'd be freshmen girls with bronze bodies and blonde hair, too drunk to know what was happening. He could see it clearly. And why not? He'd lived it, hadn't he?

He wondered what might have been if he hadn't won that drinking game and stumbled out into the night. If he hadn't been too out of it to see that a freaking wolf was heading right for him. If he hadn't blocked its teeth with his forearm. He studied the jagged line marring his skin; the light red ridge looked like a scar any reckless male might carry, perhaps was tame compared to some. But that little ripple was nothing. Nothing compared to the storm it set off. Nothing compared to the destruction to come.

"I can't believe you're punking out, dude," Mark whined. "What the crap am I supposed to do at the beach without you?"

"One of these days, you're going to have to learn to make your own negotiations, Malone," Logan replied.

313

"But you've been a member of the walking dead for the past two months! How was I supposed to hone my skills without my mentor?" Mark's social life had probably taken a nosedive while Logan was hanging with Lillie.

" You've got the Italian Stallion, remember?" Logan couldn't help but smirk.

"But he never shares the wealth, man!" Mark threw up his hands.

"Sorry, Mark. Really. But I've got a thing with the parents this week, and I can't really get out of it since I'm living off Dad at the moment." Logan looked at his roommate and had to work hard not to pity him. "But if I can duck out early, I'll try to catch up." The latest offer did little to placate Mark, since he left Logan in the living room without a word.

Logan held out until the day before his thirteenth phase. Keeping the space that seemed to desiccate him. It was she that ended the depravation, and he was too parched to prevent it. He was walking to the study room, and it was as if she had strategically taken her five minute break.

"Hey, Logan," she said as she walked up to him.

"Hey," he smiled.

"It's tonight, right?" Lillie looked right at him, and he had to remind himself that he hadn't just left her bed.

"Yeah." He looked down, hoped he wasn't regressing.

"You driving to the state park again tonight?" Her voice was soft, warm. *Crap but I'm thirsty!*

"I haven't decided. The last two times I was farther and farther from my car. I don't want to wind up so far

314

away that I can't find the Camaro." *But I don't want to be too close to you either.*

"Especially since you'll be naked," she snickered.

"There is that," he grinned, "but I was thinking more about not having a cell phone to call for help with," he chuckled too. *Be careful. It would be so easy.* He made a show of checking his watch. "Gotta go sign in," he let his fingers brush hers as he moved away.

"Be careful," she whispered and surprised them both when she caught his lips with hers. After a long pull, she stepped back, slid her hand down his arm, and left him dying for another drink.

She answered the knock that afternoon and found Logan on the other side of her door. He knew he was unexpected. "It's been a while."

"I know," he watched his feet.

"Is there something you want?" she refused to let any emotion into her voice, and he was glad.

"I came to . . ." but he couldn't finish. He gave in to himself and kissed her. *What could it hurt to let himself taste her one last time?*

"Maybe I should ask you to be careful more often," she smiled.

"You won't have to, Lillie. I came to say goodbye," he told her, and his last image of her was watching that smile disappear.

~

Lillie watched the wolf from the safety of the tree she'd crouched behind the night of their unsuccessful attempt to trap it. She knew that if she kept still enough, it wouldn't bother her. She was not inside its territory, and she posed no threat where she was. It was distracted at the moment anyway, sniffing at some raw meat that she supposed came from its latest kill.

315

Her studies had taught her that wolves needed several pounds of meat a day, and she had no doubt that what she was seeing was only a snack.

She settled in to wait for its feast to end until she saw that the wolf was dissatisfied with its food and had nudged it aside in favor of stalking some small animal it could see and she couldn't. She thought the behavior odd, but it wasn't like she was a forestry major. She could predict patterns in most humans' behavior because she knew her subject well, but she could no more predict the wolf's actions than she could Logan's of late.

~

Logan arose from the darkness and was in 317. He had never been more miserable. Not even when he had no idea what was happening to him and thought he was going to die of an aneurysm at any moment. *How the freak am I even alive?* He couldn't do anything right. He couldn't catch a wolf. He couldn't let go of Lillie. He couldn't kill himself, and he sure as hell couldn't gather fire wood if his life depended on it. He tried to think of a new plan, but antifreeze in the ground round had been his only idea. He had a little less than twenty-four hours, and by then, whatever he was going to do had to be done because his life didn't depend on it, but hers did.

~

Lillie had to work fast. She'd gone to three antiques stores, but she'd finally found a silvered mirror that was large enough to serve her purpose. She tried not to think about the expression on Logan's face when he left yesterday. He was more lost than she'd ever seen him, even in the beginning. She knew the consequences of suicide and wasn't willing to let him damn himself to

316

that fate, but death by another's hand was different. In that case, his sins could eventually be absolved. If ever a soul could be prayed out of purgatory, she would make sure his was. She also tried not to contemplate the effect her part in his death would have on her own soul. Still, purgatory would be better than knowing Logan was experiencing eternal damnation.

She got Courtney Hunter who worked the circulation desk right after her to come in a little early that afternoon. Courtney was a bit strange, but she was polite and always helpful when Lillie asked for anything. "I can't thank you enough for covering for me," Lillie pasted on a smile she hoped made her look excited rather than loony.

"No big deal. What's twenty minutes compared to the promise of a Double Shot?" Courtney grinned. *Caffeine* **would** *be nice*, Lillie thought before she could stop herself, but she couldn't drink coffee again until she got used to sleeping alone or . . . *Maybe after he's cured, he'll stop feeling like he's a danger to me and come back . . .* but she forced herself to remember that even if he survived tonight, the chances of that happening were slim.

"Say, Courtney, do you happen to know any guys who might be able to help me carry a large mirror into the woods? I'm helping a friend with this art project and—"

"I know some people who know some people. What time's this going down?" Courtney reminded Lillie of some sort of secret agent, but she was taking too much joy from the impending mission to actually be employed by the CIA.

"Well, I was hoping to get it done soon, since I want the mirror in position in time for sunset. . ." Lillie made sure to sound casual.

"Consider it done. We can discuss terms of payment later," Courtney nodded, as if business was concluded.

"Um . . . Does that mean you want two Double Shots?" Lillie was beginning to fear that she might have to come up with an insane amount of cash in unmarked, nonconsecutive bills.

"I'm thinking I'll want to upgrade to an espresso *and* a scone," Courtney answered before turning to the customer waiting behind the counter, who was now more than a little intimidated by the piece of conversation he had overheard.

~

After a few hours, it became clear to Logan that finding arsenic or cyanide in a store would not be an easy task. Apparently, a person had to be cleared to have access to those types of chemicals, since they were so poisonous and had been such popular means of killing people in the past. The next best thing would be rat poison, and he could only hope that it would be as odorless and tasteless as arsenic was reputed to be.

~

Lillie was satisfied with the way Courtney's guys situated the mirror. It was laid on the ground, covering a hole that was six feet deep. The guys Courtney had recruited weren't as weirded out at the prospect of digging a hole that was deep enough for a grave as she thought they'd be. *Then again, they are* **Courtney's** *friends.* She made sure the mirror was just out of range of the wolf's territory, and that the terrain around it

318

would be easy enough to negotiate quickly in the darkness. Her life and his both depended on that.

She returned to her hiding place just after dusk and waited for darkness to fall. In less than half an hour, she saw the wolf searching the wood for food. Lillie held her breath. *Please, God. Please let this work.*

The closer the wolf came to her, the more impatient Lillie became. She was anxious to run, anxious for it all to be over, but with only one chance, she had to be patient. Had to wait until the wolf was so close she could see its fur shifting with each step it took. Until she could see the sharp points of its teeth and smell its sweat. When it was an arm's length away, she took a deep breath, said a Hail Mary and dashed into the path in front of him.

She didn't need to hear the throaty growl behind her to know that she was in trouble. She could feel it in every fiber. She knew enough from her research that wolves hunted by tiring out their victims, so she didn't run as fast as she could. She paced herself. The mirror wasn't too far away, but she knew from her last encounter that she didn't have the option of taking her chances.

She tried not to look behind her as she moved, but she concentrated on the ground in front of her and what she was passing. It was very important that she didn't take a wrong turn or stop short. If she didn't lead the wolf in the right direction, neither of them had any hope. From the corner of her eye, she saw that the mirror was coming up on her left, and she double checked to make sure.

When there was no doubt, she decreased her speed and turned sharply from the path. The wolf was a few yards behind her. Lagging behind purposefully so that

319

she would spend all her energy trying to increase the distance, and when that happened, it would move in for the kill. As she suspected, the wolf sped up when it lost sight of her, but by now she was a stride or two away from the mirror. She pushed herself as hard as she could, praying that she would reach the tree with enough time.

She gripped the rope she'd tied to a branch previously and used it and her legs to crawl as quickly as she could up the trunk. She had to be in position by the time the wolf reached the mirror. Each step up the bark seemed to take hours, but she made it to the branch and swung her leg over so that she was straddling it. She took a deep breath and leaned forward so that her face was visible in the glass beneath her.

Lillie had just let herself relax after completing the worst of her plan when the wolf appeared and walked right up to the tree. It approached carefully, not wanting to spook its prey. It could smell her, and knew that she was near, but had not yet located her. She watched its eyes searching the darkness around it and didn't dare breathe. The wolf took another hesitant step and recoiled as its paw landed on something unfamiliar. It peered curiously at the mirror for a moment, debating. The wolf eyed the shape in front of it with wonder. As it moved slightly, so did the shape. Wariness seemed to shift to recognition with each second that passed, and the wolf seemed mesmerized at viewing itself. Suddenly its gaze found hers, and it lunged. The wait was over.

A beat later she heard a thunderous crash. In her mind, she'd imagined the sound would be horrific but brief, and in reality it probably was. But to her the noise was protracted, a continued cacophony of shattering and struggling. And then there was nothing. No crunch, no tinkle, no growl, no whimper. Nothing.

When she had crouched in the tree so long that her legs were cramping, and there was still silence beneath her, Lillie crawled carefully down from her perch and looked. All she saw was a heap of dark fur. The closer she got to it, the louder her shoes crunched the bits of glass beneath them. The wolf was dead. She was certain as soon as she knelt beside it, even before she laid her hand on its side to feel its breath. There was no movement. No intake or exhale. She wanted to check for a pulse, but couldn't remember where the lupine pulse points were.

It would have growled, if it was alive. When she touched the snout, it was wet and cool. *It's finally over! Thank God, it's finally over.* For a moment, she was overjoyed, and her laughter rang through the pines. *It's over.* And suddenly she wasn't laughing any longer. Tears were streaming down her cheeks, and she was sobbing. *It's over.* And it was. The wolf was dead. Lillie laid her head against the soft fur and ignored the sharpness she felt against her knees. His heart was motionless. *He's gone. He's gone.* The thought multiplied in her mind until she couldn't think, couldn't breathe. She gasped in desperation and wondered how she was still alive if her own heart was frozen in her chest.

Lillie awoke with the sun. It was rising in a brilliant orange. She picked her head up from the soft fur it had rested on, so she could watch dawn break over the horizon. Like the light, it all came pouring onto her. She looked down at the cold, stiff body and the pools of dark crimson, the sparkling shards that glinted like jewels. *I can't leave him. I can't just leave him like this.* But she did. With hands that were covered in a mixture of her own dried tears and his dried blood, she removed what was left of the frame and as much of the glass as she could and put it into the trash bag she'd brought with her to hold anything she could clean up. Then she turned from the body and left him there.

She gave herself the rest of the day Saturday to cry. She slept the entirety of Sunday. By Monday, Lillie made herself get back to life. If she wasn't as cheerful as before, if she wasn't as focused, she worked to correct those deficiencies. Her loss was her own. She wasn't about to share that with other people. And when she considered it, she was glad that Logan had kept her separate from the rest of his life. *It seems all he did was protect me.*

It had been more than a week since he had gone, and Lillie didn't even have to work at smiling anymore. She just did it automatically when she encountered an external stimulation in spite of the sadness that still hobbled her inside. She was stuck behind the circulation desk, but passed the time by reading ahead of her syllabi. She was mid-paragraph in one of her textbooks when she thought she heard the other girls close to her say, "Hi, Logan."

She couldn't help the snap reaction that made her look up from her book, though she told herself logically, *There are thousands of students on campus. Any number of them could have that name. You know it isn't the same one. After all, it is April Fool's Day.*

322

Still, in the moment that she first looked up, she thought she saw him. She shook her head, knowing that his body didn't even exist in that state anymore, so there was no way it could be him. Yet she looked again, and her eyes and heart overruled her brain.

It was him. She'd know that frame anywhere, and by touch besides. It was the same set of the shoulders. The same dark hair. She couldn't stop herself. "Logan," she called to him. And he turned. He met her eyes with ones of that steel gray she saw so much in her sleep. Then he smiled and ripped her insides apart. It was the same smile he gave the cashier at Hill of Beans or the pizza delivery boy. Not the one he gave her when he hadn't seen her all day. Not the one she got after a kiss. Not the one she saw when they lay together, spent and breathless. It was the one he gave her so long ago when he first came to her section and pretended to be doing medical research. The practiced smile he kept for strangers.

"Hey. I'm sure we've met at one time or another, but I can't remember your name. If you don't remind me, I'll be kicking myself for days." Even now he was charming, though he was twisting the knife.

"I'm sure you will. Give me a call if it ever comes back to you," she sent him a practiced smile of her own and took a bathroom break.

It was another two weeks before she noticed anything. In all that had happened, she hadn't been too concerned. But before she had always been almost perfectly punctual, and now she was more than two months late. *It's only stress. It's only stress,* she told herself as she waited for the results to appear.

Lillie Thackery sat in her assigned seat. Her undergraduate career would officially be over the moment she received her diploma. Her life in the Thackery family would officially be over the moment she told her parents about the baby. *They won't understand.* They'd want her to go away for a while to have the child, and then give it away. *But I could never do that. I could never give up the one part of Logan I still have.*

She heard the announcer say, "Philip Logan Michaels," and watched as he walked up to the stage, crossed to where the chancellor was waiting with his diploma to shake his hand, and then left the stage to return to his seat. *Is it my imagination, or did he catch my eye? It may be the last time you see him. Doesn't he have a right to know?* But there was nothing she could say. He had no knowledge of her at all. He'd lost twelve months when the wolf died, and in that span, their entire relationship. *There's no possible explanation*, she decided and wiped a tear away before anyone else could see it.

~

He took his seat and tried to comprehend what just happened. He was a college graduate. It would have been hard to believe, even if he hadn't woken up naked and in a hole in the woods near Lake Raleigh one morning with absolutely no memory of the last twelve months, at least that's what he told himself. There were moments when he hated the blankness he found when he tried to remember anything between the beginning of Spring Break his junior year and the end of Spring Break his senior year. He'd been to doctors—his father made sure they were the best in the state—and they'd all come up with nothing other than the theory that he'd experienced severe head trauma. There was no cure for the amnesia, they said, but it shouldn't have an adverse

324

effect on his life. It didn't really seem to bother anyone but him. As long as he wasn't on drugs or dying, his parents were fine. His roommates thought it was creepy but were still unconcerned. "After all, you didn't miss much," Mark promised.

Still he felt uneasy. It was almost like having the answer to a question on the tip of his tongue and not being able to recall it. He was always sure he was one step closer to remembering, but fell short. The more he thought, he only came up blank save a pair of forest green eyes. He had been on the lookout for them since he was able to pull them out of the fog that was his mind. He turned in his seat to scan the crowd of students in caps and gowns. He had the uncanny feeling that those eyes had just been watching him. He pushed the thought away. Logan Michaels was never one to believe in superstitions.

Epilogue

Ann Arbor, MI, 2021

Perhaps he never did learn to believe again. Perhaps he never remembered the name of the girl behind the circulation desk or the significance of those green eyes. But Lillie remembered for both of them. She remembered and recorded as she had been taught. For someone who loved stories and keeping them alive, none was more important than this.

That is why when I awoke this morning in my bedroom floor, totally naked and covered in mud, she was calm. She took the day off work, helped me get cleaned up, sat me on the couch, looked straight into my gray eyes and said, "Lo, my love, there's something you need to know."